Family Bedrock

Irene Radford

I0614611

Book View Café
304 S. Jones Blvd. Ste #2906
Las Vegas, Nevada 89107

Table of Contents

Copyright 1

More books in the world of Tess Noncoiré 2

Dedication 3

Acknowledgements 4

Family Bedrock 5

PROLOGUE 6

Chapter One 13

Chapter Two 23

Chapter Three 31

Chapter Four 37

Chapter Five 43

Chapter Six 50

Chapter Seven 55

Chapter Nine 61

Chapter Nine 67

Chapter Ten 75

Chapter Eleven 84

Chapter Twelve 91

Chapter Thirteen 99

Chapter Fourteen 106

Chapter Fifteen 112

Chapter Sixteen 122

Chapter Seventeen 130

Chapter Eighteen 136

Chapter Nineteen 144

Chapter Twenty 153

Chapter Twenty-One 160

Chapter Twenty-Two 167

Chapter Twenty-Three 174

Chapter Twenty-Four 184

Chapter Twenty-Five 192

Chapter Twenty-Six 200

Chapter Twenty-Seven 208

Chapter Twenty-Eight... 216
Chapter Twenty-Nine 223
Chapter Thirty 228
Chapter Thirty-One.. 235
Epilogue.. 242
About the Author.. 247
Other Book View Café Titles by Irene Radford 248
ABOUT BOOK VIEW CAFÉ 250

Copyright

More books in the world of
Tess Noncoiré

HOUNDING THE MOON
MOON IN THE MIRROR
FAERY MOON
FOREST MOON RISING

The reason there have been no valid demon sightings in the last fifty years is that they are all hanging out at Cons winning costume awards.

Dedication

I dedicate this book to the wonderful and welcoming community of fandom, especially those who attend Science Fiction and Fantasy Conventions. Not only do you support authors and buy their books, attend our readings and panel discussions, but you come to chat with authors at their book signings and kaffeeklatsches. Without you I would never have achieved anything, let alone a moderate level of success.

Thank you one and all!

Acknowledgements

F andom may create and run Science Fiction/Fantasy Conventions, "Cons," but forgiving hotel staff keeps them anchored and on track. Bless the housekeepers who come up with irons and ironing boards for last minute costume corrections—and sometimes even pins. The wandering staff members who jump in to help maneuver wobbling luggage racks that don't roll in a single direction have saved many a sales booth in the vendor's hall, as well as art show displays. Emergency catering for an impromptu party happens. Extra pillows and blankets, no problem. And one must not forget the wait staff who take care of us splendidly in the café. They keep us on our feet with coffee and calories and fulfill the weirdest of dietary restrictions with a smile.

We thank you all.

Family Bedrock

Irene Radford

B ook View Café
304 S. Jones Blvd. Ste #2906
Las Vegas, Nevada 89107

PROLOGUE

L ouis Metcalf peered at the widely spaced individual pixels on the enlarged photograph. It had landed on his desk in a plain, unmarked envelope, no name or address. His office building was equally obscure—not even a number out front. But the URGENT tab, just a pre-printed post-it in the shape of an arrow outlined in red, on the plain manilla, nearly shouted for attention.

Who knew why? The anonymous courier had come in the middle of the night when no one should have been in this part of the building, except maybe Lou if he had a thorny problem. The courier had collected Lou's signature on a digital clipboard and handed him the thin package.

During the entire procedure, the messenger had kept his hat brim pulled low over his eyes and never once engaged Lou's gaze. No words either, just a grunt of acceptance of the signature.

Standard procedure.

Except, few couriers delivered material after midnight. Even the clandestine services rarely delivered so late, especially if they needed a signature.

Lou had tossed the ubiquitous brownish, yellowish envelope atop a file of vague UFO reports that obviously needed no further investigation. Beneath those reports lay an untidy stack of satellite photos needing a report. Most of them looked strange on the surface only to end up having rational explanations.

But Lou couldn't leave a UFO report alone if his life depended upon it. All of his colleagues knew that. It was his job, as well as his passion, to examine those reports and photos pixel by pixel and then either dismiss them or hand them to seasoned investigators. When he had the time, he joined the hunt.

Even a few outsiders now associated his name with proper and complete investigations of possible alien aircraft. He'd never done an interview or appeared on any of the exposé TV shows, but still, people, including his government and his employers at the UN, acknowledged him as the leading authority in his field.

Maybe the universe meant for him to see this particular digital image because no one else would understand the implications of four costumed individuals. People. Not UFOs.

Only he could find a connection when no one else knew where, or how to look.

On his computer with the forty-two inch plasma screen, he outlined a small section of gray dots, to the right of center on a male chin, and reduced the magnification so that the weird dots shrank together.

A lozenge shape took form. Clearly this discoloration appeared to be a very strange birthmark.

He didn't think so.

"Wow!" He had to sit back and shove his glasses to the top of his nearly bald head, blinking rapidly while he pinched the bridge of his nose and stroked the sides of his grey-touched beard. Then he replaced his glasses and focused on the adjacent section of pinker dots. He combined them to equally sized sections.

He found a pattern. The pink bled into the gray seamlessly without a definite edge.

The time and date stamp in the lower left-hand corner of the original photo told him it had been sitting in the files for nearly twenty years and couldn't have been subjected to modern computer manipulation. Now someone had sent it to him for digital scanning and analysis.

He looked again at the post-it note stuck to the top right corner of the 5X8 photo. The handwriting was barely legible. The signature less so. Not unusual in this section of the secret agency world.

"The director says this has to be a skin anomaly, like dead skin from a frostbite burn," he read the sticky note attached to the photo out loud, trying to make better sense of the words. His instincts told him differently. And why had it come to the director's attention now?

Someone in this lab must have found the file and passed it up the chain of command. Not the first time he'd been bypassed by an ambitious underling. Nor the last either. Usually, a lowly minion was hoping to go alien hunting while the higher ups had grown bored with the speculation.

But for now, Lou was almost glad he had the opportunity to chase down the photographer and the people the camera had captured.

He went back to the original photo at 100% magnification. A face emerged on his screen. Dark hair and almond eyes of a rare moss green color gave him the impression of someone of Asian ancestry. Or possibly Amerindian. But the person was tall, half a head taller than his companions.

"The rumors are true!" he gasped, rummaging through files on a different computer screen for a report he'd been trying to ignore.

The companions in the photo gave him the clue he needed to supply their location. One was dressed as an iconic television version of a spaceship captain. Lou had loved that show and binge-watched the series, and all of its spin-offs, every winter. The uniform was accurate down to the holstered energy pistol. Behind him stood a male and female pair dressed in the silvery jumpsuits of movie space aliens. That cheaply made, badly directed movie had become a cult classic. Lou owned it on DVD and watched it every three months. A young woman at the side of the gathering wore a chainmail bikini (he hoped she'd lined the metal garments to avoid painful sunburn beneath it) with a plastic broadsword sheathed across her back. The thing was so long she'd never be able to pull it free. But she still had the bright yellow twist tie around the grip indicating a peace bond—her oath not to draw a weapon during the convention. Her escort wore a top hat with multiple drop-down lenses on goggles, the uniform of the Steampunk movement.

This combination could only take place at a science fiction and fantasy convention. The tall man with the scale on his chin wore a rare costume, not part of the media-dominated genre. "Stone-colored, overlapping scales covered his body, except for the face. That wasn't a costume. The scale on the chin emerges from the skin. It isn't a separate piece affixed with special effects glue!" Lou chortled.

He'd seen the phenomenon before.

He'd also been sworn to secrecy.

Pieces of information he'd been gathering for ages began to fit together in a complex jigsaw puzzle of his mind.

He'd been waiting a long time for this to surface.

He laughed out loud, mirth rising from his paunch to consume his heart and brain with satisfaction and tremendous relief. He laughed so loud his assistant dared breach protocol and open Lou's lab door without invitation.

Damn, he'd been here all night and the earliest staff had reported for duty already.

"Sir?" Stella asked. She stashed her own glasses in her lab coat breast pocket and focused her long-sighted eyes on him.

He knew from experience that she could spot a fly across a room but couldn't make sense of her own fingers held in front of her eyes without those glasses.

"Stella, we are going to another convention. Grab your camera and pack a kit. We'll need to test DNA samples," he said, picking up his original print of the photo and waving it at her.

"You've found something interesting, sir." Her voice sounded flat and bored. "That photo is nearly twenty years old. It's not even digital. It can't be accurately analyzed, not like modern ones."

How did she know that? He'd talked to no one since the clandestine delivery.

Lou peered at her suspiciously.

"I came in early to tidy up a few things before... I peeked at the contents of the envelope before waving the courier in to get your signature."

"Before what?" Lou searched his overloaded brain for any hint that Stella planned something outside the normal schedule.

"I'm taking two weeks of accumulated vacation time before I lose it, sir." She stood straighter, chin lifted in defiance.

"Vacation? You never take a vacation." Confusion turned his vision grey.

"Which is why I have so much of it accumulated. Stevie—you know the man from accounting I've been seeing?"

"Yes, yes, I know who he is." He waved a gesture of dismissal.

"We are going to the Bahamas and getting married. Tomorrow. I won't be going with you."

"We'll see about that." He paused while he cleaned his glasses, trying to think up an excuse to keep her at his side. He'd never survive the chaos of getting to their destination without her organization skills.

"Cheer up, Stella. This isn't a wild goose chase. I've found evidence of aliens. Real aliens living among us in disguise. Where else can they hang out in their natural form and be themselves but at a convention where costumes rule?"

"Sir, we've been this route before. You are supposed to be debunking UFO reports. A convention is usually just an excuse to hook up with your ex and see your daughter."

Lou dismissed her allegation with a gesture. But her words did bring warmth to his belly in fond memory of the woman he'd once loved and now considered among his closest friends. Their brief marriage happened only because she was on the rebound. They didn't *belong* together.

But he did love and miss their daughter.

"I don't need the spaceship if we find the aliens." He placed the photo in a file folder and added it to the stack he intended to pass on to the director when he completed his report.

"Sir, is this about the rumors coming out of black ops that a terrorist group has been doing genetic experiments to produce warriors who grow their own stone armor?"

"Yes. But I do not believe genetic experiments of this magnitude are possible at the current state of science, let alone twenty years ago. These are genuine aliens with the innate ability, or maybe a device, that triggers the armor to grow from a single scale embedded in the skin. Now where did I put my camera?"

Stella crossed the room and plucked the device from his worktable where it always awaited him, in plain sight. "We know about the teens with costumes resembling stone armor," Stella said. She tapped her chin in consideration.

"Costumes only," Lou replied too quickly. "I debunked them with your help." But there were holes in his report. Only an astute analyst would notice them, Lou hoped.

They are the adopted children of my old friend Bryce Maxwell. I can't betray them.

He accepted the camera from Stella, slinging it over his shoulder by the thick strap. Then he stared at it in a moment of confusion. Something clicked in his mind, so he collapsed the extended lens. It became a discreet and compact rectangle he could secrete in his shirt pocket.

"But you are right. This photo is nearly twenty years old, so it can't be Rod or Sprite who are still teenagers." Stella had only been his executive assistant for twelve years, so she hadn't been around when this photo was taken.

Stella had helped him write the report five years ago that debunked the idea of the twins being anything other than normal teens wearing unique costumes.

Looking at the entire photo again, he realized something else. "The woman draped around the Asian man is Jacquelyn Johnstone, the birth mother of the Maxwell twins. She's well known for 'bagging' more aliens than anyone in con history. There's a club of middle-aged sexually frustrated women. They keep journals and rack up points." Though in the photo, Jacquie had barely been eighteen and President/Founder of the club. Now she was still under forty.

Could this photo have been taken the weekend the twins had been conceived?

"Sir, may I remind you that you have a request from the White House to find the best wording for a new Executive Order concerning the UFO proliferation? You can't leave on an unauthorized field expedition until you compose the EO related to this case. You don't need me for that. I'm going to the Bahamas."

"Confound it, Stella, I don't have time for such nonsense. This EO didn't come from the president. I'd bet money that Senator Desdaganet is behind it. It's illegal to kidnap people, even if they are aliens. Nor can we conduct lethal experiments on them. I will not be a part of such activity. Besides we have to have proof of their existence before we can turn the black ops troops loose on an innocent population." Though he was pretty sure he had the first bits of evidence in those photos. By the end of the weekend, he'd have proof and know what to do about it. But he wouldn't write that damned EO.

His best friend Bryce Maxwell could ensure the success of any black ops mission. Or sabotage it completely, so he didn't think the EO would do much good.

"Sir, the White House believes these people are real and they must be brought under our control so we can exploit their natural... um... talents before someone else finds them. Every army in the world is looking for them." She sounded as if she parroted the memo that had come with the EO request.

"All the more reason for me to find them first and organize their legal and physical defense."

"Sir, can't you word the EO so that detaining these aliens is so wrapped in legalese the order itself will be tied up in court for years? Long enough for you to figure out how best they can help our government?"

"I'd rather sign a treaty with them." Lou bent his head to his computer screen again, bringing up a series of photos for comparison. "Treaty! That's the key."

"Very well, sir." Stella backed out of the lab. "I'll make the travel arrangements for you, and you alone, before I leave on my honeymoon. I believe the photo shows the subjects pointing toward the BeachCon sign."

BeachCon. Next weekend. The third weekend in June.

Bryce would be there with the twins. And most likely so would Lou's ex and their daughter.

"I already have my plane ticket, hotel reservation, and membership," Lou said, proud that he'd remembered to do all that back in February when the Con Committee had announced that they'd open for certain this year with minimal pandemic protocols in place.

"I'm going to visit my daughter and take her to look for student housing at the university of her choice. She's already been accepted to three of them. She's so smart, she must get it from me."

Chapter One

Three weeks prior:

"Hurry up and take the damn picture!" Rod Maxwell groaned through gritted teeth that were supposed to be a big smile.

"It has to be perfect!" Sprite, his twin sister, complained. "This is for Dad, and we have to show as much of our graduation gowns as possible. Which is impossible because you are a full foot taller than I am. Scrunch down."

"Oh, let me do it," Rod said, grabbing for the selfie stick.

Sprite yanked it away from him. "No, you'll cut me off at the bottom of my cap.

"Why don't you just let me take my own picture," a gravelly male voice said from behind them.

"Dad!" they shouted in unison. Rod whirled around, then he and his twin sister flung their arms around the man in the grey off-the-rack suit, white shirt open at the collar and no tie. They were careful not to dislodge his carefully angled black leather, broad-brim hat and pandemic mask. Strangers tended to only see his ordinary wardrobe and dismissed Bryce Maxwell, if they noticed him at all. Few looked close enough to notice the stretched, too smooth skin grafts that marred the left side of his face.

The shadows cast by his hat and the mask obscured most of the ugly details.

"You came!" Sprite sobbed with happiness. "I told you not to bother. This ceremony is just one more hurdle to get over so we can get on with the rest of our lives. And Senator Desdaganet's speech went on forever and said nothing interesting. But I'm ever so glad you did come."

"I couldn't desert you two on a day as important as high school graduation. And yes, the senator is a bore."

"He did say some creepy things about us grads, who are now adults, being constantly vigilant against the enemies who walk among us, trying to subvert our wonderful government." Rod shook his head in disapproval. "More likely he and his friends in the military-industrial complex are the enemies of the people."

Sprite shivered in the June heat. Something about the guest speakers...

She checked all around to see who might be watching them, before speaking. She didn't like the senator who'd been in office too long but couldn't be ousted.

"We're safe, Aphrodite Sarsaparilla," Rod whispered. He knew she'd stick her tongue out at him for daring to use her real name. Their biological mother had given them both hideous names and made it a condition of adoption that they not legally change them.

They'd turned eighteen last March and could cast off this last remnant of Jacquie Johnstone in their lives.

"Safety is ephemeral. For now, everyone's too consumed with their own families to notice ours, Android Spartacus." Sprite retaliated. Then she stuck her tongue out at him.

"Careful, I might steal that." Bryce Maxwell made a pretense at grabbing her tongue with gloved fingers, his own playful way of trying to curb her bad habit. Mostly he'd cured her.

But there were times Rod couldn't resist taunting her.

"Are you okay, Dad?" Sprite asked, changing the subject.

"Yes, I am. Now stand back and let me take about a hundred of my own photos." Bryce crouched a little to get them both in the shot from his own phone.

Rod stopped teasing and pulled his sister close. He bent his head so that the corner of his mortarboard touched the top of Sprite's. His dad touched the screen of his phone about a dozen times before gesturing them to change poses.

The twins each held up their right hands, thumbs up. Their moss-green eyes sparkled with joy. "See, Dad, we made it, all the way through, just like we promised. Now you have to keep your promise," Sprite said.

Rod nodded his agreement.

"Okay, okay, in a couple of weeks we drive to the coast for BeachCon—newly returned and improved with post pandemic protocols in place. I knew you two would squeak through high school, pass all your exams, and write all your papers in time to graduate."

"Does that mean you already bought our memberships and reserved a room?"

"You mean you don't want to camp on the beach?"

Rod's heart beat a little faster in eagerness. "Can we?"

"Ewwww. Dad, we haven't had to camp out since we were five!" Sprite grimaced. "Though I do love the bonfire on the beach Friday nights." She hugged herself with a dreamy smile on her face. "Patrick said he'd drive down from Seattle to join us."

"You mean that using the cool evening air as an excuse to snuggle with Patrick is what you love about the bonfire." Rod had seen them share their first kiss by the fire three years ago.

"And you with Liz." For once Sprite didn't stick her tongue out at her brother. Romantic relationships were too new to both of them for either to fall into teasing mode. He had some great memories of his first kisses too.

He wished that Liz could have come to this graduation to witness his greatest success so far. His chest swelled a bit. He'd finally graduated, despite his mediocre grades, and he wanted to share it with his girlfriend. But she had her own commencement to attend today, in Cave Junction, hours south of here.

But Cave Junction meant Liz and her mom lived almost local to BeachCon.

"Dad, are you well enough to camp?" Rod asked.

"On the beach where I can breathe clean, moist air, yes. But I'm not going to risk it yet. I made the hotel reservations. I even sent my costume to the dry cleaner." He straightened up slowly.

Rod reached a hand to balance his father. He didn't have his cane with him today.

"I'm okay," Bryce said, shaking his head at the offered help. He gathered the twins into another brief hug and aimed them toward an exit. "I think we'll grill some steaks tonight out by the pool. I found some first of the season corn at the market earlier. But first, my little Sprite, there are ice packs in the cooler in the back of the rig."

Both Rod and Sprite covered their chins with a hand. Rod's scale didn't itch. He could barely feel the difference in texture from his regular five o'clock shadow. Sprite on the other hand looked as if she had a glowing red rectangle of a pimple about to explode. The afternoon early-June heat and excitement had stressed her control.

"I'm okay," Rod whispered. "Where's the car? I'll bring it around."

His father looked down at his left leg and tested his weight on it. "You're moving faster than I am these days." He patted all of his pockets, jacket and trousers.

Sprite intervened and pulled the keys out of his front left pants pocket and tossed them to Rod. "We'll wait in the shade of that oak." She pointed toward an elderly giant of a tree across the drive, rooted in an island between parking lanes. Its shade offered the most sought-after parking places in the acres of pavement around the college gymnasium that had hosted the commencement exercises.

The good parking spots, including the handicapped spaces, were full when Bryce had dropped the twins off several hours ago. More so when he returned just in time to hear the opening strains of *Pomp and Circumstance* and watch Senator Desdaganet lead the procession of graduating seniors as if the music had been composed just for his own inflated ego.

PO DUC WRENCHED OFF his tie as he lowered his long frame into his wife's hybrid sedan. He hated the formal wear required by lawyers and courtrooms, and only had one tie—a very nice silk one that Mimi had given him when he received his Master's in arson investigation. After a few moments of deep breathing and feeling almost human again, he looked at the text that had just come through his phone. Expecting notification of the jury findings of the arson trial where he'd just testified as an expert witness, he was surprised at the caller ID— Po Luc, his older brother, and chair of the family foundation.

FAMILY BEDROCK

Rogue element of Homeland Security has ordered Louis Metcalf to write an Executive Order making us "illegal" citizens. Kidnap, torture, extreme interrogation now legal. He refused and returned the order to POTUS. Speculation Pres didn't know about it. Manipulated by Desdaganet. Emergency meeting tonight 7:30.

Duc narrowed his eyes and read the message twice before replying that he'd be there. Damn, damn, damn!

The foundation needed to find all of the paranormals in the region and make certain they had sanctuaries. That was why his parents and grandparents had poured their life savings and much energy into protecting first themselves and the family, and later, other talented people, giving them places to stay until a violent neighborhood calmed down, and sometimes, new identities and relocation for the persecuted.

Life often got ugly for people on the edge of society. That's why his people kept showing up at science fiction conventions where they could assume their natural forms and call them costumes. Or display paranormal talents dismissed as con games.

Maybe it was time to start taking his girls to the cons so they'd have a place to get used to their armor when it manifested. Today, in mid-June, it was nearly hot enough to trigger his own armor. He started the car and turned the AC to full blast.

Another text chimed.

Please pick up milk and bread on your way home. M

His wife was always polite, even when extremely angry or in simple family requests. That was a trait his grandmother had instilled in him, and Mimi picked up from exposure to his sprawling family. Politeness had saved more than one tense Thanksgiving dinner from erupting in verbal abuse, and once, a fist fight between his father and uncle.

Dad, the younger brother, had inherited the stone-people gene. Uncle Jin had not, and resented it.

Some families shouldn't be forced to spend time together during the holidays. He knew what had inspired an anthology of horror holiday stories he'd read last winter. Sometimes zoning out in front of football games wasn't enough to soothe frazzled nerves.

How many house fires had he fought that started with fisticuffs that knocked over the Christmas tree which landed in the brightly burning fire?

Time to put the trial out of his mind. Let the lawyers and the jury figure out the verdict. There'd be another one next time some of the college kids got drunk and started setting fires in trash cans. This last one had spread through a homeless camp and killed two, badly injuring five more. Duc had been called in to rule it an accident. But the deliberateness of the way the fire spread spelled pre-meditation in his book.

Now to go home to his wife and daughters and the glimmer of hope that maybe Mimi was pregnant again. His parents kept telling him it was the white woman's fault they had no precious grand*son* to ensure the family line.

He gave up listening to them ages ago. Any new baby was a blessing.

"YOU DIDN'T BRING YOUR cane," Sprite said as soon as Dad settled with his back against the tree trunk.

Bryce shrugged. His well-worn hat tipped forward as he rested his head against the tree.

"You're tired. Why didn't you bring your cane? Or use the handicap sticker to park closer?"

"Pride."

She tucked herself up against his side and placed his left hand on her shoulder, letting him use her for support in place of the ebony cane with a silver handle shaped like a dragon's head. His body was warmer than she liked.

She opened her sky-blue graduation gown and shrugged out of it, revealing a short and floaty sun dress of the same color. A sigh of relief escaped her. Her stone scale lost some of its heat and itchiness.

In silence she neatly folded the gown before placing it on the grass at her feet. Her cap went on top of it, squared up with the edges of the neat parcel.

"Feeling better?" Bryce asked.

"Some. I still need an ice pack, though. What about you?""

"Breathe deep," he coached her. "Long even breaths. Calm. You need to be in a cool and calm sea with moonlight soothing your eyes."

She fell into the lulling rhythm of his voice. Her body temperature lowered. Her racing heart slowed. The burning itch surrounding her scale faded.

Dad mimicked her practiced meditation. His muscles relaxed and he leaned less heavily on her.

"How are you feeling?" she asked. She couldn't monitor him and herself at the same time. She wished Patrick had come. Not only did she want to share today with him, as a pre-med major in Seattle, he'd know how to help both her and her dad.

"Tired. Not feverish. It's been a very full day. I got some good work done wrapping up a project. The check should be in the household account next week. I'm very glad you and Rod decided against the Senior Party. I wouldn't sleep properly until you got home tomorrow morning."

The Senior Party would be boring without Patrick.

"It's supposed to be alcohol free, but the kids always find ways to sneak in booze or pot and do nothing more interesting than get drunk or high. The whole thing is run by the jocks and cheerleaders, the same kids who bully us for not being as beautiful or privileged as they are—and for never participating in their drunken binges. We don't like them."

"Understood. And you are as beautiful as any of them. Let's hope they never encounter you two when you have had a few drinks. You could bash in their skulls without thinking, just to push them out of the way."

"I hate losing control. I'm glad you let us experiment with a few drinks at home, under supervision."

"Paranormals have a reputation for weird and unpredictable reactions to alcohol."

"Rod's coming. I can see the car at the end of this lane." She pointed along the left-hand lane of the parking lot. The small, pearl white SUV—not the cliched black monster Rod wanted, Sprite wanted red—moved slowly, allowing for the mass exodus of cars trying to escape the ceremonies. Four big tour buses idled next to the building to take some of the graduates to their final party. Four more waited at the entrance.

"If it takes Rod a few more moments to get here, then the air conditioning will be working full blast to cool you down," Bryce said. He opened his eyes, reset his hat, and straightened away from the tree.

"You don't always have to think about us, Dad. You need to think about your own health more," she said. "Two years ago, when you caught pneumonia, your lungs came close to collapsing. The pandemic patients strained the hospital staff and resources beyond capacity so they couldn't admit you. That really scared me."

"Bossy little mite, aren't you?" He chuckled.

"Someone has to keep us organized and moving forward. Now about your costume, I think you should let me glue some sequins around the eye hole and rim of your mask."

"I'm the Phantom of the Opera, not a harlequin. No sequins."

"Hrmf." Sprite disagreed with him. Sequins would draw attention and make his scars look more like artful makeup than the aftermath of a horrible fire with toxic smoke that had nearly killed him. Getting him out of the inferno was the first time the twins had manifested full armor. They'd been six at the time. The fire hadn't touched them, and working together, they were able to free their dad from the inferno. "No one at the con cares what we look like," she added.

"I know. Which is one of the reasons we go to so many. We can all be ourselves. But I still feel more comfortable hiding my scars."

"If you hide the outside scars, you think you are also hiding the inside ones."

He winced. "Another reason to go to the beach, moister air to soothe my lungs. And none of the local pollens that irritate my breathing."

"Did you take the new consulting job? The money will cover about six months of mortgage payments."

"I'm still thinking about it. I don't like organizing black ops missions in central Africa. And the job I just finished is enough. And... there's something else we all need to discuss before we go to the con."

Then Rod pulled up alongside them, interrupting the tsunami of questions she needed to ask about the "something else."

Both twins helped Bryce settle in the shotgun seat where he could stretch out his long legs. He accepted their assistance with grudging grace.

Sprite climbed in behind Rod, folding her legs beneath her. Her father was nearly as tall as Rod and both of them had their seats pushed way back, leaving her little leg room. But this gave her access to the cooler on the seat beside her—after she dislodged Rod's heaped graduation cap and gown. She grabbed three bottles of water and an ice pack. She handed two bottles forward. After gulping half the water in her own bottle, she held the pack against her chin until the scale stopped throbbing with heat.

Crisis averted, she allowed herself to breathe deeply. Then she moved the ice to the back of her neck to help cool her entire body while she folded her brother's robe. "We have to return these to the rental shop. You might show a little more respect for them," she grumbled.

"It's always cooler at the beach," Bryce said, capping his now empty water bottle, and neatly terminating another argument. "The climate will do all of us good. The valley's heating up earlier than usual this summer and releasing pollens in heavier doses. Maybe we should move to the coast."

"Not close enough to specialty clinics," Rod replied. "Do you need a pain pill? There's both OTC and Rx stuff in the glove box."

"The community colleges on the coast suck," Sprite chimed in. "We wouldn't be able to commute to the city for better classes." At that thought she grimaced. Both her grades and Rod's had suffered these last three years as it became harder and harder to control the demands of their scales when facing bullies. Being out in the world and keeping their paranormal talents hidden exhausted them both. They hadn't bothered to apply to any four-year colleges. By the time they'd taken the SATs it was too late.

"I read your SAT scores, kids," Bryce said. "One year at community college to figure out what you want to do with the rest of your lives. Then perfect 1600s will open a lot of university doors for you."

"Any university besides Portland State is out of the question," Rod insisted.

"We have to be able to stay near home and take care of you, Dad," Sprite added.

"I'm disabled, not a full invalid. I don't want my health to get in your way."

"We'll see about that."

"Now about that consulting job..."

"I'll make a decision after the con. We are going to enjoy your joint graduation and your belated birthday celebration without a thought about mortgages and tuitions and getting a second car."

Chapter Two

Bryce checked an incoming text while Rod and Sprite unloaded the back of the pearl white SUV onto a rolling luggage cart. They didn't need supervision. Still, he kept an eye on the suitcase oxygen condenser that he hated using.

Drinks in the bar. 5. LM

He smiled to himself. "Hey, kids, Looney Moose is here!" he called as Sprite counted the number of hangers inside the dry-cleaning bag. Six. He'd counted them too.

"Cool," Rod replied. He disconnected the car key from the rest collected on his ring and reluctantly handed it to the hovering valet. "Wonder what his costume will be this year?"

Satisfied that the hotel employee wouldn't steal or, worse, scratch his beloved vehicle, Rod helped his sister maneuver the hotel's rolling luggage rack into alignment with the ramp to the lobby.

Bryce had bought the rig for the family to begin with. He had the idea that when the twins began commuting to college next fall, he'd buy a smaller vehicle for his own use. Rod had a lot to say in that decision. Sprite didn't care.

He turned his attention back to the family. Then he plucked his duffel off the top of the teetering mounds of baggage.

"Uncle Lou will wear the same thing he always does: a too-large T-shirt celebrating his favorite SF movie of the week, khaki shorts and a brown, billed cap with felt moose antlers," Sprite grumbled at the family friend's lack of costume imagination. "You, as always will be the Phantom of the Opera."

"Boring!" Rod said. "Since Uncle Lou loves the movies so much, he should dress as one the starship captains. He's more fit and would show off the uniform better than most of the pudgy imitators."

Rod's phone pinged an incoming text. He stopped in the middle of the drive to check it. "Liz and her mom are half an hour out. She wants me to reserve some swim time before the gaming room opens."

Bryce had to smile at that bit of news too. He hadn't seen Lou's ex and daughter in far too long.

"Patrick is here already." Sprite beamed at the news of her boyfriend's presence. She punched an answering text into her phone. "He'll meet us at con registration in half an hour." She pocketed her cell and returned to counting luggage, again, then nodded in satisfaction.

"You know we can swim for at least an hour before the game room opens." Rod had to skip the last two steps across the hotel's porte cochere to avoid a van that was ready to pull out.

This con was good for both the twins, offering their two favorite past times, ocean swimming and computer games. Pools were good, almost a necessity to help them regulate their body temperatures. Networking with never-met friends while playing at home were also good for them. But the open ocean and being in the same room with other gamers provided the best experience for them.

"Dad, will *she* be here?" Sprite asked. She chewed her bottom lip and her scale reddened. Her eyes strayed toward the inviting ocean waves rolling in on the long sandy beach behind the hotel.

"She's not on the membership list as of last night," Bryce replied. He pocketed his phone to give him a free hand to squeeze her shoulder and still clutch his cane. His hat continued to shade the left side of his face until he donned a pandemic mask. At least he'd stuck a jaunty sea gull feather in the hatband to brighten up his appearance.

With just that little bit of reassurance, Sprite calmed down and proceeded to take charge of moving them into the hotel. She used her copy of the family credit card, signed where indicated, collected three keys and pointed her family toward the proper elevator.

The fine hairs on the back of Bryce's neck prickled. The kids were taking over his life. Damnit, he wasn't helpless. Yet.

He'd always involved them in household decisions, preparing them for the inevitable when he couldn't fend for himself, or worse, died. His injuries slowed him down, but he still earned a better than decent living, collected an apologetically huge pension, and tried his best to be a good father.

But then he was also proud that his children were so capable of fending for themselves, and well-grounded in reality, despite their grades. He valued the art of balancing a checkbook over being able to name the finest painters in the art museum.

Reality had a very different definition in their normal lives than here at the con.

"Any glitches?" Bryce asked Sprite when the elevator doors slid silently together.

"Nope. Just that Didi Desdaganet was checking in at the same time, flashing a very ringless left hand and laughing a lot about being 'Shut of her pompous ass of a father-in-law.' She shuffled her Tarot cards repeatedly—almost nervously. And awkward without the weight of her rings. And she said that my aura was off kilter so she wants to do a reading for all of us."

She paused and shook her head in puzzlement. When she lifted her head, her eyes were bright and focused again. "The hotel staff remembered us from three years ago, the last time we were here—pre-pandemic. We get the same corner suite overlooking the beach on the fourth floor every year." She punched the button for their floor. "Single king in the bedroom, two fold-outs in the living room, less than ten steps to the exit. Full bath off the bedroom, powder room off the living room. Private balcony overlooking the ocean, minifridge stocked with mineral water and protein bars, personal safe big enough for your weapon and laptop, and air conditioning cranked up to Arctic."

"First dibs on the shower," Rod muttered, rubbing his chin. In the last year his dark beard had become a lot thicker. If he had his way, he'd shave three times a day to keep it under control.

"Are we agreed, no costumes until after we register for the con?" Bryce asked as they exited the elevator and turned left. "And ocean swimming only in daylight and only with a partner. No solo stuff."

Both twins sighed heavily and replied in unison, "Yes, Dad."

Rod pushed the luggage rack while Sprite guided it. At the door, Bryce paused while Sprite unlocked it. Out of habit he counted the three seconds until the green light blinked and he heard the latch click. Rod held the door while Bryce entered. He twisted the dragon snout on his cane handle and held it up while he turned a slow circle. The crystals embedded in the dragon's eyes remained a clear, pale green, not blinking or brightening. He ripped off his pandemic mask and sighed in relief at his easier, and cooler, breathing.

"Okay, room's clear of bugs," he called and stepped out of the way while the kids stormed in and began staking out their own corners to unpack and stash things.

"Dad, you can come away from the windows now," Sprite said. She tugged lightly on his arm to make sure she had his attention.

The sound of water running in the shower and Rod's absence from the room signaled just how long he'd stared at the waves, trying to separate himself from his past.

"Regrets?" Sprite asked. She knew him too well.

"Not really." He hugged her tightly. "If I didn't have you two, I wouldn't be alive right now."

"There was a time when you didn't feel alive if you weren't out in the field chasing bad guys and predatory demons."

"That has passed. I'd rather have you two and the life we've built together. It's not fast or a continual rush of adrenaline. It's a different kind of adventure every day."

"Speaking of adventures," Rod said, exiting the bedroom, draped in a towel and smelling of his favorite shaving cream. "It's nearly three and the line at registration will be getting long and we have a date with Looney Moose at five."

"Correction, I have a date with our favorite clown. You two are on your own for dinner." He retreated to the bedroom where he found Sprite had laid out his costume for him, complete with the white Phantom mask, now edged with a fine line of black sequins. "At least they aren't red," he muttered.

"Don't forget to eat!" Sprite called after him.

"Two beers only. You'll be needing pain pills by eight, after a six hour drive," Rod added.

Bryce closed his eyes and smiled, now that his back was turned to them. He'd raised them to be thoughtful and considerate, not his nannies.

"No armor until you get your badges!" he called back.

"I'm swimming with Patrick as soon as I get my badge!" Sprite added. "The tide is out and the wind light."

"Liz should be here by then. We'll swim with you," Rod called after her retreating back.

PO DUC OPENED THE CAR door and stretched his legs outside almost before turning off the engine and releasing his seatbelt. Three hours driving from Eugene, Oregon through the twisted Coast Range left his shoulders tight, his neck a knotted mess, and his knees aching. Mimi's compact hybrid was designed for city commuting, not long mountainous drives by a tall man. But Li'l Red, as the girls called it, got a lot better mileage than his extended-cab, Dodge Ram pickup that was tricked out for wildfire fighting.

Luc, his older brother, had tracked Louis Metcalf, who knew more about UFOs and paranormal incidents than almost anyone in government employ, through plane and hotel reservations to BeachCon. As a sheriff's detective for Lane County, he had access to databases normal people didn't.

Duc had a long weekend off after the ordeal of investigating and then testifying in three arson cases in a row. He'd rather spend the time with Mimi and the girls. But the family foundation business had to come first sometimes.

Confronting Louis Metcalf was the top of his to-do list.

This latest threat from Homeland Security—rogue or normal—needed attention right now.

The convention hotel—part of a mid-priced national chain that catered to convention gatherings of all sorts, not just the Sci-Fi crowd—was fully booked from Thursday night to Monday morning. The luxury hotel next door was just too expensive. So Duc opted to pitch a tent in a campground one half mile on the other side of the con lodging. Running water, showers, and enclosed fire pits made it comfortable compared to bare-bones backpacking when he was called out to fight wildfires. Every summer of late he'd joined the Hot Shots in the bigger forest fires that required expertise in controlling. He didn't like to think about how often his stone armor had helped him save the lives of his team.

He and his family were part of a special gene pool that had evolved to protect and evacuate villagers from volcanic lava and ash in the islands of the China Sea. Or so family lore claimed.

After a few stretches to unkink his back, he set up his rudimentary camp and started walking back to the hotel along the beach. He planned to buy a membership and start looking for Louis Metcalf. He had to find out who was pressuring him to write the illegal and immoral Executive Order outlawing all paranormals.

Half an hour later, Duc tucked his driver's license back into his wallet and accepted his laminated badge, still warm from the printer, from the con volunteer, a young woman with short green hair styled into tufts with thick gel. Not an unusual look from the few cons he'd attended in high school and college.

"Say, Ducky," she used the con name he'd selected, "you any relation to Rod Maxwell?"

"I don't recognize the name," Duc hedged.

"Tall, Asian guy, about my age. He just came through the pre-registration line with his sister Sprite. They're regulars along with their dad. Dad always registers as 'Phantom of the Opera,' and dresses like the character. His real name is Bryce. We have to put legal names on the badge, just like I know the little, tiny print off to the side of your con name is Po Duc. The kids wear this weird beige chain mail that looks more like sand than metal."

Duc looked quickly over his shoulder to see if anyone was close enough to overhear this conversation. This early in the convention, most of the members had already registered and needed only to pick up their badges. Last minute attendees probably wouldn't show up until dinner or later.

He fumbled with attaching a lanyard to his badge and pulling it around his neck.

"No, I don't believe I've met Rod and Sprite."

But everyone attached to the foundation knew the name Bryce Maxwell. He'd dropped out of sight ten or twelve years ago. Before that he'd led many missions to take down predatory and dangerous paranormals—or demons as his U.N. agency labeled them. Why had he resurfaced here and now with two Asian children in tow?

Duc had to say something to this chatty, wide-eyed con volunteer to satisfy her curiosity without answering her question. "You know we Asians all look alike." He cocked a silly grin at the girl as he threw the old cliché at her.

"Yeah, funny. You might keep an eye out for them, cause Rod looks just like you, same green eyes." She returned her focus to her computer screen.

With no one behind him in line urging him to move on, he took a chance, asking his own question. "The one person I'm looking for is Louis Metcalf. His con name is Looney Moose. Has he collected his badge yet?"

"Lemme look." Green-hair tapped her keyboard and moved her scroll pad mouse around a new screen. "Yeah, the Moose is registered but hasn't checked in yet. He's another mainstay here. Funny you know him but not the Maxwells. They're all best buds along with Liz and Ellie Buchanan."

Duc returned her smile, nodded acceptance of her information and moved off.

A ubiquitous, potted Ficus tree stood at the entrance to the room designated "Con Ops." He took up a position there, pretending to read the program book. Mostly, he needed to think and study the list of pre-registered members.

Memories of an earlier con, nineteen years ago, overrode his current reason for being here. Was Jacquie Johnstone a regular here as well? He didn't think he wanted to meet her again. Her sexually predatory life-style had made him wary, and he hadn't attended BeachCon, or any other SF convention since. But what if...

He didn't know if his wild, one night stand at a science fiction convention had any consequences. Jacquie hadn't contacted him, though he'd given her his phone number before he realized the relationship could not survive their one night together.

Duc didn't know anyone outside the family who could protect themselves from intense fire and volcanic lava with such an armor that snapped into place instinctively when heat enveloped them.

Apparently, the Maxwell twins wore that armor as a costume that wasn't really a costume, but a part of themselves.

"It's just folklore from Viet Nam," his anthropology professor from the U of O had proclaimed. If he'd gotten any kind of positive response, he might have stayed an anthro major and not switched to Fire Engineering and then on to an MA in arson investigation.

"My family brought the gene with them when escaping the old country at the end of the Viet Nam War," he mumbled.

Up until Duc's generation, the gene only appeared in one child in a family, and often skipped a generation or two—only enough "mutants" to protect small villages. Now all of his siblings and first cousins manifested the mutation.

A clear sign to him that, with all of the really bad wildfire seasons, results of climate change would require more and more of his kind to protect an expanding population.

And now he'd passed it on to more than just his two daughters, Lily and Monique, ages four and six. They both showed tiny rectangular birth marks on their chins, similar to his own. They had yet to expand the single scale to full, overlapping, stone plates of armor.

He and Mimi took pains to keep their little girls away from large fires that might trigger their armor.

He wondered if the Maxwell twins were the result of that wild one-night stand and had inherited his talent as well as his green eyes.

Now that he thought about it, he realized that Jacquie had not noticed him until the Friday night bonfire on the beach, at that long ago con. The towering flames had drawn him in, pulled him away from friendly companions from the University. He'd gotten too close and triggered his armor. Only then did Jacquie pounce and lure him to her bed.

Chapter Three

"Hey, wait for me!" Sprite called to her brother and Patrick as they splashed into the waves, long legs carrying them toward deep water. A pang of regret stabbed her in the gut, that her boyfriend hadn't waited for her.

She finished laying out her beach blanket and placing her towel, dark glasses, and sunscreen in a tight grouping on the upper corner. As she always did. Compulsively.

Then she took a moment to smooth the decorative skirt of her swimsuit and tug the elastic leg band a little lower to cover the burn scar on her upper thigh.

When Dad had rescued her and Rod from Jacquie's negligent attempt at care, Sprite had developed second degree burns from diaper rash. She still bore the permanent markings of that neglect which she took pains to hide from outsiders. Including Patrick.

Rod, as usual, had just dumped his towel on the sand and run off. Patrick had done the same.

She guessed they both needed to stretch their entire bodies and burn energy—testosterone—before acting like civilized human beings around their girlfriends.

"Sprite, wait for me!" Liz Buchanan called. Tall and long legged, the strawberry blond strode purposefully down from the small bluff that marked the boundary between the hotel grounds and the public beach. Her flip flops made small slapping sounds with each step. But her two-piece swimsuit in bright red made her lithe figure stand out among the scattered occupants of the beach.

Sprite's friend could have been a model if she'd wanted to pursue a career. Instead, she'd always been a science nerd and frequently used her math and logic skills to win computer games. She was the only one of their gamer acquaintances who could routinely trounce Rod.

He always lost to her with a smile. Which made Sprite wonder if he deliberately lost to her to bolster her confidence and break through her shyness barriers.

Liz spread her own beach blanket next to Sprite's and laid her towel atop it. "I'm glad you waited. I don't like swimming alone."

Sprite hid a wince. Liz was not a strong swimmer and would hold her back when Sprite wanted to stretch her arms and kick strongly to master the waves. She had energy to burn, and the ocean offered her just the challenge she needed.

She turned her head to watch the boys' progress. They'd already found a proper depth and turned to swim southward parallel to the shore. Sprite would give Rod one lap. When he turned back toward her, she'd summon him to companion Liz while she stroked northward, with or without Patrick. He was a decent swimmer, but not as strong as she or Rod.

"How was the drive through the mountains?" Sprite asked, stalling to give the boys time to come back for them.

"Long. Mom is such a cautious driver, it took us twice as long as it should. We had to keep pulling over to let lines of traffic pass," Liz complained.

"We took the easy road and drove south on 101 from Lincoln City."

"Easy but longer," Liz replied. "You'd have saved an hour at least to drive south on the freeway and then cross over to Florence."

"But by coming south along the coast road, we stopped three times for brief swims and a great breakfast and gourmet lunch. Dad knows all the best places." Sprite began walking toward the tide line. It had reached its lowest point. The next big wave would mark the turning and the beginning of dangerous rip tides.

"You must have left home at dawn. Which at this time of year is way, way, too early." Liz lagged a little behind Sprite. She didn't seem eager to embrace the cold ocean waters.

"Do you think they'll finish building the bonfire in time to light it at sunset?" Sprite asked, to fill the time Liz needed to get wet. She pointed to a spot near the bluff where some volunteers in bright yellow safety vests placed dead branches and neatly cut firewood.

Too near the bluff, Sprite thought. And not nearly tall enough to burn all night as in years past.

"I guess they don't want to have to haul the wood further than they have to," Liz said grumpily. "I kinda don't blame them. There's not much in the way of driftwood this year and they have to supplement with cord wood."

Sprite stood at the edge of the water, allowing a lazy wave to caress her toes. Her feet acclimated to the coolness rapidly. She needed more. The wind came in from the west, enticing her with vague racial memories of a different shore in more tropical climes.

Why did Liz pause so long, just inches from the water?

The heck with her. She might be a long time con friend, and Rod's sorta long distance girlfriend, but Sprite *needed* the ocean water to complete her soul today.

She abandoned Liz and ran the few steps through the water until she dove into the next wave, the one that marked the transition of the tide. She came up long enough to shake her short dark hair out of her eyes. Liz was only knee deep and hesitating about what to do.

"Rod's coming back now, you can swim with him!" Sprite lifted her feet from the ocean bottom and struck off heading north.

Breaking all of Dad's rules to swim alone, but she knew not to drift too deep, and she always swam parallel to the shore rather than out. Besides with the incoming tide she'd have trouble getting out beyond the surf line.

This! This was what she was born to do, to let the ocean currents embrace her with loving support, and become one with waves while scouting the shore for...

She didn't know what she was looking for, only that she needed to note who played in the surf, who basked in the sun, and who approached the beach and from what direction.

And why only one hundred yards north the beach was littered with logs, uprooted trees, and branches that had drifted in with the last tide. The con beach had been stripped clean of debris.

DUC'S PHONE PINGED while he still sat on the floor contemplating his past and the convoluted relationships among those on the registration list. He stepped out of the con ops room and retreated to a quiet alcove near the elevators. "Hello, Chief. What do you need?" he answered, recognizing the caller I.D.

"Po, the forest fire south of Klamath Falls is getting worse. National Forest Service is calling out the Hot Shots," the gruff voice of Grady Baxter, his boss told him. His vocal cords had roughened prematurely from breathing too much smoke from too many fires, domestic and wild. High tech protection and breathing gear hadn't come into regular use early enough for the chief. He was only in his fifties, and looking at early retirement and disability. Duc thanked whatever divine powers watched over him that by the time he came on the line, modern equipment protected first responders better.

Duc sighed. He'd have to assign the mission to deal with Lou Metcalf and his poisonous Executive Order to another member of the foundation. He was needed on the first line of defense against that fire.

"As of this moment you are on official medical leave. You are not to respond to the call!"

"Sir," Duc protested, "They need every trained..."

"You are useless to them and to me if you fall asleep while on the front line. You are exhausted from fighting the blazes as a first responder and then the investigation into that chain of arsons."

"I will not fall asleep...."

"You did while waiting to testify yesterday. I'm granting you an extra week of medical leave. Now rest and relax until you heal mentally and physically. That firebug has been classified as sociopathic. I don't care if he is a privileged frat boy or not. If they don't execute him for murder, they'll certainly give him life in a max security asylum. You are off duty, Po. If you show up on the line, I'll throw *you* into an asylum." Chief Baxter hung up on him.

Duc frowned at his phone, willing his boss to come back on line so he could argue his point. "But they need me!"

No answer. His gut sank in resignation as well as relief. He was tired. Mentally as well as physically.

"Okay. I'm needed here as much as on the line. Wonder if the twins will show up at the bonfire?"

ROD WAVED TO LIZ AS he and Patrick waded out of the deep water toward the tide line that was creeping closer toward their towels and the bluff that marked the end of the public beach and the beginning of hotel landscaping. He hastened his steps, lifting his knees high to break free of the sucking sand and enveloping water.

He drank in her subtle curves highlighted by Liz's daring two-piece outfit. Not like her at all to wear something so eye-catching. Had she chosen it just for him? Like maybe she'd allow him a few more liberties with her body this year?

At last, he could wrap his arms around her in an all-encompassing hug. She laughed as he spun her around, the sound tickling his ear like a half-forgotten song that had implanted in his brain and wouldn't let go. Slowly, he let her slide down the full length of his body until she stood firm on her own two feet again. Then he kissed her, long and hard.

"That was some welcome," she breathed, still clinging to his shoulders as if she needed him to steady her balance.

He felt a bit dizzy himself.

"Is that Sprite bobbing around out beyond the surf line?" Patrick asked. He'd turned his back to give them an illusion of privacy, but also to stand vigil waiting for her return. "She's wearing black if that's her. But I can't tell if she's human or a seal."

"She's wearing black with pink highlights," Liz said. She'd notice that sort of thing, while it all blurred together for Rod.

His sister was his sister, no matter what she wore, so her clothing was unimportant.

The same didn't apply to his dad, however. What Bryce Maxwell wore, and *how* he wore it, signaled his mood, his energy, and his state of health. Both Rod and Sprite needed to be constantly alert to that.

"Here she comes," Patrick chortled.

Rod continued to hold Liz close to his side while they watched Sprite touch down and angle her steps toward them.

Patrick eagerly strode out to meet her when she was still knee deep in the waves, which had increased in power and surged further and further up the beach.

Sprite eagerly leaped into Patrick's arms and kissed him long and hard. The incoming tide still swirled around them. Patrick lost his balance and fell backward. Rather than let go of Sprite and flail for an even footing, he kept his arms wrapped around her waist while they both landed in the water.

"He's very protective of her," Liz said, leaning her head upon Rod's shoulder.

"Yeah." The last bit of anxiety over Sprite's welfare, without Rod standing beside her, evaporated. Patrick would take care of her, come hell or high water.

Speaking of which...

He made to move forward and drag them both away from the waves.

"Leave them be," Liz said, laughing and pulling him backward. "She's half fish and he's studying pre-med. They'll be fine."

"And so will we." Rod kissed her again, lightly, as he dragged her away from the tickle of the next wave on his toes.

As he turned her back toward the hotel, he noticed a tall Asian man watching the growing bonfire stack. It was too scanty to become a proper bonfire that would burn all night. The volunteers still had a few hours before sunset. Only days away from the summer solstice, the sun lingered in the sky until after nine. Still, plenty of time to finish the bonfire. But it should stand closer to the high tide line than the bluff where it was now.

Was that a hint of smoke on the shifting off-shore wind? Not unusual this time of year. But his chin scale began to itch.

Chapter Four

Sprite concentrated on the maze on the computer screen. Patrick, sitting at the terminal beside her, moved his character hard on her heels and in danger of pushing her aside to forge forward. She'd be back in the dungeon again if he did that.

Trap! Rod warned her from his own terminal beside the game master who'd set the pattern of the maze and the pitfalls.

She smiled to herself, hiding it behind the overlapping stone scales across her chin. Her paranormal suit looked akin to a hooded chain mail shirt. But where chainmail fit loosely over padding, her armor fit like a second skin. Because it was.

Also, unlike chain mail, her second skin was more akin to pumice than heavy metal, or stone. She could swim in her armor but hadn't today. Her pixie cut hair had just started to curl around her ears as it dried beneath the armor.

Her dark brown curls had to be a legacy from her detested mother, where Rod's thick, straight, coal black hair must be from their Asian, and unknown, bio-father.

She allowed her gaze to flit ahead and to the right of the avatar on the screen. The last trap had been far left. This one should be near right, or... or directly in front of her.

Aha! She'd found the pattern. She side-stepped the trap and hastened toward the prize at the center. She'd never been able to beat Patrick honestly before. She wiggled in her chair, not daring to show her excitement.

"How'd you do that?" Patrick demanded, half standing.

"I saw the pattern," she replied, trying not to gloat.

"Well, that does it. I'm done for now. Want to grab a pizza?" He moved to stand very close to her. His fingers entwined with hers.

Warm joy filled her.

"I... um... Let me see what Rod wants to do." She ducked her head so she wouldn't have to meet Patrick's gaze.

Go ahead, Rod replied. *Liz and I will catch up.*

Sprite scanned the gamers filling the room and waiting impatiently for a terminal. Some of them had brought laptops to plug into the network. Ah, there was Liz Buchanan at the end of the long library table where Rod sat. After their time on the beach, she'd taken care to change into her Amazon warrior costume. She bristled with tough, touch-me-not plastic weapons that shouted a statement of her independence.

Does she know she's going on a double date with you? Sprite sent to her brother.

Implied. He flashed her a grin, then turned his gaze toward the fierce young woman pounding the table beside the keyboard.

"Hey, Sprite, look, your dad is picking up Honor Harrington!" Patrick called. He'd wandered over to the wall of windows overlooking the mezzanine and the bar below.

Both Sprite and Rod scooted out the door to lean over the wrought-iron railing.

Her dad sat in an armchair with a tiny, round, pedestal table slightly to his left. That gave him room to extend the leg that didn't bend as well as it should. The table also kept intruders from tripping over his vulnerable knee. He tapped his cane against the floor as he constantly surveyed the gathering crowd, neatly avoiding engaging the stiffly upright female hovering near him.

She wore a dark blue business suit and carried a briefcase. Her cropped hair and erect posture nearly shouted her military connection. No wonder Patrick had thought her a con member in costume suitable to his favorite fictional spaceship captain.

The younger man standing just behind her left shoulder could only be her subordinate, also wearing a subdued suit and carrying a briefcase. He could be as invisible as Dad could when he wanted.

Trouble.

"Yee haw! I can picture the fan fiction: Phantom of the Opera vs. Honor Harrington. Smack down Saturday night at the Masquerade." Patrick chortled. "But why is Didi Dogooder so interested?"

Sure enough, Didi had shifted her own little round table six inches closer to Dad. She had her trusty her crystal ball on a three-pronged brass stand on her right. Her brightly-colored Tarot cards—the witch and cauldron and set—she dealt an elaborate fan directly in front of her. She appeared to be studying her props rather than listening.

Sprite didn't have to say anything. She and Rod dashed toward the spiral staircase leading down to the bar area sunk three steps below the level of the lobby.

She took a deep breath and began withdrawing her armor. Rod did the same. By the time they fetched up flanking Bryce they were back in their ubiquitous jeans and long-sleeved tees sporting the con logo.

Sprite picked at rough skin on the back of her left hand. Not good. Her instincts wanted that armor fully engaged. This was more important than the vague whisper of smoke on the wind—the hotel air conditioning filtered out most of that.

"It's 7:30, Dad, where's Looney Moose?" she asked, hands braced on his armchair, whispering into his ear.

"Have you eaten, Dad?" Rod asked mimicking her pose on the other side of the chair. No way would Miss Priss get to their father without going through them.

"General Maxwell, sir, I insist we have a word in private." The female military entity held out a business card.

Sprite grabbed it from her since Dad kept his hands occupied fiddling with the grip of his cane. Trouble, big time.

"Major Marjorie Arbuthnaught," Sprite read out loud. "Homeland Security."

"Around here we call you people *Gnomeland* Security," Rod added.

"Cute costume, ma'am. I almost believed you to be Honor Harrington," Patrick said. He must have followed the twins down the stairs and come up behind and to the right of her. "I *know* he's the Phantom, proved it often enough. Mr. Maxwell, ask her if she can sing. Please, oh please, I'm dying to

39

hear her answer. I've already got the skit for the Masquerade outlined in my head."

Major A whirled on him, a snarl on her angled features. Nothing cute about her.

Her comrade reached for a weapon tucked into the back of his waistband.

Rod stepped in front of Dad.

A ghost of a smile tugged at Dad's mouth, even on the left side which was a lot less mobile than the right.

"No, Major. We get no more private than this." Dad looked up at her. Then he did the unthinkable. He took off his mask, revealing the full extent of the overstretched, smooth skin of plastic surgery over the worst of the warped skin of burn scars.

The major gulped and remained stiffly in place. But she did avert her attention from Patrick. She kept her features well-schooled. Obviously, she'd either seen worse or knew what to expect.

Not so the younger male. He turned his head away and placed a fist in front of his mouth. His throat worked as he swallowed bile. Repeatedly.

"This is what happens when I allow HS to set the rules." Dad replaced his mask.

They all breathed a little deeper and easier.

"I was told that you got caught in a fire fight, sir," Major A said. "I presumed automatic weapons with terrorists."

"You presumed wrong." Dad shifted his weight as if preparing to stand.

Rod was right there offering his arm for support.

For once Dad didn't refuse and leaned heavily on Rod while bracing on the sturdy cane.

At least he couldn't draw the fifteen-inch blade from the depths of the ebony cane while putting that much weight on it. BeachCon had a strict "No Weapons" policy.

"Did you order dinner?" he asked, engaging Sprite's gaze.

"Sub sandwiches in the room?" She pulled her phone out of her back pocket and sent the order. She knew that Dad was not terribly fond of pizza, having eaten too much of it when he couldn't cook for the twins, and responsibility for meals fell to their teenage appetites.

"Sir, this is important," Major A interrupted.

"Not as important as me having food in my stomach before I take Class A prescription drugs for pain."

"Sir, Louis Metcalf has been kidnapped," the younger officer spoke for the first time.

Oh, no! Not Uncle Lou. Sprite's gut clenched in apprehension. Her father's best friend and a constant in their lives for many years. She couldn't imagine who would kidnap him. Or why. She searched in vain for Liz. Uncle Lou was her father, after all.

The tall girl had remained in the gaming room, avoiding any kind of confrontation. As usual.

Rod needed to break the news to her.

"He texted me about three, four hours ago. That's too soon to even know he's missing and deploy you two." Dad straightened to his full six feet of height, only a finger width shorter than Rod. Even though he'd lost a lot of weight and muscle mass since the fire, he still made an intimidating figure.

Major A and her companion looked around with wary gazes.

The rest of the crowded and noisy bar seemed to have retreated, their attention on the news flash on the big screen above the impressive array of expensive liquor. A wildfire east of them, near Klamath Falls, had just exploded from a containable fifty acres to over six hundred acres with a rising east wind.

That explained the whiff of smoke.

But not the absence of Lou Metcalf.

The fire tugged at her heart like... an overwhelming need to armor up and protect while evacuating those in the path of the firestorm... just like the night that Dad got caught in a burning house when she and Rod were six. It was the first time their scales had erupted and covered their entire bodies.

"We have a ransom note, sir. They want all of Mr. Metcalf's UFO files and a private jet fueled and ready to fly to a destination of their choosing, and $10 million cash by dawn." Major A held up a small tablet in landscape position with enlarged text on the screen.

Sprite jerked her attention away from the compelling wildfire on the TV screens. Her back itched with the need to dash to it and help suppress it. She wouldn't know where to begin with that chore.

Her Dad's needs also tugged at her. She could almost feel the wheels churning in her father's mind. More like she knew his facial expressions too well. He'd worked with Uncle Lou before the fire that changed their lives. Somehow, he was involved with U.N. black ops. Just like Dad. They rarely talked about that work, but she and her twin knew about it.

She and Rod exchanged thoughts faster than she could put them into words. Jointly they put pressure on Dad's side, urging him toward the elevators that would take them up to the suite.

General Bryce Maxwell, retired, shook them off. "May I study this a moment?" He handed his cane to Rod and reached for the tablet.

"I'll transfer it to your device, sir."

Bryce held up his phone with a sensor pointed at a similar spot on the rim of the tablet. He and Major A touched screens in unison, exchanging a complex code.

Patrick's eyes went wide, and his mouth gaped.

"You will forget you ever saw any of this," Rod snarled at him.

Patrick bobbed his head.

Sprite touched his jaw to make him close it. "This is a con. Role playing games don't stop for reality. It's all a game. This one is adults only." So much for a make out session at the bonfire. She doubted that Dad and the major would wind up their business before the event.

"Yeah, sure. A game. That explains it all." Patrick scooted three steps away. Still there. Still observing.

Sprite hated lying to him.

Two blinks from lights on each device and Bryce brought his oversized phone closer to his face. Then he handed it to Rod. "What do your younger and stronger eyes tell you?"

"You need food and your secure laptop."

"My boss has spoken." Bryce nodded to Major A and began the march toward the elevators, without using his cane or a limp.

How much did that display of bravado cost him? With retired General Maxwell one never knew which image he projected was real.

Chapter Five

Bryce rubbed absently at his left thigh while studying the screen of his phone during the elevator ride. He trusted his kids to get him back to the room without compromising their security. They waved and chatted with people getting on and off the elevator, friends from previous conventions, and gaming companions they kept in touch with.

A party of five stayed with them all the way to the fourth floor. Bryce swallowed nervously, then really looked at their clothing. Jeans and tee shirts, parents and adolescents. The father even had the Gnomeland Security collage on his shirt.

Regular con members. He thought he might have met them before.

They turned left along the long corridor. The twins steered him right. This time he opened the door himself and turned on his scanner before entering. The dragon eyes began glowing red almost immediately. He cursed silently as he signaled the kids to stay outside. Then he drew the blade from the ebony cane sheath. The shaft of the cane made a second weapon in his trained hands.

Slowly he drew in a long breath, held it for three heartbeats, then released the pent-up air. He'd turned off the AC before leaving. The wind had shifted to offshore and had turned cool and moist. Now the HVAC unit rumbled and strained to keep the room colder than even the twins liked. He turned off the AC from the thermometer on the wall beside the door. Without the mechanical noise, he heard someone else breathing and smelled the rancid sweat of a nervous man. Only male testosterone smelled like that.

Without thinking he let his training take over. He yanked open the louvered doors of the closet, pulled a stranger into the room. A quick flick brought the shaft of the cane across the windpipe. The cloth hand loop stretched and anchored one end of the tube while he grabbed the loose end on the other end, keeping up the pressure on his captive's airways, while pricking the man's ribs with the blade through a camouflage uniform.

This could be a con prankster.

He didn't think so. Not after learning that Looney Moose was missing and being held for ransom.

"Who sent you?" he whispered and shoved him into the main room of the suite, keeping his punishing hold on him.

"*Nyet,*" the blond man spat. He was as tall as Bryce and more muscular, but powerless against the pressure on his throat and the knife tickling his ribs through the thick cloth of his uniform.

Behind him, he heard the click-clack of scaled armor snapping into place. Damnit! He didn't want the kids exposed to foreign mercenaries.

"I speak Russian but my bodyguards don't. Who sent you?" he asked again. This time he let the knife penetrate the first layer of skin. The scent of wet copper penetrated his senses.

"Homeland Security," the man replied in heavily accented English.

"Bullshit." Bryce pushed his blade an eighth of an inch deeper.

The man's Slavic pale skin blanched further.

"They hire mercenary."

Possible. "More bullshit." The knife went in another eighth of an inch, almost to the muscle wall.

"My government."

"Russia. Why am I not surprised? Why are you here?" He eased up a fraction on the cane pressing on the throat apple.

"Mr. Metcalf. You know where he is. *You* know what he seeks. We seek too."

Proof of space aliens.

"Get Honor Harrington up here now," Bryce barked to the kids.

"'Onor 'Arrington? What is this?" the Slavic mercenary asked. He relaxed a bit. Planning something.

Bryce pushed the blade again. He felt the slight resistance of muscle. Damn, the man didn't have an ounce of fat on him.

Time was, Bryce didn't either. He hadn't gone soft, just a bit paunchy. Physical therapy and swimming with his kids took care of average fitness, but he wasn't as honed as he needed to be to continue this for much longer. His left shoulder already ached from the unnatural angle.

Sprite scooted around him, back in jeans and tee. Maybe, if they were very lucky, the Russian merc hadn't seen the stone armor.

"Now talk or I turn you over to the real Homeland Security. She's not nearly as gentle as I am." He gave the blade another little push and downward slice.

The odor of dripping blood filled the room.

Sprite handed him a coil of nylon rope. He raised his eyebrows at her. She shrugged. "Never know when it might come in handy."

Thank you, JRR, for that lesson, he thought

"Rightly so. Bind his hands behind his back, then pass the extra length around his throat. Secure it back to his hands in that knot I showed you back in Girl Scouts."

She grinned like a feral cat about to pounce on an exhausted mouse.

Bryce heaved in a deep breath, admiring the quiet efficiency he'd instilled in both of his children, and afraid of what he might unleash into the world if he ever let them go.

STILL IN ARMOR, ROD ran up to Major A. She'd taken over Dad's chair in the bar, sitting back as if viewing her queendom. Her gaze shifted from group to group. A paunchy, middle-aged man in a black pseudo military uniform, complete with a beret and patch, wandered over with two bottles of beer in hand. He offered one to the lady.

"Captain Harrington, so good of you to join us this evening." He kept a straight face and never broke character, though his eyes appraised her with pleasure.

Rod almost laughed at the hopeful stranger. He didn't have time for con games.

"Who are you and why are you bothering me?" Major A managed to look down her nose at the man. Not Honor Harrington. She looked more like a displeased Queen Elizabeth I.

Rod choked back a laugh. Then he decided to end the charade. He took up a position immediately in front of Major A. "You are needed upstairs. Now." He turned on his heel and sprinted toward the stairs.

Major A sat, waiting.

A screeching wail erupted from the back of the bar. In full kilted gear, a phalanx of bagpipers marched out to begin a circuit of the lobby around the sunken bar.

The major and her unnamed minion bounced up and followed Rod without further question.

This time of night at a con, four flights of stairs were faster and less congested than the bank of four elevators.

The HS officers proved as fit as he. No panting, no slowing. Straight up they went, taking the turns at each landing with a minimum two steps and proceeding.

"What?" Major A asked as they faced the door to the fourth floor. Rod used his room key to gain access to the restricted area. "Russian mercenary," he spat.

The HS officers drew their weapons. "They're all effing crazy," Major A muttered.

"There's too much at stake to take a chance," her junior reminded her.

They followed Rod cautiously, in that smooth sideways shuffle, keeping their weight forward toward the balls of their feet, prepared to sprint or dodge as necessary. Rod barged ahead, confident that if his armor withstood an inferno of a burning house, a bullet would have to work hard to penetrate overlapping layers of stone.

The scene in the living room looked too placid. Dad sat in the armchair in front of the desk, laptop open and connected to the hotspot on his phone—not the open signal provided by the hotel. Sprite cleaned her nails with the fifteen-inch blade from the cane.

And a blond stranger wearing green camo knelt on the floor between them, a length of sturdy nylon rope running from his wrists bound behind his back, around his neck, down through his legs and refastened to the wrist. The knots looked professional and slick.

"I coated the knots with clear nail polish. He won't break free soon," Sprite said, returning her attention to her... um... manicure.

"Wait a minute, these guys never travel alone," Major A said, inspecting the knots and nodding in approval.

"His companion is on the balcony, debating jumping from the fourth floor onto a concrete patio, filled with bar patrons carrying drinks and hot hors d'oeuvres, or facing a disabled old man and two teens," Dad said.

The younger HS officer, who never had been introduced, ran to the sliding doors, peered through the tiny gap in the curtains, then looked to his boss. She held up three fingers, and silently lowered each one in turn. The man threw open the window as the major rushed through, weapon pointed, finger on the trigger.

Muffled grunts and groans followed.

They returned a moment later with a second mercenary, shorter than the first, but just as muscled and blond, in tow. The major held her pistol to the back of the head of her prisoner and twisted his arm up behind his back. "Call for back up," she barked.

"Why not just shoot them?" her subordinate asked, keeping his weapon trained on the merc as well.

"Because they'll tell us where to find Metcalf," she snapped.

"Doubtful," Dad said, closing the laptop and pushing the chair away from the desk. He stopped rolling when he was between Rod and the Major.

Rod wanted to push him aside so he could keep an eye on the action in the center of the room.

"If they know anything about Metcalf, they wouldn't need to confront this crippled old man and his teenage children," Dad said. "Rod, change out of your costume, then help the major take out the trash. Sprite, you go with them." He pushed against the floor with his toe and rolled to her side. He retrieved the cane from her grasp but did not reassemble it.

Then Major A's gaze riveted on Rod. She almost dropped her grip on her prisoner's arm. He struggled to escape. Sprite tripped him with the ebony shaft of the cane.

Major A looked from Rod to the mercs and back again.

"Um... maybe I should change out of costume," Rod said, edging his way toward the bedroom. He hated shifting in public even though it had been necessary earlier while approaching his dad and the two HS officers.

"Don't bother. With you and your sister, we don't need Metcalf, or these two prisoners," the major said, eyes narrowed in calculation.

"That tells me more than you intended to reveal, Major," Dad said. "Now tell me why you find my children a substitute for a highly placed photo analyst with a security clearance a lot higher than yours, or mine, for that matter?"

"You don't have the security clearance to know why."

"Wanna make a bet?"

The major gulped. She had to be running multiple plans through her head and discarding most of them.

"Sprite, call your boyfriend and tell him that the Phantom is about to throw Captain Harrington out on her ass." Dad stood up to his full intimidating majesty and slowly removed his mask and cape.

Rod giggled. "The video will go viral in about twelve point three seconds."

"Ten, if I have anything to say about it." Sprite grinned, as she punched one number on her phone.

"Wait. Wait just a minute." Major A held up one hand, palm out in a universal sign to halt. "I get the phantom reference. But who in the hell is Captain Honor Harrington?"

"Google her. I have a feeling you will have a lot of time to read at least a dozen novels from your holding cell waiting to be debriefed as to how and why you allowed your face to be plastered all over the internet. I'm not sure if the old rules still apply. You might get lucky and receive only a courts martial and dishonorable discharge along with loss of your security clearance. Or they might just shoot you. That's quicker and less messy," Dad said.

Rod took the opportunity to escape to the other room and collapse his armor in record time.

As he emerged, he heard his dad say, "Sprite is filming you. Now I get your promise, and word of honor, that you will forget my children exist or this video of you capturing two foreign terrorists will go viral. I will retrieve my friend Louis Metcalf with my own team, but only if HS and all the other agencies keep their distance."

Major A opened her mouth as if to protest, then clamped it shut again. "Very well. But we will be tailing you."

"For your own safety, stay out of sight, and keep your distance. You do not know what you are dealing with."

"Do you?" the major snarled.

"Yes. And contact Lou's assistant. She was probably the last person to see him alive."

Major A ushered her companion and two prisoners out the door into the arms of six armed military police. Rod closed the door on their hind ends, and engaged the deadbolt. He wanted to kick the door symbolically but decided against it as too childish.

"So, I guess Looney Moose's crazy conspiracy theories about alien contact with the government finally got him into trouble," Rod mused. "Who do you think has him?"

"I think our dinner has arrived. I don't know about you, but I'm a bit peckish," Dad said as he cleared the desk of his laptop and peripherals.

"What are we going to do, Dad?" Rod asked as his father dealt with the delivery guy and brought three bags of redolent sandwiches into the room.

"We need to start packing. We leave by midnight."

"But the con has just started!" Sprite wailed. "And Tess Noncoiré and her kids are singing in concert after opening ceremonies—in about an hour."

"Sorry about that. But you know what I used to do for a living. You know that only something as important as your lives would drag me out of retirement." He eyed them both.

"Okay." Rod sat and began eating. He knew the rules. Eat when you can, take a pee when you can. Sleep when you can. Because you never know when you'll get a chance again. That was one thing every spy movie or action TV show got wrong. Those heroes went days without eating or sleeping and then never stopped to pee. They just dove into a fight without a care.

He'd be different when his chance came to succeed his father in the adventures ahead. "Where to?"

"First step is one I swore I'd never take," Dad said around mouthfuls of a redolent meat ball sandwich.

"No," Sprite gasped.

"Are you sure, Dad?" Rod added.

"Yes. We need to go see your mother.

Chapter Six

"Interesting," Duc muttered. He twisted his barstool around to face the hovering bartender. He'd spotted the teens, he now knew to be twins, on the beach, and then again, an hour earlier when they exited the elevator on the mezzanine. They'd worn ordinary swimsuits and board shorts outside the con precincts. But when they entered their chosen venue playing computer games, they wore full stone armor.

He remembered the relief at being able to shed his tight control over his human body when he attended his last convention. Everyone assumed his armor was just a clever costume.

His back itched with the need to head east to fight the fire splashed all over the news. His reaction was worse outside where he actually smelled the smoke.

But the need to stay here now that he had little doubt he'd sired those two teens also tugged at him. A surge of masculine pride surged through him. A smile spread from his webbed toes to his straight black hair.

He needed to find out more about the twins and why they hovered around Bryce Maxwell so attentively. Protectively.

He grabbed his beer from the bar and found the quiet alcove near the elevators. From there, he could watch the Maxwell family while he informed Mimi of his latest discovery. Eight o'clock on a Friday night, she'd be halfway through her shift at the hospital, a nurse in the burn unit. Their daughters would spend the night with Mimi's parents since he was out of town.

"Hi, sweetheart. Miss me?" he greeted her when she answered on the first ring.

"Of course." She paused. "Baxter called me," she whispered.

"Me too. I promise to stay away from the fire."

A rustle of movement by the elevator made him turn his back on the woman who rushed furtively toward con ops. She wore brightly colored leggings in a splashy tie-die pattern that did nothing to hide her jiggling thighs. Her overblouse in the same loud yellow as the dominant color on her lower half, hung in asymmetrical lines that didn't disguise her sagging belly. Not someone who took care of her fitness level.

Then something in the tilt of her head and the avaricious squint of her eyes looked familiar. Jacquie Johnstone!

He gulped, trying to think of a way out of the alcove without attracting her notice.

"Duc, are you still there?" Mimi sounded a little panicky.

"Yes, darling. There's something I need to talk to you about. Do you remember I told you about the last time I attended BeachCon?"

He couldn't help but watch Jacquie approach the suited man who'd been part of the confrontation with the Maxwells. Dang he wished he'd overheard that discussion. As it was, he felt like he was one of the looky-loos hanging around a fire. Fascinated and horrified at the same time by the disaster.

"You got him?" Jacquie stage-whispered loud enough for people in the noisy bar to hear if they listened. She'd not been discreet nineteen years ago either.

"Yeah, Lou's nicely locked up, and not talking. We'll break him though," the suited man said quietly.

"I don't care about the Looney Moose. I found him for you, now pay up!" Jacquie spoke in normal tones while shaking her fist in his face.

The minion's knuckles turned white under his tightening grip on his briefcase.

"I paid you half up front. The rest will be in your account when he talks." He pivoted with military precision.

"You'll pay me tonight, at the bonfire, cash, or I spill it all to General Maxwell."

"I'll call you back when you get off shift. I love you," Duc whispered into the phone.

The con always needed volunteers and having a professional firefighter run safety at the bonfire was a bonus they'd not likely turn down.

BRYCE'S PHONE CHIMED just as he chomped down on the last potato chip that came with his meatball sub sandwich. He'd really eaten too much, but his kids fussed if he didn't clean his plate. Too many times in the past he'd lost his appetite for weeks on end and lost valuable weight and muscle tone. They feared that if he fell into that state too often, he'd continue to decline rather than rally and regain health.

He pulled the mobile out of his pocket and stared at the screen a long moment. A grin tugged one side of his face upward. "Speak of the Devil and she shall appear," he grunted after he'd answered the call. He knew that Jacquelyn Johnstone heard his comment.

Sprite edged her chair backward, her head turned right and left, seeking avenues of escape. Bryce's heart wrenched that his children *feared* their bio-mother. Jacquie hadn't been alone with them since she'd relinquished custody to Bryce when they were two.

Rod left his chair to stand beside his sister. He rested one hand on her shoulder, as much in comfort as to keep her in place. In the way of twins, they shared their energy and comfort, drawing strength and calm from each other.

Bryce could tell when the boy spotted the portable chain ladder that could hang over the balcony. It was meant as a fire escape but offered solutions when other things threatened.

"Jacquie," Bryce said flatly as he pressed the screen to activate the speaker.

"Bryce, my darling, where are you? I thought for sure you and my babies would be in line for opening ceremonies and stay for the concert." The woman's breathy voice sounded squeakier than usual. He didn't have to see her face on the screen to know she pouted, full lips pursed to make them appear kissable.

He knew better.

"What do you want?" As much as he needed to speak to her, he couldn't vary his routine disapproval or he'd raise her suspicions—or her hopes of more access to the twins.

"We aren't babies any more, Jacquie," Rod chimed in.

"No, no, I guess you aren't. But I still remember how sweet and beautiful you both were..."

"All two-year-olds appear sweet and beautiful. But they cramped your lifestyle, so you gave them up," Bryce reminded her. She never had publicly admitted her addiction to sex, but Bryce had made a point of keeping track of her, and all the signs were there: clinging to a different man each day of a con, booking hotel rooms with a king bed and a jacuzzi, always leaving her blouse open and unbuttoned below her bra line, the way she stood with one hip thrust forward as if opening the availability to her crotch. The list went on and on. The kids knew about her and didn't like any of it.

He shuddered at the memory of the filthy, crying, hungry toddlers, and their soiled diapers. Jacquie had left them alone in her hotel room with a box of cereal to feed them for three days and the television set blaring cartoons to drown out their screams of fear and loneliness.

Sprite had figured out how to wiggle out of her tight legged diaper when her rash turned to second degree burns. In effect, she'd potty trained herself and her brother that weekend.

Jacquie considered convention parties and hook ups with exotically costumed con members—especially if they were true paranormals—more essential than the welfare of her children.

Jacquie met the accusation with silence. She had no defense.

Normally Bryce would have ended the call right then and there, but he needed her skills.

"How'd you find me, Jacquie?" He finally broke the intense silence.

"You know me. I can find anyone if I set my mind to it." She did have that unique talent, which made her very useful in her day job as head of the canine search and rescue department for a mountain county. He refused to even think about how close she lived to his Portland home lest the kids move out on their own for his deception that she lived in another state—far, far away from them.

"Care to tell me where I can find Louis Metcalf?" he asked the woman.

Another long silence. Then, "Who? I don't think I know him."

"Looney Moose," Rod said.

Sprite still hadn't spoken.

"Oh, him. The clown with sagging felt antlers attached to a Forest Service billed cap, and movie T shirts."

"That's the one," Bryce confirmed.

"I haven't seen him here yet. Is he registered? Maybe I can suss out his hotel room for you. The desk clerk is delicious looking and very vulnerable. He's young enough he might be a virgin. And you know how well I like innocent..."

"Cut the crap, Jacquie. You never did care if you corrupted your children."

"They are just babies..."

"We're eighteen and high school graduates!" Rod protested. "I've registered for the draft. We've registered to vote."

"Oh." Her voice lost the seductive breathiness. "How time flies."

She had seen the children several times over the years, but only at cons when they knew their dad was close by to step between them and their bio-mother. Bryce made sure he could separate his children from her until they were old enough and angry enough to defend themselves.

"We need to talk, Jacquie. Lou isn't here. He may have been kidnapped. I need to know who and why as well as the where."

"I'll be right up."

"No. We will be down when we've finished our dinner. Wait for us outside the ballroom. I have little interest in the opening ceremonies, but I do know Sprite and Rod want to go to the concert afterward. They've made friends with the teens in the Celestial Vines band." He ended the call, not mentioning how much the kids were looking forward to the bonfire later. It had become a ritual for this con, one they'd all been deprived of during the pandemic.

"I guess that means we don't have to leave the con before it truly gets started?" Sprite finally spoke up. She had her priorities.

"For now. I'm keeping our plans fluid."

"I'll be in the gaming room if you need me." She flounced out, halfway transformed to armor before she opened the door. She'd only eaten half her sandwich and none of her chips.

Chapter Seven

Sprite found Patrick waiting for her in the gaming room. He idly played a solitaire card game while watching the glass door. He smiled so brightly as he caught sight of her that Sprite blushed. The weight of her personal gloom lifted from her shoulders and made her feet want to dance.

It was so easy—almost too easy—to rush into his outstretched arms and let his strength enfold her in a tight hug. He was still dressed in his trademark bright turquoise shorts in a wild island print that highlighted the dark gold of his con T shirt. Almost a costume.

For the first time she could remember, her second skin of overlapping scales of rock-hard pumice felt too heavy and uncomfortable. She didn't want the barrier of her paranormal origins between them.

Without thinking, she allowed the scales to flow back into her body, ready to protect... she wasn't sure what she was designed to protect against, but for now settled for keeping her bio-mother away from her.

"You don't usually do that..." Patrick said. He stood back from her, his hands on her shoulders the only point of contact between them. His gaze travelled up and down her body, now covered only in a light, tie-dye gauzy skirt and her own old-gold colored con T-shirt.

Of course, she had revealed to him her true nature, three years ago when they'd first kissed. At cons, three or four a year in different locations, they were a couple. The rest of the year he lived in Seattle and attended the University of Washington, majoring in pre-med. She lived two hundred miles south of him while she finished high school.

Their dating life consisted of texts, video chats, and online games.

"My bio-mother is here," she replied. The gloom descended, but not as heavy as before.

"Have you considered confronting her?" He'd taken a couple of psych classes and talked about becoming a psychiatrist specializing in criminal cases. Jacquelyn Johnstone, as well as other con goers who played out their violent fantasies in costumes with fake weapons fascinated him.

"I've written her five letters since we first talked about this."

"But did you mail them?" he asked, cocking his eyebrow. Tall and lanky, he looked too much like Mr. Spock to not be in costume.

"No, I burned them." She hung her head, not wanting to admit her shortcomings.

"Well, that's a start. At least you have expressed your feelings and gotten them out of your head, temporarily."

"Can we just play a game until the concert starts?"

"Avoidance?"

"Yes. My dad is meeting her at the opening ceremonies, and I really don't want to be there. She'll want to hug me and fuss over me like I was a two-year-old again. When she was on the phone with him, she called Rod and me her babies and acted as if sixteen years hadn't passed since she gave us up for adoption."

"What I can't figure out is why she waited so long to give you up." He escorted her to the table where the computers they'd used earlier were paused on the game, right where they'd left off.

Like Jacquie had paused her emotional life right where she had left off with her children.

"Dad says that her primary goal in life is to have sex with as many paranormals as possible. She keeps a record book of them all. It's a game with her, and she saves all her money to attend cons because she knows that 'demons' hang out where they can wear their normal skin, and no one notices."

"Like you and Rod?"

"Yeah. Most of the time we have to fight the instinct to armor up, especially when it's hot out. That's why we have a pool instead of a backyard. Anyway, Jacquie knows that a paranormal sired us, and she was afraid that whoever might adopt us wouldn't know how to deal with us and end up throwing us away." Sprite played with the trackpad on the computer rather than look at him.

"Now, that's almost funny, ironic in a terrible way. She neglected you two beyond the point of abuse while thinking she was protecting you from potential abuse." Patrick leaned forward to peer at his screen.

Neither one of them had activated their game.

"Fortunately, Dad swept in and rescued us. He knew all about 'demons' and convinced Jacquie he could protect us better than she could."

"That's almost too much of a coincidence," Patrick mused. He swung his highbacked chair so he could face her, keeping his left hand near the keyboard but not playing.

Sprite appreciated that he wasn't so addicted to gaming that he couldn't focus on her.

"Well, Dad was a... an investigative journalist who'd been on the trail of a murderous demon. That's when he figured out that the bad kind of otherworldly paranormal creatures hang out at cons, as well as benign ones who just want a few days of letting our guard down."

"And I'm glad he sees fit to bring you and Rod to the cons. Otherwise I'd never have met you."

Before she could react beyond a smile, five other teens crashed into the room. All of them were in middle school and high on caffeine, too busy shoving each other to get to the best terminals first to notice Sprite and Patrick.

They seemed to suck all the air out of the room.

"Let's go to the concert," Patrick suggested.

"Stay close?" She pleaded with him.

He bent his head and kissed her lightly. "Of course."

ROD SAT CROSS-LEGGED on the floor behind an ubiquitous Ficus tree near the double doors leading to the Grand Ballroom. The pebble filler in the square, raised planter kind of matched his armor in color and texture. Unless his dad and Jacquie were actively looking for him, they shouldn't spot him.

He had to remember to stay very still. One of the first lessons in survival his dad had taught him was that color and movement attract the eye.

Sprite was better than he at this stillness thing.

"I need to hear what *that woman* has to stay," he whispered to himself.

Sure enough, within a few heartbeats, Jacquie wandered toward the closed doors. She'd gained weight since he last saw her. Her too-tight leggings and floppy over-blouse gave her a doughy appearance he found unflattering. At least she'd lost the fake red hair dye and now kept her natural light brown locks cropped to chin level and combed sleekly. Sprite got her vertically challenged genes from her.

From inside the ballroom came the raucous sounds of the Master of Ceremonies cracking jokes and prancing around like a maniac with sound effects that never quite crossed the line into not-family-friendly territory. He was such an exuberant personality, dressed in khaki shorts and loud flowered shirts, wild blond hair pulled back into ponytail, and neatly trimmed goatee, few noticed his obesity or remembered his real name. He was just the Master of Ceremonies. At least that's what his con badges always named him—without the legal name printed in tiny letters on the bottom left corner.

Dad had chosen the right place for a private conversation. The noise from the ballroom should mask any listening devices except closely listening ears.

Dad approached from a different angle, leaning heavily on his cane. The dragon eyes glowed a reassuring green. No electronic listening devices.

Rod didn't like the way Dad leaned so heavily on his artificial support. They'd had a long drive to the convention on the southern Oregon coast, then the trauma of Honor Harrington and her crew, plus the Russian mercenaries. How many pain pills had he needed to take? Rod shuddered at the idea that his near-indestructible appearing father might have resorted to a morphine injection to get through this interview. The man was still full of tricks, but more and more he resorted to tricks because his strength failed him. Good thing Rod was nearby to lend a supporting arm if needed.

"I want to see my babies," Jacquie said the moment Dad was within earshot.

"If I let you see them, will you help me find Lou Metcalf?" Bryce stopped three long paces away from the woman. Then he shifted his grip on the cane. It became a weapon in waiting.

Rod braced himself, ready to launch himself through the tree if necessary.

"How do I know that you will live up to your promise?" Jacquie asked. She studied her long, polished nails rather than look Bryce in the eye.

"You don't, any more than I know you will come through with a location while Lou is still alive. You've been known to sell out to a higher bidder or even withhold information until too late if the price is right."

"I would never..."

"What about that plastic surgeon lost on the glacier three years ago? He was known to work with organized crime and was about to go to the FBI with photos of convicted criminals he'd help to change their identity."

"What about him? He loved mountain hiking. Not my fault he fell into a crevasse."

"Autopsy results proved he'd lived fifteen hours after the fall, and you, the legendary finder of lost hikers, were within ten feet of the crevasse rim. You *should* have heard his cries for help. You sent the dogs and your teams two miles in the other direction." Bryce started tapping his cane in agitation.

If Jacquie had any smarts at all, she'd have noticed how Bryce now carried his weight equally on both feet. The cane was just for show, feigning weakness, as much a part of his costume as the cape and mask. Rod settled back against the wall, more willing to watch than intervene.

"He was as much a criminal as the mob bosses he protected. For a half mill, you'd have left the man lost. I keep track of your financials. You're struggling to make your mortgage payments." Jacquie defended herself.

Rod had to smile at that. Sprite kept the family accounts (she found beauty in neatly ordered columns of numbers) and knew how much Dad stashed into trust funds after every job for U.N. black ops teams. The mortgage was also a cover. They could pay it off at any time if they chose and still have enough money for college, for both himself and Sprite.

"I would never exchange the life of an innocent for mere money, and you know it. Besides, a half million dollars is peanuts for the mob. You should have held out for more or reported the payer to the FBI."

They engaged in a long moment of silent stubbornness.

Jacquie caved first. Rod could see it in her less than rigid posture.

"I'll need a photo of the Looney Moose, without his costume hat. Anyone could wear that hat, and few would know the difference because all they see is the hat, not his face."

Bryce produced a three-by-five print from his inside jacket pocket. Jacquie grabbed it away from him and studied it for several long moments before tucking it into her belt pouch.

"Now when can I see the children?"

Rod almost snorted. So, he and his twin had graduated from "babies" to "children" in the space of two minutes. He shifted his concentration to the woman's face, needing to see her shock and despair when Dad produced his next revelation.

"They have both gone into hiding. You'll have to dig them out of whatever cave they've crawled into."

She snarled. "You knew that before you promised."

"I can find them. If motivated. Find Lou Metcalf and I might be motivated."

"Okay, okay." She paused and sniffed the air as she turned a full circle. Something in Rod's direction caught her attention. He didn't think it was himself. She'd never seen him in full armor, and he knew his body chemistry, and therefore his smell, changed along with his skin so she shouldn't detect him.

"Metcalf isn't at the con," Jacquie said. "But he is in the region. I'll know more in an hour." She stalked off, still sniffing and turning back toward Rod's hiding place.

Chapter Nine

S prite and Patrick, holding hands, crept into the back of the ballroom through a side door. She made sure Dad and that woman didn't see them from the main entrance. The Master of Ceremonies was winding down his spiel about keeping safe, no weapons—real or fake—in view, and finding a designated driver. Behind him, a blond woman and five teenagers, three male two female, tried to be quiet about setting up their instruments and sound equipment. The girls had dyed their scraggly locks vibrant green. A good look for Phonecia and E.T. who claimed dark forest fae genes. They'd been slightly tipsy at a late-night con party last year in Idaho when they sensed paranormal genes in Rod—with whom they flirted outrageously—and confessed all to him. He, of course, shared everything with Sprite.

At the next con, in Seattle, Sprite had introduced herself to Phonecia and E.T. They'd become con friends—little contact in real life. Lately they'd texted and video chatted more often, preparing for final exams and graduation—though Phonecia was home schooled, never having gotten the hang of schedules and academics.

A number of people started leaving the ballroom, not fans of filk, the folk music of science fiction/fantasy. A lot of it was parody, putting new genre lyrics to old songs. This group, Celestial Vines, tended toward more rock rhythms, heavy on the bass and the drums.

Phonecia pounded out a lot of her internal anger on those drums. E.T. was better on the light and floaty notes of a set of pan pipes.

"Here's some seats," Patrick tugged Sprite's hand to lead her to a row of empty chairs in prime territory up front—recently vacated by the Guests of Honor.

Sprite eagerly followed him, spreading her skirt over the seat on her other side. Sure enough, Rod slid into the empty chair and placed a hand on the one next to him. Dad claimed it within seconds. "Do I need earplugs for this?" he asked before he nodded a greeting to Patrick.

"Maybe," Sprite replied. "Oak goes a little wild on the bass when Tess isn't looking."

Dad fished in his jacket pocket for some foam plugs. Before he could insert them, Rod nudged him with an elbow. "Dad, you know Liz and her mom?" He gestured to the woman and teenage girl across the aisle and one row behind them.

Despite the age difference, the women looked remarkably alike, with the same nose, chin, bright blue eyes and sandy blond hair, though Ellie had some professional highlights to mask the few grey hairs creeping in.

"We've met," Dad grunted.

Actually, Sprite knew he'd introduced himself to Ellie last year when Rod and Liz had begun a friendship that looked to be growing into something deeper. It was something parents did, sizing each other up to judge the 'safety' of teenage liaisons.

He'd done the same thing with Patrick's parents at a Seattle con.

"They've invited me to come stay with them for a few days after the con," Rod continued. "You know they live in Cave Junction, just inland from here. And they have a pool." Considering how Rod and Sprite reacted to heat by growing stone scaled armor, a pool was essential in summer.

"It's more than a bit inland from the coast, but yes, I know where they live," Dad said in a lazy drawl.

Sprite hid her giggles behind her hand. She and Rod both knew that their father occasionally hooked up with a woman he met at a con. Rarely the same one twice in a row. She didn't know if the women broke it off once they'd seen his scars, or if Bryce found something in his background checks of them he didn't like.

He and Ellie were still in the circling stage. Both Sprite and Rod, and probably Liz, too, hoped they'd just get on with it.

This year, this con might not be a good time for them what with Uncle Lou—Ellie's ex and Liz's father—missing.

Dad rose slowly to his feet, using his cane for leverage. Patrick started to rise to assist him, but Sprite dragged him back to his seat, shaking her head. "He's tired. It's been a long day," she whispered. "He doesn't like to depend on anyone."

Patrick nodded and settled, taking her hand.

Dad limped over to sit beside Ellie, making a wide flourishing bow with his cape.

Liz popped up and scooted over to sit beside Rod. "Maybe this year," she whispered with her hand resting intimately on Rod's thigh.

Sprite nodded agreement.

"NOT MANY WOMEN OF OUR generation can pull off the Cat Woman look, but I must say, Ellie, you rock the outfit," Bryce said, keeping his hands to himself and his eyes on the family band on stage.

"You always were an outrageous flatterer," she replied. "You know who still has a great figure, is Tess up there on stage. Five teenagers and a five-year-old, and she still looks barely thirty."

Bryce shifted his gaze from Tess Noncoiré back to Elizabeth Buchanan. "She's a Warrior of the Celestial Blade, she has to work out to stay fit."

"That's her con persona."

"Of course." Bryce knew better. It had been his job to know who was fully human and who wasn't—before the fire, or BTF as the kids referred to it. Tess hadn't been active back then, she'd been an overweight, mid-list fantasy writer who hung out at cons to help sell her work.

He'd maintained his connections, especially those involving paranormals and cons. They'd alerted him when Tess's semi-autobiographical novel hit the best seller lists, and she showed up at a WorldCon, fifty pounds lighter, walking with a confident swagger, and carrying a unique double crescent-bladed staff over her shoulder.

The blade verified her connection to the Sisterhood of the Celestial Blade, who guarded portals to demon dimensions.

"Besides, all of her children are adopted; the two oldest boys. Cedar and Oak, live with her stepbrother. The youngest boy, Doug, bounces back and forth between them. She hasn't had to deal with baby fat." Though Bryce knew that she and her husband, known only as Gollum, had been trying for a couple of years to get pregnant.

He wondered briefly if the imp flu that had been part of her initiation ritual prevented her from conceiving as well as immunizing her against most human ailments.

Ellie jerked away from him.

"You've had eighteen years to work off your baby weight gain. You're looking good. Too good for the likes of me."

"Don't sell yourself short, Bryce. With the lights out..."

"Why'd you ask Rod to visit you and Liz?" He had to change the subject quickly.

"Because Liz wants him as a boyfriend. I want them to spend enough chaperoned time together that he's no longer an exotic toy she only sees two or three times a year for a weekend. If they are still attracted at the end of next week, I'll stop putting obstacles in her way of going to school in Portland, near your house."

"Good idea. But Sprite and Rod are twins. They do everything together. If Rod visits, so does Sprite."

Ellie half turned to face him. "Why? What are you up to?"

"I need to go to New York for a job."

She slumped in her chair. "You're still working."

"Special case. Normally..."

"Normally you'd take them with you because you are a family and you do everything with them, like cons. If you are dumping them with me, it means danger and you don't want to involve your children." She looked away and swallowed deeply.

"Can't think of anyone I trust more." He flashed her a big smile, knowing full well she could only see the unscarred half of his face.

"Shut up and listen to the concert."

"Yes, dear."

Three long sets later the band took a water break and changed their sheet music. The audience rustled, shifting in their uncomfortable folding chairs. Bryce took the opportunity to lean over and whisper, "Homeland Security doesn't want me to tell you, Lou has been kidnapped. I'm going to New York to search his lab and his apartment for clues."

Ellie gasped and looked like she'd faint. He made sure he had an arm ready to hold her upright if she passed out.

DUC CIRCLED THE BONFIRE site wearing his own hard hat and fluorescent yellow safety vest. Enough split logs had been neatly stacked in a lopsided tee-pee shape, and kindling stuffed between, to set the fire ablaze, but only enough to sustain it for an hour, maybe two.

The circle of wood had a diameter of about six feet. The protective ring of rocks showed signs of scorching in odd places, like they'd been used before and moved to this location recently. They rested a good meter away from the wood.

This was not the towering monstrosity he'd watched burn until dawn the last time he attended BeachCon. This was little more than a campfire.

And it was now too close to the six-foot-high crumbling cliff that separated the hotel property from the sand. Wooden steps offered convenient access to the beach and receding ocean. The rise in elevation would provide some protection from the wind, not enough to warrant the move to an area too close to civilization. A big bonfire would send sparks high and wide onto vulnerable structures.

He looked up and couldn't see the hotel. Too close to the bluff to get a proper line of sight. Too close indeed.

At least this area had been cleared of debris and flotsam. Often huge rafts of logs chained together for transport overseas broke apart and careened on shore, providing more fire hazard for the unwary.

He checked the loose sand around the structure. Too many scuff marks, bare feet and shod, to determine how many people had been a part of the arrangement of logs and kindling.

Whoever had set up this bonfire, on the far south boundary of the hotel's beach—almost to the edge of his campground, had experience but didn't truly understand fire.

Duc understood fire. He identified two subdivisions of arsonists in his mind, those who needed fire to cover a crime, often to collect too much insurance on a worthless property, and those who loved fire for the sake of watching it burn and follow its natural path of destruction—regardless of what, or *who* got caught in their glee.

And this arrangement wouldn't work for long for either of those motives.

He needed to talk to the ConCom and find out which amateur was responsible for this. If he were the local fire marshal, he'd never issue a permit for this fire.

He grabbed the first out-of-place log that leaned to the left and the base was further away from the center. He meant only to straighten it.

No sooner had he dislodged the piece of wood than his armor began snapping into place even though he detected no heat and smelled no smoke. A man's hand, bruised, with dirty nails flopped out of the confining space. The cuff of a forest camouflage uniform shirt rode above a broad ligature mark.

In the fading light as the sun neared the western horizon, he knew for certain this fire would not burn tonight.

He backed away and called 911. Then he hailed a passing couple, out for a sunset stroll along the beach and asked them to notify the hotel.

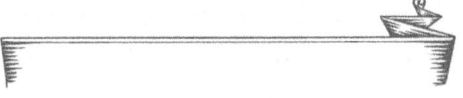

Chapter Nine

We've got a dead body on the beach.

Fear clenched Bryce's heart. He dared not breathe. *It can't be Lou. Please, God, don't let it be Lou.*

Caller I.D. showed Major Marjorie Arbuthnaught.

The concert was nearing its close, with a rousing battle song that had been featured in a recent space opera movie. The entire audience joined in, standing, and raising their fists in defiance of an imaginary enemy.

Bryce had barely noticed the vibration of his phone with all the noise surrounding him. Even Ellie stood and shouted the words.

She never could sing.

"Damn," he muttered as he eased out of his uncomfortable chair, leaning on his cane too heavily. *Just stiff muscles from sitting awkwardly too long,* he told himself.

Ellie looked at him with questions written in her eyes.

In reply, he lifted his phone, without letting her see the screen. "I've got to take this. Keep an eye on the kids." He mouthed the words rather than speak aloud. Ellie would understand him.

She always had in the past.

Even as he eased his way through the raucous crowd, Bryce typed a reply to Major A.

Is it Lou?
Unknown.
Meet me there.

Bryce's vision blurred as he stumbled his way across the lobby to the French doors that opened onto the patio and led to the stairs down to the beach.

Couples and small groups filled the scattered round tables, with umbrellas tilted to protect them from the setting sun. They sipped drinks, ate finger food, and chatted quietly, unlike the concert goers inside.

He kept moving.

A circle of spotlights, pointed inward, showed him where on the open sands he needed to be. Already local police officers, and possibly firefighters, crowded around the now scattered bonfire. He picked out Major A's stiff posture standing on the fringe. A stranger in a hard hat and safety vest seemed to direct the photographer in camera angles and placement.

Bryce took a deep breath and slogged himself through the soft sand beneath the cliff where the hotel sat. He'd spent too many years behind a desk and not enough time pushing his muscles to do more, building fitness layer by layer. He had to do this for Lou.

Lou deserved all of his attention and expertise.

He arrived at the edge of the crowd, beside Major A, hardly breathing deeply at all, with only a minor leg ache.

A thought crossed his mind briefly: *How much of his disability resulted from him succumbing to the overwhelming need of his children to take care of him?*

Then he dismissed the idea. He needed to deal with the crime in front of him.

Two uniformed EMTs lifted a black body bag onto a gurney that had been modified into a sledge to get their burden across the shifting sands, up the stairs, and onto pavement where the ambulance waited. They must do this often enough to make the adjustments to their equipment worthwhile.

He raised his hand, palm out in the universal signal to halt. A flash of a badge, a few authoritative words and the man at the head of the gurney opened the bag's zipper. A face emerged, mouth open, eyes wide with terror. Not a pretty or easy death.

Blond hair, high cheekbones, and a square chin bare of beard sent a wave of relief through him.

Not Lou.

Instead, the Russian mercenary, who had hidden in the closet, stared at death beyond a horizon that remained hidden from the living.

"Cause of death?" he barked in his best drill sergeant imitation.

The first responders snapped to attention.

"Ligature marks on the throat suggests strangling. Looks like duct tape on wrists and ankles restrained him. Tape was removed, taking body hairs with it." The stranger in the hard hat had followed the EMTs and answered Bryce's question.

In the uncertain light, Bryce couldn't determine much to identify the man. But something in his vocal tone and posture reminded him of someone.

"Flashlight," Bryce ordered Major A, holding out his hand for the tool.

As expected, the Homeland Security Officer responded to his superior rank—even though he had officially retired.

The new light showed a second, fainter bruising lower on the deceased man's throat; a mark made by Bryce's cane, non-lethal. The darker and broader bruising looked more like they were caused by human hands.

"Takes a cold-hearted bastard to strangle a restrained man with his bare hands," Mr. Hard Hat growled.

"Have the ME check for traces of black leather gloves," Major A added.

Bryce nodded and gestured the EMTs to continue their grisly job. They closed the body bag's zipper and trundled their conveyance uphill.

"Body temp and lividity suggests he died little more than three hours ago. And he was moved," Mr. Hard Hat said.

Damn, he sounded familiar. Where had he met the man before?

That put TOD, time of death, shortly after Homeland Security took him into custody.

Bryce turned his attention toward Major A.

She'd disappeared. Chasing her would do no good. But he knew highly placed officials in D.C. and New York who could locate her quickly.

He sensed the stranger moving away.

"Do I know you?" Bryce asked Mr. Hard Hat. He looked and acted like a professional. But he caught a glimpse of a corner of a con badge tucked beneath the bright vest.

"We haven't met, sir. I'm Po Duck, an arson investigator out of Lane County. Reliving my misbegotten youth in returning to this con." His words took on an almost foreign inflection... like his first language might have been... Asian?

"In your professional opinion, will the bonfire happen tonight?" Bryce kept his gaze moving, searching for Major A or her minion, or anyone who looked like an HS officer. Someone had to know how the Russian went from their security detention to murdered and dumped.

"Nope. And not in this spot," Po Duc replied. Now he sounded purely American, all traces of an ethnic origin had vanished.

"There's the ConChair," he pointed to a tiny woman in her fifties, dressed in a flowing green gown with a lace up bodice that looked vaguely like pagan ceremonial robes. She was a fixture in organizing and running various conventions throughout the Pacific Northwest. "Explain it to her. I'll see if I can stall the crowd inside until a formal announcement can be made and postings throughout the event rooms."

"It's been awhile, but in my day, the bonfire was the only way to pry hard core gamers out of their room," Po Duc replied.

"Not much different now. My twins turned eighteen last spring and seemed to have outgrown the hardcore gamer status overnight. They only spend half the con in the gaming room instead of all the time now. Their friend Liz is on a panel about the pros and cons of genetic manipulation, and I heard something about a panel discussion on 'Diverse Voices.' Cons have been too lily-white until quite recently."

Po Duc shrugged. "I noticed you limping." He stared hard at Bryce's cane.

Bryce wondered if the man could see through the dense ebony and locate the fine electronics inside.

"Do you need assistance back to firm ground?"

"No." Bryce tried hard not to clench his teeth. "I can learn a lot during a slow trudge alone." He nodded abruptly and turned away from the growing crowd on the edge of the clifftop.

A uniformed police officer stationed at the top of the steps was having a hard time keeping people off the beach. Typical of con goers in full rebellion mode, at least ten younger people defied authority and simply went around the officer to a spot where the cliff dipped and dropped to the sand. Thankfully they stayed outside the hastily strung yellow "Crime Scene" tape.

But they all had their phones out recording the business of mopping up after a murder.

Bryce whipped out his own phone and texted to the only two people he truly trusted, Rod and Sprite.

> *STALL!*
> *Keep people off the beach.*
> *Bonfire tomorrow night.*

SPRITE EXCHANGED A plan with her twin, telepathically.

He nodded and stood up with his hand raised. "Tess," he called before she could acknowledge him. "Will you take requests? We haven't heard you sing *Bimbo* in quite a while."

The audience applauded approval. *There's a Bimbo on the Cover of My Book,* sung to the tune of *Coming Round the Mountain,* was a longtime favorite.

Sprite used the moment of distraction to scuttle across the aisle to where Gollum, Tess's husband, sat with their smallest adopted child. She flashed him the screen on her phone with the message from Dad. "Introduce the family and how you all got your names and nicknames. Involve the audience. Keep them here."

She returned to her seat, crouching low so she didn't block those on the stage.

Patrick raised his eyebrows at her in question. She showed him the text message as well.

"Guess tonight we are all international spies." Then he pointed to a couple standing with their backs against the far left wall. They seemed to be whispering angrily to each other while pointedly not looking at each other. "Isn't that Honor Harrington and her minion? Why aren't they with your dad if things are going strange out on the beach?"

She shrugged. "I don't see a way to get close to them to hear what they are saying without attracting their attention."

A round of applause drew her attention back to the stage. Gollum had joined Tess at the microphone along with a diminutive five-year-old with a mop of dark girls. Like Phonecia and E.T. she wore new crisp jeans and a con T Shirt. Her membership badge proclaimed her name to be "Soapy."

The little girl held her arms up to her mother and shouted "Hug, Mama."

Tess complied. Who could resist such a charming temptress?

"Audience I'd like you to meet our youngest, Soapy. Say 'Hi' to everyone, Sweetie."

The little girl waved shyly at the crowd.

"Gollum and I adopted her when she was just a year old. She couldn't talk well enough to pronounce Sophia. But she could run. Never did bother with crawling or walking. She just transitioned from creeping to running. And catching her was like trying to pick up a bar of wet soap in the shower... so Sophia became Sofie became Soapy."

The family continued a well-practiced spiel of how each of them came into the sprawling family. Only a few in the audience knew that the elaborate tale of the teens growing up in the wilderness raised by a Dark Elf was true. To most it was just another story by a best-selling novelist as well as favorite singer.

Sprite jabbed Rod with her elbow and pointed toward the lobby.

Seconds later, he, with Liz in tow, slid out of their seats and headed to the back of the room. Sprite followed them with Patrick. As they passed the officers from Homeland Security, she quietly told them, "Go ahead and take our seats." Then she positioned herself and her boyfriend so the suspicious couple couldn't go around them and leave.

With a roll of her eyes, Major A complied. Her minion flipped Sprite the finger. He mouthed "keep your nose out of our business," then also sat front row center, where a hasty exit would attract a lot of attention, something neither would want.

On to meet Dad, in the lobby by the patio doors. He stood there looking stern and ushering people away from the exit. He flashed his official shield at anyone who tried to defy him, but he never let anyone look long enough, or close enough to read the U.N. logo. Tonight, he was just an ordinary policeman.

FAMILY BEDROCK

THROUGH THE WALL OF glass overlooking the patio, Rod noticed the ring of police spotlights just beyond the drop off to the beach. Uniformed figures moved in and out of view as the cliff shadowed them or blocked them from his line of sight.

"What's happening?" he asked his father, dropping Liz's hand from his grip as he instinctively took a wider stance and bent his knees. His weight shifted to the balls of his feet. Fight or flight.

"The Russian merc was found strangled to death beneath the bonfire framework. Major A left the scene surreptitiously."

"She's inside with the minion. Sitting where we were a few minutes ago," Rod replied.

"She seemed angry but needed to blend with the crowd. What's she hiding from?" Sprite butted in. She too had taken on a wary posture.

Patrick stood at her shoulder, half-turned to monitor activity in the lobby.

Liz bit her lip and knotted her fist. Ellie joined them. She took Liz's arm and pulled her close. She whispered into her daughter's ear. "Dad?" Liz said. "Why would anyone kidnap my dad?"

Rod captured her hand again and squeezed it with as much reassurance as he knew how to give.

"We are working on that, Liz," Bryce said. He pulled his roving gaze back to their little circle. "Right now, I need you all to act normal. The Master of Ceremonies is on stage, announcing the change of the bonfire. He will light it tomorrow night, right after the Masquerade. For now, the hotel will keep the pool open an extra hour, until eleven tonight. The local authorities need to examine the area more closely at least until then. Rod, you and Sprite need to step up and be leaders instead of loners. Keep as much activity inside as possible."

"How?" Rod felt bewildered.

"Start a game of water polo," Patrick replied. "Gamers vs costumers."

Ideas brightened Rod's mind. "Trekkers vs gamers." He tugged on Liz's hand and led her toward the central courtyard surrounded by the hotel wings. Along the way he grabbed one of the younger gamers as he drifted down from the computer room on the mezzanine.

"Any way we can project a movie onto that blank wall on the north side of the pool?" Sprite asked.

"Let's find out. We have enough computer wizards among the membership to figure out a way to stream something through a laptop onto the wall," Patrick enthused. He grabbed Sprite's hand and led her in a different direction.

"I'm sorry about your dad, Liz." Rod pulled her close and kissed her temple gently. "But you know *my* dad. He'll move heaven and earth to save his best friend. We poor mortals just won't know what he's doing and how he's doing it behind the scenes."

"I know." Liz leaned her face into his shoulder. "The hard part is waiting and not knowing. I want to tear the hotel apart looking for him."

"You heard my dad. We need to act normal and let him do his thing."

"Look at him," she whispered. "He and my mom are clinging to each other like they belong together. Maybe something good will come of this."

"Provided they find the Looney Moose alive and well," Rod said, as he slid an arm around her. "If anyone can do that, it's my dad. He used to be a superhero, you know."

"And my dad was his sidekick." She sighed and rested her head on his shoulder.

Chapter Ten

Ten thirty. Duc raised his arms high to stretch out his back and shoulders. Bones and muscles and cartilage began shifting back into place. He pushed through a modified Tai Chi routine to rebalance his body. His veins and arteries began channeling blood into nearly forgotten nooks and crannies in his body, bringing them back to life. When he felt like his entire being began to sing in harmony with life, he stood still and just breathed for several long moments.

Now that the local authorities had turned off the spotlights and tagged and bagged all the evidence, they could find he didn't feel needed at the crime scene. There wasn't much left to offer clues.

4 He had begun building the new bonfire a proper distance from the cliff.

"No more tonight," he told himself as he crawled into his little tent. With the front zipper closed, he shucked his clothes and lay flat on his sleeping bag. Thank all the gods in the universe, he'd remembered to inflate his air mattress when he set up camp this afternoon. His back and shoulders cracked and shifted as he stretched a bit more.

Even when he was so tired he was almost sick with dizziness, the fire raging to the east called to him. He personally needed to bring it to heel and keep it away from people. His boss wouldn't let him.

His massive body aches told him every night that his years as a fire fighter diminished. Every summer when wildfires gobbled up more and more forest land, he felt the need to throw all of his energy and resources into the fight. And every season robbed him of more of himself.

How long could he keep this up?

He would always be needed, but few people kept up the arduous work beyond the age of forty. Two more years. Surely he could last that long.

His eyes drifted toward closed.

"We have to move him, *now*. This place is too crowded and people will complain and call the police next time he screams!" a feminine voice shouted.

"Quiet. You are drawing attention." A more masculine voice this time. He screamed almost as loudly as the woman.

Duc's eyes opened wide.

"Okay, okay. We'll move him again. Later. When people are asleep and won't notice." The woman spoke again.

Duc tried to triangulate the sound, as he would if he heard a cry for help in the wilderness with a wildfire creating its own unique cacophony.

He put the arguing couple closer to the road than his own snug tent. He heard the crash of waves very close. He'd chosen a spot almost on the beach.

"We move him now!" the man said.

A diesel engine roared to life.

Duc's whole body cringed. The beastly motor would need several loud minutes to warm up enough to move out of the campground. He resigned himself to the inevitable, counting down from one hundred. The motor kept idling.

Maybe he should call Mimi. He'd promised to catch her when she got off work on the swing shift.

No. He wouldn't be able to hear her over the RV.

Was that a scream of pain?

Duc couldn't be sure. The scale on his chin nearly exploded. He clamped down on the instinct to engage his armor in the face of danger. He mastered it. But he certainly wasn't going to get any sleep now.

Reluctantly he pulled on his jeans and stuffed his feet into sandals, not bothering to pull up the heel strap. He opened his tent, stuck his head out of the opening and assessed his surroundings.

The RV was just ahead in one of the pull-through parking slots. The headlights came on, nearly blinding him.

"Enough!" He stomped over to the massive vehicle the size of rock band tour bus. Sleek and black with minimal silver trim and tinted windows, the vehicle shouted money. It didn't fit in this aging and minimalized campground.

"Excuse me," he said when he came within five feet of a man in a dark, bespoke suit bent over and reaching into the luggage compartment beneath the RV.

"What?" he snarled at Duc.

"You are making too much noise! Quiet hours started two hours ago. If you don't stop yelling at your partner and shut off that motor, I'll have to call the police."

"Get out of my way you redneck yokel!" The man slammed the compartment hatch down and swung around to face Duc, raising one fist while he reached for a weapon with the other.

Duc raised his hands and backed off, warily searching for something, anything to hide behind that was more substantial than his nylon tent.

Then the tone of the diesel engine changed.

"Get in here, you slimeball. I'm leaving now, with or without you," the woman called from the now open door of the rig. She shifted into gear and the engine's rumble changed again.

Duc stood his ground as the man swung himself inside, even as the RV started moving. It moved slowly, at the 10 MPH posted speed, around the looping drive of the campground. He followed it at a discreet distance. At the exit, he watched it turn north onto the highway without signaling. The noise diminished a little as it sped up and turned left into another driveway—the entrance to the expensive hotel.

He returned to his sleeping bag, shaking his head in wonderment. Only then did he allow himself the luxury of calling Mimi.

"Hello, my love. Did you miss me?" he said softly when she answered.

"Always," she replied on a sigh. "This house is too damn quiet without you or the girls here to brighten things up."

He could picture her stretched out on the sofa in the living room, watching something silly to help her shift from the intensity of work to the nurturing calm of home. He didn't ask her about her day. She'd talk when and if she wanted to. Most nights she didn't need to relive the events of the burn ward. Just as he didn't always want to taint their normal and cozy home with the details of following the scientific clues to the disturbed personality of an arsonist.

"So, is the con everything you expected?" she asked.

"Well, Tess Noncoiré is here. I enjoyed the bit of her concert that I heard."

"When's her next book coming out?" Mimi asked breathlessly.

"We haven't exactly engaged in conversation, but if the opportunity arises, I'll ask."

"Oh, good. She did leave the last one on a bit of a cliffhanger."

"There have been a few strange developments, love."

"Like what?" She sounded wary. She should.

"Do you remember what I told you about the last BeachCon I attended?"

"Just that you were celebrating your acceptance into the Fire Engineering program after two years of Journalism and Asian Studies."

"And the nature of the celebration?"

"You hooked up with some bimbo who was making the rounds of men in cool costumes." Now she sounded terse and disapproving.

"That was before I met you, and I'd had a few drinks... to celebrate. You know I don't handle my liquor well. That Asian thing about lacking the enzyme to metabolize it."

"Excuses. Is she there?"

"Yes. I've seen her, but I don't think she knows I'm here. She's concentrating too hard on the Master of Ceremonies and collecting money for something secret, and possibly criminal." The puzzle of activities began to shift into a new pattern...

Jacquie demanding money for finding someone... the voice of the man sounding very like the one who'd just left in the RV... the Maxwells searching for someone... and Louis Metcalf being missing....

"And...?"

"There are a set of twins, eighteen years old, boy and girl, and they've both got a scale on their chins."

There. It was out there. He had to finish the story.

"And?"

He took a deep breath. "The girl, Sprite, looks like a clone of Grandma Po. The volunteer at registration said I looked the spitting image of Sprite's brother, Rod."

"Oh."

"What's even stranger is that their mother was incredibly neglectful—to the point of serious abuse. She gave them up for adoption when they were two to avoid prosecution and probable jail time."

"And...?"

Mimi hadn't demanded a divorce yet. He breathed a little easier.

"The man who adopted them is none other than Bryce Maxwell."

Duc held his breath while she digested that little bit in silence.

"Isn't he the guy your dad warns our recruits to avoid at all costs? He hunts down and destroys paranormals without discrimination."

"Yes."

"And that woman gave up her children to that monster? Do we need to rescue them?"

"Um... yes... and no."

"But."

"He's incredibly gentle with them and they adore him. He's physically broken, badly burned, limps, and carries an oxygen condenser. The kids drop everything to take care of him. Gossip says that Bryce was caught in a fire when the twins were six. They manifested their armor and worked together to drag him free."

"That's more than loyalty. That's love beyond measure." Her voice quivered. "Were the kids hurt?"

"Nope. Their armor protected them, even from breathing the toxic smoke that nearly killed him. He has some scarring and always wears a hat and/or mask in public. His con character is the Phantom of the Opera."

"It's a wonder he survived."

"Yeah. They saved him from more than the fire. I had Luc do some quick research. Maxwell cut back his field work when the twins came into his life. Then he retired completely after the fire. Except..."

"Except what?" Now Mimi sounded awake, alert, interested, and concerned.

"Deep in Luc's search, he found suggestions that Maxwell keeps a hand in planning the tactics and logistics of some black ops missions all over the world. He's an enigma. And there's some kind of clandestine activity going on. I've got a line on Lou Metcalf but he seems to have been kidnapped and no one knows why."

"You need to talk to the twins. We can't let them flounder without guidance through the world of paranormals. Their lives sound like a mine field."

"I don't know."

"If they are truly your children, you know where they will be at dawn."

"Returning to the womb of life. Swimming in the ocean."

"Same place you go whenever you are close enough to smell the salt in the air."

He smiled. "You know me too well, my love."

"I should. We've been married for almost ten years. And I intend to stay married to you for the next forty or fifty. Now get some sleep. Dawn is less than seven hours away."

"I'd sleep better if you were here. Take the next couple of days off, grab the girls and join me. We can camp out, cook steaks over an open fire, and swim in the ocean as a family."

"Let me sleep on it. I love you."

"Love you too."

"MIDNIGHT CURFEW," ROD grumbled as he fished his key card out of his damp swim trunks. "I'm eighteen and... and shouldn't have to cut things off just when they got interesting with Liz." He'd managed to get her bikini top off and explored her nipples with three licks. His groin tightened painfully. Then his watch had chirped and the dim lights around the hotel pool blinked twice at eleven.

Then he walked her back to her room. Ellie wasn't there so they'd indulged in a little more hard-core making out before his watch chirped again.

Rod didn't fight the curfew. He never had, because when Dad had a bad coughing fit, or muscle cramps, or just pain, it almost always happened at night.

Actually, he'd been surprised that Sprite and Patrick hadn't joined the crowd in the pool where the cool water kept activities relatively chaste. The hot tub, on the other hand, had deeper shadows and the warm water enticed couples to break a few rules.

But the water in the hot tub was too... hot for the likes of Rod and his twin. He didn't want his armor to start sprouting just when things got interesting.

Besides the hot tub was getting too crowded for his taste.

The lock on the suite door buzzed acceptance of his keycard. Then raised voices inside set his senses tingling and his chin scale vibrating a warning.

That dampened the last of his lingering lust for Liz.

He eased the door open a foot, no more, and slipped inside the tiny entrance way. Closet to his left, fully closed. Small bath to the right. That door remained open a crack, letting the night light illuminate where he placed his feet. He saw one of Sprite's clunky boots just in time to avoid kicking it noisily.

Just like his sister to set a trap for him so she'd know when he came in and she should shut up.

"No, Dad, you are not going to New York alone. It's more dangerous for you than it would be for either of us if we aren't there to protect you." She'd already changed into jeans and a normal tee—the one with a big red butterfly spreading across the front.

"I don't need protection!" Dad shouted. "I was running black ops in central Africa before you were born." He too was back in jeans and a black polo shirt.

"I've never been to New York. When are we leaving?" Rod asked, as casually as he could. Uncle Lou lived and worked in New York, near—but not in—the U.N. building.

"Both of you are staying for the remainder of the con, then going home with Ellie and Liz. I've already talked to her about it," Dad said, pulling his suitcase off the top shelf of the closet in the separate bedroom.

"Visiting friends can wait. Rescuing Uncle Lou and keeping you out of trouble won't," Sprite insisted. She had her own suitcase out and tucked her clothes into it, still neatly folded. Even in agitation she kept her life tidy.

"Commercial airlines, or is Honor Harrington providing a military flight?" Rod asked.

"Major Marjorie Arbuthnaught to you!" Dad snapped back. "I thought I taught you two to respect your elders."

"Only if they deserve it," Sprite snarled back at him. "Right now, she looks like a bully of the worst kind."

Dad paused long enough to suppress a chuckle.

Rod used the distraction to grab his own duffle bag and start throwing his clothes in, starting with the stray sock on the floor. If his father and sister were already packing, he guessed the flight would happen soon. Before dawn anyway when light would glimmer on the horizon about five hours from now. Tiny airport in Brookings with a puddle jumper to Eugene. Then either a short flight to Portland or Salt Lake City for the direct flight to the east coast—probably with a layover in Chicago. He checked his phone for flight times and seat availability.

Sprite closed her suitcase, pointedly jangling a set of keys, her pinky finger hooked into the ring of the keychain.

"Um... Dad, what are you planning to do with the car?" Rod asked.

"I'm leaving it with you and Sprite to take with you to Cave Junction," he replied, concentrating on sliding a garment bag over his Phantom costume. "You can hang this in the back of the car and take it home with you..."

"Um, Dad, stop and think about the logistics of this. That's your strength; it's what you do for a living. Your old boss pays you a great deal of money to get the details right for the most efficient execution of the plans," Sprite said. She faced her father with feet planted and hands firmly on her hips.

Rod knew that pose well. Even with his superior height and weight, and years of martial arts training, he could not knock her over when she took that stubborn stance. Dad was in trouble, even if he didn't recognize it. Yet.

"And your point would be?" Dad faced her with a totally blank expression.

"That unless Major A has a military helicopter revved up and waiting for you, if we take turns driving, two-hour shifts we can be back in Portland in the same amount of time it will take to fly there."

"It's a six to eight-hour drive," Dad protested.

"Factor in security hassles, luggage checks, lay overs, weather delays..." Rod checked the weather app on his phone, added a couple of zip code adjustments, and showed it to his father. "Heavy rain all along the coast and T-storms over the central Cascades. The local airport is postponing all flights starting now—minimum two hours. Add to that understaffing at all points along the way and we are looking at fifteen hours to Portland International."

"But you two aren't going."

Rod and Sprite glared at him.

"You have been overruled." Sprite set her bag on the floor and extruded the handle. "I'm ready. I'll bring the car around. Rod, please arrange for check out. We'll meet out front."

"I suggest we ask for check out Sunday morning. We let Patrick and Liz cover for us so no one goes looking for us until we're already in New York," Rod added. He shouldered his own duffel and grabbed the garment bag.

Bryce just shook his head and closed his own suitcase. "I trained you too well. I'll call Ellie and make our excuses for missing breakfast together."

Rod grinned at his sister. "Maybe next year they'll get together."

Chapter Eleven

"General Maxwell, you need to stay here," Major A said from the now open suite door. She held a keycard in her hand.

Bryce needed only a glance at the red border on the card to know it was a management master key. No official wearing the red blazer with the hotel logo embroidered on the outside breast pocket stood behind her. Which led Bryce to conclude that Major A was not authorized to use that key—access to any room. Had she invoked Homeland Security or stolen it?

Her minion was missing. Which led him to the next conclusion, the by-the-book subordinate didn't know she had come, nor that she did so without authorization.

"Why?" he asked her. "Why must I stay when my best friend has been kidnapped? There is valuable evidence in his lab and his apartment."

"My people have searched his lab and his apartment..." Major A replied.

"But none of you know the Looney Moose like I do. You wouldn't recognize something that doesn't belong there, nor if something is missing." Bryce shifted his weight for better balance and leverage. "And why isn't his assistant here to help look for him? Stella knows more about his work life than we do. His work is his life since his divorce."

"Bryce?" Ellie pushed her way into the suite. She held a cell phone out toward him.

Major A hadn't closed the door. Sloppy.

"What, Ellie?" He held his hand for the phone, never taking his eyes from Major A.

"It's the kidnappers. They have changed the ransom demands," Liz said quietly.

"Why did they call you?" Major A sneered. Her gaze raked Liz from crown to toes. Her assessment must not have come up positive from the way she lifted her lip and returned all of her attention to Bryce.

Her glance slid over the twins as if they were insignificant. Big mistake.

Bryce felt safe in scrutinizing the cell phone screen. Liz had paused the call. The caller I.D. was blocked.

"Why in Hell did you even answer this?" he snapped at Ellie. At the same time he flashed a coded gesture to the twins to trace the call. Major A turned her back on the scene and followed Rod and Sprite to the hallway. The kids already had their phones pressed to an ear. The trace would happen faster with them each calling his two emergency contact numbers.

Ellie shrugged. "I hoped it was Lou."

Bryce answered her with a curt nod. Then he activated the call and put it on speaker. This was not the time for privacy. "Maxwell," he barked into the phone.

The screen sprang to life with the image of a haggard and bruised Louis Metcalf. Swollen bruises closed his left eye and marred the other. A split lip distorted his stained and off-center beard. Blood dribbled a streak down from his temple to his ear. More blood and dangling flesh from where his earring, made from his beloved wedding ring, had been ripped out.

Ellie gasped. She covered her mouth with a quivering hand to muffle any further outbursts. She wore an identical earring to the one Lou was missing. Their divorce had been amicable.

"I need proof of life, or this discussion ends now," Bryce said, swallowing his own revulsion.

"This is your only proof." A raspy and obviously disguised voice scratched through the ether. No telling if a man or a woman spoke behind the electronics.

"That's a still photo. Not proof of life. I won't ransom a dead man." Bryce fought to maintain his harsh demeanor as a professional military commander. His heart raced and sweat broke out on his brow and chilled his spine.

The photo went black, replaced almost immediately by a live image of Lou sitting on a folding chair, duct tape covering his mouth, longish hair dirty and tangled with mats of blood.

But it was the dull, resigned eyes that made Bryce's throat clench.

His best friend had given up.

He couldn't let the situation continue.

"What do you want?" he finally choked out.

"You can keep the $10 mil. I want your children."

SPRITE KNEW THAT CHAOS would follow the call even as her father took the phone from Ellie.

What did she need to do?

Her first priority had to be Dad. The moment the screen changed to show a live video of Uncle Lou, she reached for the oxygen machine and dragged the nose canula free of its holder. She'd turned the beast on before she draped the clear tubing over her father's ears. He stuffed the nose piece in place even as his knees sagged.

She had no brain space to acknowledge anything else happening in the suddenly over-crowded room.

Movement in her periphery told her that Rod too had leapt into action, catching Ellie before she hit the floor in a dead faint. But Liz was suddenly there, holding onto her mother while tears fell.

"I got your dad," Patrick whispered from behind Sprite. "Deal with Major A."

Where had he come from?

Sprite didn't care. He appeared when she needed him. Maybe that was his paranormal talent. He deftly monitored the machine settings and the flow of clean air into Dad's lungs.

"Follow Major A, you and Rod," Dad said. Not the gasping raspy voice she expected. "Take weapons."

Patrick raised an eyebrow at her.

"Sometimes it's an act so people will underestimate him. Sometimes he's really in trouble." She rose from her crouch, searching the room for signs of her brother.

There, already near the door. Sprite reached into the depths of her suitcase, now laying on its side and pushed aside by too many feet needing too much of the limited space. Frantically she thrust aside basic undergarments and spare shorts until her fingers closed around the slender wand of a collapsible cylinder.

"Rod!" she called over the confusing noise of panic.

He paused long enough to glance in her direction. She tossed him the weapon. He grunted something and flipped his own duffel open. Inside he found a set of num-chuks and held them up for her.

She was on her feet and lunging for him.

"I meant a gun," her father grunted.

"Zero tolerance for projectiles at the con," Patrick replied. "They shouldn't openly carry those blunt force pieces either."

Sprite barely heard them. "Major A," she said to her brother, just catching sight of a dark blue jacket hem flaring out as the wearer sped around a corner in the direction of the fire exit.

They raced after the fleeting image. Five steps and they heard the distinctive clang as the heavy fire door shut.

Rod yanked it open, only a step ahead of Sprite. Armor already snapping together as she swung the num-chuks open and ready.

The stairwell remained empty and silent. Major A hadn't had time to descend out of sight or climb upward to the roof. Any feet on the metal steps should have resounded in the enclosed space.

Sprite and Rod stared at each other in puzzlement.

"She out-foxed us," he whispered, barely louder than mind speech, which seemed to have deserted them both.

"Trap?" Sprite asked soundlessly. She'd spent enough time in computer games to recognize a pattern she associated with the major's domineering personality type. Intelligent, sneaky, blind to suggestions outside her narrow-minded thinking...

"Dad!" the twins said at the same time, even as they shifted balance and changed direction.

Rod seemed to have trouble holding the door open, his arm muscles bulging beneath the short sleeve of his T-shirt.

Sprite dashed through the narrow opening, wondering why her brother hadn't sensed danger and fully changed to armor that would add to his strength and stamina.

She'd barely cleared the door and found her footing on the industrial carpet of the hallway when a change in the air pressure told her that a different fire door at the other end of the hallway opened and then closed again, noisily.

"She played us," Rod said inspecting the hinges on the door that had tried to close on him. He held up the pneumatic device that normally slowed the closing of the door. It looked smashed. Someone had sabotaged it to force the weight of the portal to rush back to its normal resting place, all to give their prey more time to escape. The Major had planned ahead.

"I wish I knew her game-plan. She's Homeland Security and supposed to be on our side," Sprite mused as they returned to the suite. "But she behaves like Special Forces." She trusted Patrick to take care of Dad, but... If Major A had a gun...

BRYCE DREW IN A DEEP draught of life-saving air. The tension in his chest eased. He hated what breathing toxic smoke for too long during the fire had done to him.

An emotional shock shouldn't have laid him out flat like this. He was trained to remain calm and think clearly in a crisis.

Patrick twisted a dial on the condenser a tiny bit making the air flow smoother, easier. Bryce felt his lungs fully inflate—well as fully as they ever did. The kid knew what he was doing, even to the point of clamping the meter to his fingertip. "Good job, Patrick. Now let me up."

"I'm taking EMT training this summer. Always a need for techs. I can work at the local fire house to help pay for med-school. Stay put a moment more. Let your breathing stabilize." He sounded just like a soothing professional.

But Bryce's need to be on the other side of the room with Ellie outweighed everything else at the moment.

He'd loved her for so long, he thought he'd learned to live with the constant ache of her absence from his life.

Finally, he could stand the pain of watching her suffer no longer and yanked the machine out of Patrick's hands. He only had the strength to crawl to Ellie's side. Liz had her mother cradled in her lap, massaging her temples and uttering soothing nonsense words. Her hands moved to Ellie's shoulders, easing some of the tension building up on the cords of her neck.

"We'll get Lou back, Ellie. *I'll* get him back for you and Liz."

"Not at the expense of *your* children," Ellie snapped back with her usual spunk and acid. She struggled to sit up, slapping away Liz's hold.

"No, I'll never give up the twins. But demanding them as ransom gives me ideas of who is behind this. Knowing that gives me ideas of where they are holding Lou. This is what I do, Ellie. I'm good at it." And why he'd had to give her up after only two years of marriage.

"We'll help," Rod said from the doorway.

Bryce breathed easier, knowing his kids were safe. He'd trained them knowing this day must come sooner than later.

"No! You mustn't endanger them, Bryce," Ellie protested.

"They've always been in danger, from the day they were born."

"Jacquie wasn't that poor a mother," Ellie snorted.

"Wanna make a bet?" Sprite sneered. She marched over to Patrick and crouched down, presumably to consult on the condenser management.

Ellie cast them a strange glance. "What?" she mouthed toward Bryce. This time she managed to shake off Liz's restraining grasp and sit up.

"She'll never say," Rod said. He crossed his legs and sank to the floor beside his father. He shook his head as he looked at the machine Bryce had dragged behind him. "Dad, ease up on the air tube. It's coming loose from the fitting. You are supposed to sit still while using this thing."

"No, I'm not. It's portable so I can move around. Now stop being my nanny and let me talk to Ellie alone for a moment." He wanted to glare at all the people crowding around him but kept his gaze fixed on Ellie's face.

For several moments, silence rang heavily through the room.

"Okay, everybody *out!*" Sprite sprang to her feet and grabbed Patrick's hand. With quick efficiency she ushered them all toward the hall.

Major A stood in the doorway looking innocent and... and startled.

"You forgot one, Sprite," Bryce called after his daughter.

The twins flanked the military woman, each taking one of her arms, and escorted her out. Bryce would get a full report later. Right now he had to talk with Ellie.

"I know you love him, El. Please believe me that I hold nothing against the two of you." Even though she'd married his best friend within hours of their divorce being final.

He hadn't known that she'd already filed papers with an attorney as soon as he'd left her for that mission in the Middle East. During those weeks of slogging through deserts, then south into dense jungle in pursuit of a ruthless warlord—who employed torture and terror more efficiently than any extra-dimensional demon—that he realized how much of a barrier between them his job caused. How much he feared that his job endangered her. Better to break things off than watch her die at the hands of some mad *human* terrorist—or a demonic entity—as leverage to neutralize him.

Not all paranormals were predatory. But those that were, needed to be destroyed or beaten back beyond carefully guarded portals into alternate dimensions. Tess Noncoiré's sisterhood guarded some but not all.

His arguments with Ellie about his work flashed through his memory, as clear and as detailed as if he lived through them once again.

I hate living in New York in this dinky apartment, with neighbors watching every move we make, listening every time we make love.

And I know less about you than Mrs. Whatchamacolic on the ground floor knows about me.

I never know where in the world you are.

You never tell me when, or IF, you will be home.

I'm always afraid that the next time I see you will be on a slab in the morgue...

Their arguments could burn the ears of a casual listener. His Ellie had a mouth on her. But not since Liz had entered her life.

He couldn't read Ellie's expression. She had learned from him how to hide her emotions.

Or maybe he was just blind to her wants and needs.

He hadn't been a very good husband.

Chapter Twelve

Rod peeked through the gap he'd left between the door and the jamb. His dad lay on the floor, face in his fists, the oxygen condenser wheezing away so he didn't have to. He looked almost as if praying or pleading with his goddess.

Ellie sat upright, back against one of the armchairs. Was she crying?

Looked like it with tears leaking from her eyes.

"You damn well better find Lou and bring him back in one piece. I married him because he had a desk job and wasn't being shot at every other day. You couldn't give me that, Bryce. You still can't!" She leveraged herself to her feet and stared down at him, hands on hips, and chin still quivering.

"I don't think I was supposed to hear that," Rod whispered. He didn't think he'd spoken loud enough for Sprite to hear him.

From the way she stared at him, he guessed that she'd heard his thoughts more than the words.

"Later," he mouthed to her, then looked around at the crowd of people waiting to get back into the suite.

Finally, Major A looked at her watch and jutted her chin in firm determination. "He's had long enough to read her the entire Code of Hammurabi. I need information only he can supply." She shoved the door open, shaking off Sprite's hand.

Patrick and Rod worked side by side to get Dad into a chair. Sprite shadowed Major A. Clearly, she recognized the military woman as more of a threat to the family than Dad's ragged breathing. That had stabilized for the moment.

"Mom, whatever this is, it can wait until morning," Liz said, tugging at Ellie's arm to get her moving. "We all need rest right now. The kidnappers won't do anything more to Dad until they hear back from us on their ransom demands."

Rod had almost forgotten that *his* Uncle Lou was Liz's father and Ellie's ex. Uncle Lou never talked about them when he visited. Rod never saw them alone together, not even at cons. If Uncle Lou was with Liz, or Ellie, he was part of a large group.

Of course, Rod didn't know how they interacted when he wasn't around.

"No one is leaving this room until I get some answers!" Major A roared.

"You'll get them when we have them," Dad said calmly.

"What is so important about your children that terrorists kidnapped a very important U.N. photo analyst and investigator in return for them? What can they offer criminals that is worth bringing down the combined wrath of Homeland Security, the FBI, the CIA, the NSA, and Interpol?"

"I don't know, and I won't know until I find out what Lou was working on. The only one who can tell me is his assistant, Stella," Dad replied. He sounded calm, but incredibly tired.

"You need to be in bed, Dad," Rod said.

"Jacquie said Lou wasn't at the con, but he was close. If he checked in to the hotel, I need to see his room..." Dad said, but his attempts to stand were feeble, and he didn't bother shaking off Rod's or Patrick's supporting hands.

That alone told Rod how much Bryce Maxwell needed eight solid hours of sleep.

"He checked in to Room 215," Ellie said. "I spoke to him there when he arrived about four this afternoon."

"What!" Liz shrieked. "That room is right across from ours. You didn't tell me you'd gone to meet with him. I wanted to talk to him too."

"I know, Liz. But we had things to discuss that are none of your business."

"Like what?"

"Parent things. Money things. His retirement. Us maybe—I said *maybe*—getting back together."

Watching Liz's face go from outraged to hopeful then back to disappointed and fearful told Rod a lot about her real relationship with her father.

"All this family drama is a waste of time..." Major A tried to end the screaming.

"I need to see Lou's room and his luggage," Dad said. He tried to stand.

Rod kept him in place with a single, gentle, hand on his shoulder. "Sprite and I will go look. We'll bring back anything unusual or out of place. We know how to do this."

Dad sagged into his chair. "Okay. You know that he specialized in analyzing photos for UFOs and paranormal activity with occasional forays into troop movements. He's neat and organized."

"Only because he gets so involved in his work that he forgets what day it is. So, everything has a place and stays in that place so he can find it again," Liz reminded him.

"Do... do the kidnappers know that about him?" Ellie asked.

"We'll find out. Major A, do you still have that pass key that will open any door in the hotel?" Rod looked at the stern woman closely, trying to read her. He already thought he understood her because she had a job so similar to Dad's until the fire took him out of the field.

"I'm coming with you," Major A said, pulling the key out of her jacket pocket.

Strange, neither her hair nor her clothes looked mussed. She could have just walked out of an internet ad for the perfect professional woman.

"Of course, you are coming with us. I don't trust you to leave our father in one piece if left alone with him. Patrick, please stay and take care of him." Sprite rose on tip toe and kissed her boyfriend's cheek.

Rod remembered to do the same for Liz. "Watch your mom," he whispered. "This evening has been hard on both of you."

A lot of the earlier noise and chaos evaporated as he took the major's arm and escorted her to the elevator.

"Sprite," Dad called. "Call Tess now. Tell her as much as you know, tiny details."

"CALL TESS?" SPRITE looked to her brother for an explanation.

He shrugged and frowned.

"No, do not call anyone. Do not tell anyone anything!" Major A insisted. She grabbed for Sprite's phone even as she pulled it out of her jeans pocket.

Sprite held it away from the woman. "Orders from my father outweigh your authority," Sprite said, trying hard not to sneer—or quiver in fear. Two swipes on the screen and she found a cryptic notation in her contacts: *TN-VS* followed by a number with a Portland area code.

Dad must have put it there. Rod showed her a copy of that notation on his own phone.

Before she could call, the elevator opened. "There's rarely a signal inside an elevator," Spite muttered.

Major A rolled her eyes upward to stare at the ceiling while biting the insides of her cheeks.

"I suppose you have a device that blocks signals," Sprite accused her.

Still no response.

Dad thought of everything. Sprite engaged the white noise app on her phone that would block any blocking device the major might have. Then she used Rod's phone to call the unknown contact.

"This is Tess," a chirpy voice answered.

"This is Sprite Maxwell. My dad said to call you."

A pause while the woman hushed the noise of numerous loud voices in the background. "Okay. I know what this is about. Where are you?"

"In an elevator headed toward Room 215."

"One of us will meet you there. Two minutes." She hung up.

True to her word, a short female with a mass of dark blonde curls stood in front of the closed door of their target as they rounded the corner to the short corridor that led to a fire exit and the back parking lot.

Sprite caught a whiff of untended dumpster at the end of the hallway. She knew where that escape route led—behind the restaurant. Dad would never have taken that room because the odors drifting upward would mask the scent of anyone with ill intent who tried to hide while watching for activity in and around the room.

Dad was good with scent. Sprite and Rod not so much. Except smoke. They could smell fire from miles away.

Tess looked up from studying her phone and smiled. Then her gaze alighted on Major A and the pleasant greeting evaporated. "Who the hell are you?" she asked, studying the military posture and crisp business suit of Sprite's escort.

"I might ask the same," Major A replied.

In the subdued lighting in this secluded corridor, a red mark slashed across Tess's face from temple to jaw. It looked new, raw, and painful. Tess turned and the scar vanished, leaving smooth and clear skin, the kind that no pimple, let alone a scar, would dare mar.

The two women studied and appraised each other cautiously. Tess made certain the manilla envelope she carried remained clamped under her left arm while she allowed her hands to come forward, as if ready to bring forth a weapon. Other than a slight list of her posture to one side, she looked ready to leap into battle. Dangerous. Major A had her left foot forward so that her jacket drifted open for easy access to her weapon holstered at the small of her back.

"We don't have time for this," Sprite said, moving between the two women. Rod, she noted, had taken up a position slightly behind the major within easy reach of her right hand that was closing in on her gun.

"Ms. Noncoiré is not unknown to me," Major A said through clenched teeth. "I don't trust her. She may be in on the kidnapping."

Tess laughed with genuine mirth. "That's a stunt I wouldn't put beyond you Marjorie or any of the agencies you might work for. Still carry multiple IDs?" Her hands relaxed.

"I am authorized by Homeland Security to investigate this missing person case." She didn't shift her posture away from the defensive. Or maybe it was aggressive.

Sprite didn't care. She just wanted to search Uncle Lou's room and go to bed. Always a light sleeper, she still needed a solid eight hours a night.

"Okay, Sprite." Tess turned her full attention to her. "Your father knows I have resources he doesn't, and you probably can't imagine. This is for you and your brother to examine when you return to your room. Read it alone and then decide what to do with the information." She held out the envelope to Sprite.

Major A shot forward to intercept the missive.

Rod grabbed her arm.

Tess snatched the envelope back into her own custody.

"Manners, Marjorie. Remember your manners. Even my five-year-old knows better than to grab something that clearly belongs to someone else, and she was raised by vampires until she was a year old." Tess tsked and put the envelope directly into Sprite's custody.

"I need all documents that might relate to the disappearance of Louis Metcalf."

"Tangential information that I believe Sprite and Rod need to review first. In private." She enfolded Sprite's free hand in her own. "Now what's the Looney Moose done this time?"

"Uncle Lou has been kidnapped. Rod and I are the ransom."

"That is a problem. I'll let you get to your end of the investigation while I consult my own sources." She turned her head and focused on a point close to her left shoulder. After a moment of squinting eyes and slight chin drop in agreement, she caught both Rod's and Sprite's gazes. "While you examine that material, I shall deploy my resources. Now stay safe and get some rest. I have a feeling you are going to need it. And Marjorie, I understand that you have to monitor the situation but don't interfere. If I hear that you have anything to do with this, I shall deploy my other resources. I doubt you can defend yourself against the scion of a dark elf, and an imp attached to a Sister of the Celestial Blade." Without further explanation, she spun on her toes and stalked off, her left shoulder held half a milimeter lower than the right. "Oh, and Sprite, tell your dad I'll meet him for breakfast at seven when they open, in the restaurant. You and Rod can share a table with Phonecia and E.T."

BEFORE HE SET A FOOT inside, Rod did a quick survey of the standard hotel room from the doorway. Two queen beds, small round table with two armchairs. Flat screen TV on the long double dresser. No laptop on the desk.

That set up alarm bells in his mind. He touched Sprite's arm and pointed. She nodded and moved closer to inspect the peripherals. "Mouse and pad are still here."

Uncle Lou was notorious for insisting on a real mouse and not using the touchpad like most people.

Major A barged in and did her look around from beside the empty bed, the one closest to the bathroom. "Nothing looks touched," she said.

"Wrong," Rod informed her. "Uncle Lou will keep one bed clear of stuff to sleep there, but he'd never leave clothes, clean or dirty, thrown randomly over the spare. He'd also empty his suitcase and stow it in the closet, not leave it gaping open on the luggage rack."

He pulled open the doors and drawers of the multi-functional dresser. Empty.

"Maybe he didn't have time to put everything away?" Major A said, turning in place to inspect the mostly neat room. But it wasn't neat enough to meet Uncle Lou's standards.

"Everything has a place, and everything in its place," Sprite quoted. "It's the only way he can find things. Not exactly obsessive compulsive, but it's an ingrained habit because he is always preoccupied with sixty-five other things."

Rod moved toward the bathroom, carefully inspecting the carpet for traces of footprints. All he saw was flattened nap of otherwise thick carpet. Either someone had walked this route a number of times or someone else had deliberately scuffed through to obliterate signs of traffic.

His back and his chin itched, his armor wanted to snap into place. The room wasn't overly warm, so his instincts warned him of something...

"Any sign of his satchel?" Sprite asked quietly.

Rod barely heard her. She too must be sensing something very wrong with Uncle Lou's room and perhaps the presence of someone... something malevolent.

He diverted his path to search the not-so-secret compartment of the open suitcase. "Empty."

Then he shoved aside the sliding opaque glass door of the bathroom in the back corner, opposite the closet and luggage rack.

Again, without touching anything, he scanned the countertop and shelves below it for extra towel storage. This room looked more like Uncle Lou's domain. He opened a black, zippered bag that should contain toiletries. Rod and his dad had almost identical ones for shaving tackle.

He marched back into the main portion of the room. "Um, Sprite," he addressed his sister, ignoring Major A's useless attempt to find anything in the archeological dig of the clothes heaped on the bed. Too many clothes for Uncle Lou at a weekend con.

"Uncle Lou visits us twice a year, every year since Dad adopted us, right?" She nodded.

"He stays with us whenever Dad has to go to the hospital."

"What does that mean?" Major A asked, sounding frustrated.

"It means we see him a lot. And often. Sprite, have you ever known him to shave off his beard?"

"No!" Sprite opened the black bag wide and withdrew a can of shaving cream—an off brand with smudged labels, like it had been used enough to be almost empty. "It feels... full?"

"You have no reason to know much about shaving cream unless you are doing the weekly shopping and Dad or I put it on the grocery list."

"So why is the label faded and the sides slightly dented. I don't think Uncle Lou would buy toiletries from the 'nick and dent' shelves." Sprite shook the can as if readying the contents to foam.

The can rattled.

Sprite almost dropped the manilla envelope Tess had given her. Rod caught it before it fell from beneath her arm. He handed it back, and she clamped it under her arm once more.

"Because Uncle Lou doesn't use shaving cream. He hides things in the can," Rod said, a note of triumph coloring his voice.

"Let me see that!" Major A grabbed the can from Sprite's hand. She examined it closely with eyes and fingers. Then with a slight smile she twisted the bottom.

The can split in two equal halves along an almost invisible seam beneath the smudged and unreadable paper label.

"Betcha it's a flash drive with his latest project on it," Sprite said, grinning ear to ear.

"Sucker bet," Rod replied, giving her a high five. "We need Dad's laptop to crack the encryptions."

"We need Dad to figure out the encryptions," Sprite replied.

"I've got my own code experts," Major A said, heading for the door.

"Dad's closer and better," Rod reminded her.

Chapter Thirteen

"Major Arbuthnaught, remind me again of your security clearance," Bryce said, as he opened his laptop and booted up—not the normal procedure of most private computers of hitting the power key. No, this was an agency machine that required three levels of passwords, each one more complex than the previous one.

"Last I checked, I'm three levels above you. You are retired and inactive, therefore your security clearance is downgraded to basic," Major A replied.

Bryce bit his cheeks rather than reveal the feral snarl that sprang to his face. "Humor me. Let me see your shield." He wasn't as retired and inactive as his surface level personnel file indicated.

"Very well." The major fumbled her folder for a laminated card out of her left hip pocket. She opened the case with a flick of her thumb, giving him the briefest glance at her I.D. Then she closed and pocketed it again

"I asked to see your shield, not your badge." He'd caught HOMELAND SECURITY at the top and not much more. Good enough for most people but not for those in the know.

She glared at him, daring him to hit enter after keying in the second password. He'd go no further with her hovering behind him until he saw the opaque triangular crystal embedded in the scrollwork of an old-fashioned metal badge.

He fished his own badge out of his left front pants pocket. Slowly, lovingly he traced the scrollwork with his thumb. "I loved the work I did, making the world a tiny bit safer and knowing there were other agents and teams out there doing their bit as well. What about you, Major?"

"You loved your work so much you let a band of hashish maddened terrorists firebomb your home, with your children inside."

"You got that backwards, Marjorie." In his mind she no longer deserved her rank. She was just another annoyingly pompous paper pusher. "I set myself up as bait in a temporary rental unit. My kids were outside, in the car with two other agents and a nanny."

"Then what went wrong?" She still had not produced her shield.

"The terrorist stumbled and triggered the bomb prematurely. He and three others died because they had no plans to escape should such a contingency happen. My team captured the remaining two and got me out with no loss of life on our side." He didn't mention that Sprite and Rod had engaged their armor and dragged him out of the burning house. That was the first time he'd known about their stone interlocking scales.

The fewer people in the real world who knew about that the better.

Lou Metcalf learned about their paranormal talent hours later when he came to take care of them while Bryce recovered in the hospital. Further research—mostly by Lou until Bryce got out of the hospital—revealed the scales were as light as pumice but resistant to blazing fire temperatures.

He was pretty sure that Sprite had showed Patrick her secret, and probably Rod had done the same for Liz.

Marjorie was another matter.

Her glare induced chills up and down his spine.

He clamped down on his instinctive shudder. Whatever her clearance level, he didn't fully trust her. He just didn't know why. Yet.

"Your shield. Now," Bryce barked in his best drill sergeant voice.

Like any good soldier who'd survived boot camp, she snapped to attention and withdrew the charcoal grey, leather folder from her inside jacket pocket and handed it to him. That was a major no-no. One did not give up one's shield to anyone but a superior officer.

She'd just acknowledged that she did recognize his rank, even if he was officially retired.

Without a word, he removed the bronze-colored metal shield, embossed, scrolled, and enameled. His fingers found the slight bump of a clearance crystal on the back. He turned it over, examining every detail with eyes and fingertips for signs of anything not quite fitting. It had the proper fittings for a brooch pin. No discolorations. No extra bit of epoxy spilling from beneath the crystal. If it were a forgery, it was a damn good one.

"Blue," he said on a long exhale. "Good enough, I suppose." He made his sigh sound resigned, as if she just barely met his standards. Then he returned the shield and held up his own so she could see the nearly clear white of his own crystal. When she tried to grab it away from him, he folded his fingers more tightly around it until the metal edges bit into his skin. "You may look but not touch. Chances are, you may never see another like it again."

"Yes, sir."

"Please turn your back a moment while I key in the last password." The alpha/numeric/symbolic combination didn't matter. It was the retinal scan that gained him entry to the decryption program he needed.

The wallpaper screen came up at last, a picture of the twins at the age of eight, playing in the pool. He'd snapped that photo on the first day they'd moved into the house in Portland. Their forever home, after they'd spent almost two years with his sister's family and Lou, while he recovered. That was also the day the adoption papers became final. His favorite memory.

Jacquie had stalled and lied and played the victim for six long years. Then Bryce got word that she'd failed to find a lost skier in time and money had changed hands. The first of her criminal "failures." He'd blackmailed her into signing the papers.

But sign them she did. Rod and Sprite had become his kids for real.

Marjorie obeyed and turned back to watch over his shoulder once he'd inserted the thumb drive that wasn't an ordinary flash drive.

The computer took almost three minutes of whirring and clicking before the screen blinked. A list of file names scrolled down for three pages. He clicked on the last one, dated two days before the con started.

An old photo slowly opened, one line of enhanced pixels at a time, from top to bottom.

He recognized Jacquie easily. The other faces were unknown to him. But Lou had circled in red, a spot to the left of center on the chin of an Asian man. He resembled the twins in the shape of his nose and the breadth of his forehead, the slight protrusion of his ears... and that unnatural splotch on his chin.

The arson investigator at the bonfire.

Was he looking at a picture of the real father of his twins?

"IT'S TIME, SPRITE," Rod said quietly. They'd both gone through their normal preparations to sleep. He sat on the edge of the foldout bed in sleep shorts, chest bared, and wondering if he could nudge the AC a notch colder.

His stone scale itched, not from heat, but stress and fatigue.

Sprite looked in worse shape. Normally she was more sensitive to heat than he but handled stress better, reverting to logic instead of reacting to emotion. Later, when she had privacy, she'd fall apart and shiver and cry for a while.

"I know," she replied on a long exhale.

Dad had taken his laptop, Major A, and the recovered flash drive into the bedroom and firmly closed the door. Rod could hear the murmur of voices with tense undertones but not actual words.

The still sealed manilla envelope on the coffee table between them seemed to call to him, begging him to rip it open.

"Oh, just do it," Sprite said, sounding frustrated. "Tess would not have given it to us if she knew it would hurt or damage us. We're friends."

"I know, I know." Rod reached across the short space to the coffee table and grabbed the packet. It seemed slim, holding only a page or two inside. No bulges or pressure on the seams.

He unfolded the clasp and slid his finger beneath the sticky flap. It opened without tearing. A deep breath and he eased the papers out with the barest edge of his fingernails. By the time he had spread the pages across the table and bent to scrutinize them, Sprite was on her knees on the other side of the low table. He, too, dropped to the floor.

"Okay, we've got two pages of a photocopied archeology magazine and... and it looks like a letter signed by someone with a long name and an alphabet soup of degrees after the name," Sprite said.

"Guilford Van Der Hoyden-Smythe," Rod translated the sprawling scrawl. "Three PhDs and a professorship, a couple of master's degrees too."

"Wait, I've heard that name... Isn't that 'Gollum,' Tess's husband?" Sprite flipped the letter around and peered closely at the signature.

"Maybe."

"Phonecia and E.T. just use the Smythe surname. Tess keeps her birthname of Noncoiré." Sprite knew the girls better than he did. They texted and video chatted often. Their three brothers didn't socialize much, even at cons.

"What does the letter say?" Rod picked up the other pages, the second one had three grainy black and white photos, the first page was filled with closely written text.

"Thank goodness it's typed and not his godawful handwriting," Sprite said. She scanned the letter then looked up at him. "Mostly he says that he authenticated the author of the magazine article and verified the authenticity of the archeological dig, knows the director personally, and gives his cell phone number if we have any questions—with a note that the baby is a night owl, and he stays up with her but sleeps in the mornings."

Then he took up the pages and held them so the floor lamp shone directly on them without shadows.

He read aloud the account of recently discovered caves in Viet Nam that quickly became a tourist attraction. The native guides told tales of the oddly shaped stalagmites that looked like animals and humans crouching on the cave floor, frozen in time by the calcium laden drips from the ceiling. Anthropologists could not determine if the tales were as ancient as the caves or recently created to satisfy tourists.

"That doesn't mean much," Sprite said, sinking back and stretching out her legs. She braced her weight on her hands beside her rather than the table.

"Read the back of the letter from Gollum," he suggested, noting that the faint type on the back of the page was more substantial than bleed-through on thin paper.

Sprite flipped the letter over and squinted at the print. Then she scooted over to the floor lamp for a brighter light.

"Wow, he went to some length to make this less noticeable." With the paper held almost to her nose she read, "This may sound far-fetched, but I do believe this article is physical evidence of a tale recorded by a French antiquarian from the early twentieth century."

She licked her lips and caught Rod's gaze. "My French is okay, but this name looks unpronounceable. Closest I can come is 'Guy de la Briochement du Pechier.' Sounds made up to me. Anyway..."

Her French was more than okay. It was the one class she'd aced through three years of advancement.

Twisting the paper for a better angle of light, she continued... "According to the elderly women of an obscure mountain village, there was a time when the world was in chaos, and the gods that inhabited the volcanic craters spewed forth their dislike of humans encroaching on their lands, covering the land in lava. Many died from the ash and smoke before being engulfed in molten rock. Those who took shelter in caves were quickly smothered in liquid rock—dripping limestone. The gods of the sea took pity on humanity and gave special powers to the bravest of those remaining, men and women, hunters and fisherfolk. When the mountains threatened to erupt, these special folks grew armor of a stone that resisted the fires and toxic ash. They gathered together their people, protecting them with their own bodies until they could reach boats to flee the land now forbidden to them."

Rod fell backward until he could brace himself against the end of the bed. "Those... those are our ancestors!"

Sprite gulped, opened her mouth to speak, then clamped it shut again. She nodded in agreement. After several deep swallows. "It explains a lot."

"KIDS, I NEED YOU TO see something," Dad said from the threshold of the inner room.

Sprite scrambled to gather all three pages of information and stuff them back into the envelope. She hadn't bothered to tap them into alignment and they scrunched, unwilling to go back into hiding.

Dad, of course, never missed observing anything. He squinted and firmed his jaw.

"Marjorie, you may leave and report what your superiors need to know, including the fact that I now have the lead on this investigation."

The major snapped to attention and saluted him. "Yes, sir. You have my cell number. I will have a task force assembled and ready for you to deploy at first light."

"General Maxwell has an appointment pertinent to the case at seven in the morning," Sprite reminded them all. *Seven, two hours after dawn, more than enough time for an ocean swim before.* Tess might have said she needed to talk to Dad alone, but Sprite intended to be within eavesdropping distance. She said she had resources she had to consult about Uncle Lou. "My father will contact you after that meeting." She stood stock still, clutching the envelope to her chest as if a talisman until the major left, closing the door quietly behind her.

"Let's make this fast, I might still get a few hours of sleep tonight," Dad said, gesturing Sprite and Rod inward.

On closer inspection, he looked haggard with dark circles around his eyes and a grey pallor. She didn't need to tell Rod to grab the medication bag. He diverted his steps to the bathroom, picked up the grey bag with the discreet red cross on a white circle on the end of the canvas. The fabric folds hid the emblem from casual scrutiny. Mostly it appeared to be just another large toiletry bag.

"I don't need morphine," Dad grumbled. "What I need is for you to look at the photograph that Lou was working on before he was kidnapped. Considering the ransom demand, I believe it is the key to this whole mess."

"Along with these." Sprite held out the envelope to him. "Tess said we could show it to you after we examined all of it. Read them now." She took the chair in front of the laptop, still open to the screen Dad indicated.

Rod hovered behind her. "It's... it's like looking in a mirror!"

"Maybe for you," Sprite said quietly. She'd always known that her hair was more brown with a hint of a wave than his coal black, board-straight mop. And the shape of her eyes had less of an Asian epicanthic fold. But to see both her bio-parents in the same photo, his arm around her shoulders, felt like a sucker punch to her gut, robbing her of breath. Jacquie's young face did resemble Sprite's own. Sort of.

"Just because you look something like her, doesn't mean you *are* like her," Dad reminded her.

Sprite grabbed her dad's hand and clung tightly as her origins swam before her mind's eye in vivid detail.

Searing lava. Ash laden air. The need to guide her people beneath the towering tsunami....

Chapter Fourteen

Quiet finally reigned in the hotel room. All the extra people had left. The kids had opened their fold out beds. The con had wound down to a few murmurs of people lingering on the patio below.

And still Bryce could not sleep. He paced his room massaging knots out of his left thigh, while his mind spun and spun with problems and possibilities.

He'd called everyone he needed to notify. He'd studied every bit of evidence and supposition on his laptop. There was nothing left to do but wait and try to sleep.

A light tap came at the door that exited his bedroom directly into the corridor. He knew from experience it had no number or identifier on the exterior panel. The only way someone could know where it led was to have been inside or told where to look.

The tap came again, more like a hesitant scratch.

Bryce twisted the deadbolt and opened the portal an inch. Ellie stood there, chewing on her lower lip, and shifting her weight like she would turn away and leave.

He hadn't been home to watch her leave when she'd divorced him.

He wasn't going to let her get away again.

"What do you need?" he asked softly as he pulled the door open and her into the room. "What can I do to help?"

"Just hold me," she replied on a sniffle. "Lou..."

"It's been a traumatic day for all of us," he murmured, kissing the top of her head.

"Then hold me closer and don't let me go."

He complied as he kicked the door closed again, letting his arms enfold her. His heart rate sped up even as his breathing settled. Ellie was back in his arms where she belonged.

DAWN LIGHT PEEKED OVER the top of the Coast Range bringing sparkles to the foam as each wave crested and broke apart in the ocean's mad dash for shore. Moment by moment the water brightened from black into the dull gray of the frothing tide.

The digital clock in the hotel room had read 5:15.

The cold, wet, sand warmed beneath the sun's touch.

"Another beautiful day," Rod said, not really feeling the smile he gave his sister. She hadn't slept much after their late-night session with antique photos. Therefore, he hadn't either. Instead, he'd listened to her toss and turn, sigh deeply, and pound her pillow into a different shape. As if that would entice sleep.

He worried about her. When she confronted an emotional storm, she withdrew into herself. He ranted and raged and threw things (he wasn't allowed to throw punches like he wanted to, not until Dad bought him a punching bag and hung it in the basement).

Sprite never raged. Instead, she waited until the crisis resolved and then she exhausted herself in private crying jags followed by swimming until he feared she'd drown.

But last night... He'd found it hard to stare at his bio-father's face knowing the image was captured the same weekend, at this same beach, when he and Sprite had been conceived.

Did the man even know about his offspring?

"You know, Sis, we are eighteen now. We can legally change the names *she* gave us. I know I don't feel honor-bound, like Dad does, to keep the obnoxious monikers she gave us. I've been thinking about Rodney James Maxwell." He threw his towel on the dry sand, above the tide line, and kicked off his sandals. Anything was better than Android Sparticus.

This was supposed to be the best time for a good, long swim, to stretch cramped muscles and let their spirits soar and merge with the elements.

"I thought about that," she said, folding her towel and placing it on the sand, then lining up her sandals beside it. "What do you think about Sprite Rebecca Maxwell?"

"Much better than Aphrodite Sarsaparilla."

It struck Rod that perhaps her need for control, tidiness, and order was ingrained since the two years of chaos while living with Jacquie before Dad had found them and taken them away.

Sprite stood and adjusted the bottom of her skirted swimsuit, an habitual motion to make certain the elastic didn't rub on the burn scars that nearly encircled the top of each thigh—a permanent reminder of the perpetual diaper rash they'd both suffered as infants.

They'd dwelled on this topic too long. "Race ya!" Rod called over his shoulder as he pelted toward the retreating waves.

Sprite followed, her shorter legs pumping hard to keep up with him. They slowed only when the water swirled around their thighs. In unison they dove into the deeper water as the next wave rose into a substantial curl. Together they drowned their worries in the primal elements.

In unison they angled their long strokes until they swam parallel to the shore just beyond the surf line. Rod pushed his muscles and joints, letting the water soothe him, blend with him, let all his worries float away. The salty water supported and nourished him.

For a short time, Rod almost believed the story of their origins among the volcanic islands of southeast Asia.

They noted landmarks until they reached the next hotel, a really posh one with their own lifeguard hut elevated above the beach for better visibility and an awning to shade the guard. No one watched the waves from there today. It was too early. Dawn had barely crested the mountain ridges to the east.

But it was a good place to turn back. Together they flipped and stroked until they could see their bright red towels on the sand—and an unknown man standing beside them. He'd folded his jeans and con tee shirt alongside a thick grey towel and left them just inches away from the hotel towels.

Rod anchored his feet in the sand beneath the edge of the flowing waves. The peace and serenity of a dawn swim evaporated. He strode forward, knowing that his twin swam beside him, needing a few more feet toward the beach for her shorter legs to reach bottom. He paused long enough for her to shift her balance. All the while, he studied the stranger who eyed them steadily.

Nearly the same height as Rod, the man had a greater breadth of shoulders and chest, the same coal black hair worn long and straight to below his ears. He also wore black, tight swim trunks (almost biking shorts) and a black crew neck T. Mid-thirties, maybe as old as forty. Nothing special. And yet, something about him cast a compelling aura. Rod forgot all the rules of an action hero in the movies. He *needed* to approach him and discover more about him.

"I am Po Duc," the man called. His words carried a trace of an accent. Asian perhaps, to go with the uptilt of his... moss green eyes.

"He's unarmed. We can take him," Sprite whispered.

"I'm not certain he is an enemy," Rod replied. Her words had distracted him from his compulsion to know more. He shook his head slightly to free himself of the... enchantment.

"Do we know you?" Rod asked, gauging the distance between the red towels and the encroaching tide. How well could he and Sprite run in the soft sand back to the hotel? The shortness of his sister's legs came up lacking. If retreat became the best option, he couldn't leave her behind.

"You do not know me," Po Duc said. "I hope to remedy that."

"Are you our father?" Sprite asked. She widened her stance and moved a few steps to Rod's right. Two targets. That was her strategy if Po Duc proved untrustworthy.

"I believe I am. In my defense, the woman, Jacquie, vanished at the end of the convention. No one I asked knew where she lived."

"A one-night stand. No commitment, no regrets," Rod muttered, both outraged and understanding. He expected nothing more from Jacquie. Po Duc would have been one more exotic man to add to her long, long, long notebook list.

"Why seek us out now?" Sprite came right to the point. No silly chit chat from his logical and direct sister.

"Job burn-out, shifts in my family dynamic. A new crusade against paranormals. We need... we need help. I remembered the con from my youth. If anyone will be sympathetic to what you call paranormal, I would find them at a con. Discovering you two was a bonus." Po Duc's face remained bland, without expression.

Rod wondered how often he'd had to practice that face when he encountered prejudicial bullies. Come to think on it, he and Sprite had practiced anonymity every day at school.

"Sympathy and help are not the same thing," Sprite reminded them.

"I will exchange help for help," Po Duc said, spreading his hands out from his body indicating innocence.

"Such as?" Sprite demanded.

"I know where to find your friend. You call him Uncle Lou."

"DAD, DAD, DAD. YOU have to get up now!" Rod's voice and hard pounding of the bedroom door pierced Bryce's deep sleep. The best sleep he'd had in almost two decades.

"What?" he asked the air around him. His thoughts tangled along with the sheets wrapping his body in mummy folds. He pried one eye open trying to make sense of the noise in the outer room and the immobility of his limbs, and the comfortable weight on his chest. "Give me a moment," he pleaded with his son.

Ellie's hand flexed on his naked chest, pressing him back into their cocoon.

"Ellie?" Bryce jolted awake.

What had he done?

"Shush," she whispered. "If we are quiet maybe he'll go away." She pulled him closer to her naked body, resting her head on his shoulder. She'd showed up last night, needing comfort. A tight hug had turned into a kiss, comfort to passion... and the rest was now... never to be forgotten, or dismissed as a one-time thing.

"Dad, this is important!" Rod's voice grew louder.

Bryce peered at the depth of the light creeping around the edges of the curtains. Dawn had come, not long ago. Early morning shadows lingered. He checked the digital clock. Six, zero, two. He hadn't missed his breakfast meeting with Tess. Yet.

Some of his brain fog dissipated.

"Give me a moment, Rod." Then he lifted Ellie's hand from his chest, wishing he didn't have to separate from her once again. "I've got to go, love."

"I'm coming with you," she said. One fling of her arm and the sheets and blankets flew aside.

Embarrassment flushed Bryce's cheeks at the exposure of his scars.

Ellie paused a moment to inspect him, including his twitching manhood. "Other than your face, the burns are minimal. And I can barely see where you had a knee replacement. Get over it." She rolled out of bed and started gathering her clothing. Then she disappeared into the bathroom. The sound of water gushing through the pipes masked any further comment she might make.

Briefly, very briefly, Bryce considered joining her in the shower. His kids needed him. They had to take precedence. Besides, it sounded like Ellie washed her face at the sink rather than indulge in the luxurious shower. She'd come out when she was ready to face his family.

Clad in dark blue sweats, the only clothes he could find in a hurry, Bryce closed the door behind him as he entered the main room.

Rod stood at the end of his unmade bed—the fold-out from the sofa. Sprite smoothed her own bedding while preparing to close up the loveseat. They both showed damp hair and bright skin, signs from their morning swim.

But what arrested his attention was the tall, black-haired man with moss green eyes, the man he'd spoken to at the dismantled bonfire last night. And...

Bryce gasped. "You must be the man with Jacquie in the photo taken at BeachCon nineteen years ago." If he did, indeed, have the paranormal gene for stone armor, his chosen career in firefighting and arson investigation seemed natural.

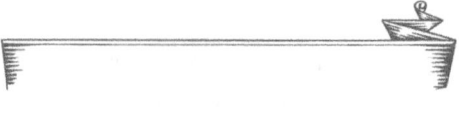

Chapter Fifteen

S prite wasn't exactly certain what she should do next.

"I think we actually met last night at the defunct bonfire," Dad said as he shook Po Duc's hand, polite and semi-formal. Two alpha males circling.

The men were still visually appraising each other when Ellie emerged from the bedroom, looking refreshed, if not exactly tidy. Yesterday's clothes bore wrinkles and her face wore no makeup. She'd smoothed down her shoulder length, dark blonde hair with golden highlights, but it really needed a shampoo, conditioner, and a good brushing. Not her usual look, but decidedly attractive in an early morning, natural way.

"Pick your jaw up off the floor," Rod whispered. "We've been expecting this. Remember?"

"Yeah, but not *this* morning, after last night, and on top of Po Duc."

"You don't need much introduction," Ellie said, approaching Po Duc with an outstretched hand. "Seeing you standing beside Rod, the resemblance is uncanny. I'm Ellie Buchanan." They shook hands. "Do you use the Asian tradition of family name first and given name second?"

"Yes, Ms. Buchanan." He nodded and bent slightly from the waist, almost a bow. "Most of my business associates don't know the difference."

"It's Ellie. I run the gift shop and tours for a winery in Cave Junction a few miles inland. We have a lot of Asian visitors. I've learned, Duc."

There wasn't much more to say about the introductions. Sprite kept glancing at Dad with his cat-who-ate-the-canary smile. She didn't think last night was a one-night stand. That pleased her.

Those emotions had to wait.

"Po Duc thinks he knows where Uncle Lou is," she blurted out.

Dad and Ellie stood at attention.

"Where?" Dad barked, already scrolling through his contacts on his phone.

"At the hotel next door to the north. Before that they were in a big RV at the campground just south of here. They moved last night around midnight. Top floor double room, not a suite. I checked this morning before I met the twins. Why leave a huge luxury rig in the parking lot of a posh hotel? A man in a charcoal grey suit and a female in black dress slacks, black silk shell, and two inch heeled pumps. Not exactly camping attire. Too formal even for glamping," Duc replied. "I'm an arson investigator and fire fighter in Eugene. I'm also on the call list for the Hot Shots when wildfires become too intense for locals. I'm trained to notice details and patterns—or a disruption in them."

"Mind if I run a background check on you?" Dad held up his phone and snapped a picture of their guest.

"Dad, is that necessary?"

"Yes, it is, Sprite," Duc replied. "I am on the edge of including myself in your family. You need to know as much about me as you can dig up. I've already done the same to you. Except for Ellie. I sense her presence is new."

Sprite shrugged her acceptance. She dropped to sit on the edge of the loveseat, lightheaded and mind reeling with tons of new information to process.

"You need to eat," Rod said. He sat beside her, elbows on his knees, and face in his palms.

"So do you," she replied.

"Okay, we have a lead on Lou's whereabouts. My meeting with Tess just became a family event. Good thing she's an early bird. You two," he pointed to the twins, "have just enough time to wash off the salt and get dressed."

"Tess?" Ellie asked.

"We're going to need her help," Dad said.

"Should I call Liz?" Rod asked. He raised his head, suddenly looking brighter. He jumped to his feet and started tossing bedding and pillows around in search of his phone.

Sprite had to chuckle. Her twin would probably never learn how much time a little tidiness saved.

"We're probably going to need Patrick too," Sprite added, grabbing her phone from the lamp table beside her foldout.

"When did this become a circus?" Dad asked.

"Probably the moment our children manifested a paranormal talent and dragged you out of a fire," Duc said. He'd done his homework too.

BARELY SEVEN AM AND the food servers had just begun to set up the buffet. Rod's stomach growled.

"I don't like crowds at planning sessions," Rod muttered to Dad as they followed the gathering crowd into the hotel dining room. His real Dad, not the bio-father who just turned up out of nowhere.

At least Po Duc seemed intelligent, educated, employed, and reasonable, unlike Jacquie.

Maybe if he thought of the new guy as Duc, pronounced *duck,* like a nickname, he'd get over the mental, and emotional, disconnect. His con badge gave his name as "Ducky" and he'd had a little sticker of a yellow duckling on it.

Maybe if they both wore armor rather than jeans and Ts he could bond with the man better.

"Agreed," Dad replied. "Too many voices trying to out-shout the rest in disagreement. At least the con-goers are barely up yet. We'll have a measure of quiet and privacy." He'd left his costume in the garment bag in the closet, but he kept his hat on, tilted to the left side so that his scars remained in shadow. The addition of a medical mask hid him nicely. Less than two years beyond the pandemic lockdown, it wasn't out of place. His lungs had suffered enough damage from inhaling toxic smoke during the big fire that a mere whiff of a respiratory ailment could seriously cripple or kill him. Most of the diners who usually wore costumes had not assumed their alternate identities yet. Actually, most of the costumers were still in bed after the late night parties. The breakfast buffet was sparsely populated. Even the wait staff still looked sleepy.

"You're the planning expert, Dad. You have to take control early and maintain it." Rod kept his eye on Tess and her two daughters. They seemed nice enough. But there was just something weird about the way they cocked their heads as if listening to someone who wasn't there, and Tess's slightly misaligned shoulders—like she carried something heavy beside her ear.

When he'd first met them at a Portland Con just before the pandemic, he found he had nothing in common with the girls, and the boys were not open to offering polite greetings, let alone friendship. They lived mostly with Tess's stepbrother and his wife, staying out of public, and self-contained, like hermits, or shy forest creatures.

Sprite, on the other hand, had instantly bonded with Phonecia and E.T., mutual paranormals with similar assimilation problems.

"Bryce has taught you well to be suspicious of everyone," Duc said. He'd dropped back from the mass of people they'd accumulated since the isolated chat on the beach. "Hiding a paranormal talent is challenging. You never know who will accept you, and who will run away screaming that you are a demon or the spawn of Satan."

"Has that happened often?" Dad asked.

Rod noticed his dad taking a warding stance, preparing to defend himself. He mimicked his father's widened foot placement and shift of balance. But so far, he'd kept his hands neutral.

"Once." Duc maintained a relaxed posture, but he scratched idly at his chin scale. "I left town and switched my career goals from TV reporter on the Asian front to firefighter. Got my masters in arson investigation rather than investigative journalism. I use my armor to fight fires. I don't like having to look pretty in front of the camera. I do that often enough when I have to appear at a press conference or testify in court."

His scratching became intense.

Rod's scale responded. But he saw only familiar faces gathered at the big table in the center of the dining room. Morning light through the large floor-to-ceiling windows overlooking the incoming tide revealed dents in the carpet where six tables had been pushed together, leaving open space all around them.

The dragon eyes on Dad's cane remained neutrally green and unblinking.

More importantly, Sprite did not scratch her chin, nor did the scale turn pink in warning. She chatted amiably with Tess's two older daughters, Phonecia and E.T.

Gollum and the five-year-old Soapy seemed to have slept in. As expected, the boys were not in evidence.

"What?" Rod asked Duc.

"There is a paranormal presence. One I have not encountered before." Now he took a defensive posture, reacting to something beyond Rod and Dad.

"Um... I think you are about to meet some good friends and valuable allies," Dad said, relaxing and moving forward. He greeted Tess with a nod as he placed a possessive hand on Ellie's shoulder. "I'd like you all to meet... a new acquaintance." He half-turned and gestured Duc forward.

Tess jumped to her feet and came around the table with her hand extended in greeting. "Po Duc, I've been wanting to meet you. I've heard about your Sanctuary. I'm Tess Noncoiré," she said. Then she gestured to the girls and continued around the table, naming each person and their relationship to the rest of the group.

"My wife and I have read your books, Tess. Enjoyable, but I prefer my fantasy on the darker side, with less romance. Mimi can't wait for the next one. When's it due out?" He grinned and shook her hand. Neither of them continued the conversation around that intriguing word "Sanctuary."

Which opened Rod's curiosity more.

"To each his own. And I think next March for the book." Tess shrugged, emphasizing her off-center posture. "At least you bought them and read them."

Rod and Sprite exchanged a knowing look. Duc was married.

Tess returned to the table and took her seat with her back to the window.

"How do you know my name?" Duc squinted toward her left shoulder. His brow puckered in puzzlement.

"Tess has resources," Dad said. "Best not to question them."

The reflection of sunlight on the waves changed the angles of bright and dark in the big room.

Duc gaped, briefly, then clamped his mouth shut and relaxed his shoulders.

Rod blinked rapidly and shook his head. He hadn't really seen the outline of... of a creature with long ears, snub nose, round belly, and wings wearing a pink feather boa sitting on Tess's shoulder. Had he?

"What do you see that I don't?" Rod whispered to Duc.

"You saw correctly." He smiled and moved forward. "You are only half Guardian, so your vision is probably shallower than mine. It just took you longer."

"But what is it?" He seated himself to the left of Duc. Sprite already sat on his right and Dad next to her. Patrick seemed relegated to the far side of the table where he could see Sprite but not touch her.

"Another form of a Guardian. They are rare outside their secluded enclaves. We'll discuss this later as well as the Sanctuary."

Tess mouthed a thank you and bent her attention to the menu.

The amorphous blob on her shoulder brightened to pale pink. Tess and her girls swiveled their heads in unison, all three staring at the arched entry to the dining room.

A slender little man with buck teeth and balding brown hair, wearing an outdated and threadbare argyle sweater over his khaki slacks stood there, surveying the crowd. A black pug dog in a pink harness with a pink leash, stood close to his ankles.

Rod couldn't tell if the dog protected the man or cringed behind him seeking protection.

Then a tall slinky blond woman, in red silk lounge pants and top, emerged from the lobby and took his arm. The man patted her hand where it rested in his elbow. They moved forward together toward a private two-person table near the patio doors.

"Ever notice how Issac the Wimp is always attached to the most beautiful woman in the room?" Patrick asked.

The women at the table bristled. Especially Sprite.

"Sorry, you are all beautiful but not showy about it," he mumbled staring at his cutlery still wrapped in a napkin.

"The dog is adorableness personified," Tess said, still staring at the couple. "That's the attraction. And I think I've just solved a plot problem in my current work in progress." The pinkish blob on her shoulder faded to transparent.

"Read her first book. It's almost autobiographical," Duc muttered with his back to the table so no one could read his lips.

"Let's just do the buffet and not waste time ordering. Most everything on the menu is included in the buffet. I'll pay," Dad said. He took Ellie's hand as he walked over to the extended heat tables along the back side of the room.

SPRITE STUDIED THE last few dabs of maple syrup for the most efficient way to sop it all up with only a single bite of waffle left on her fork. She'd noted that Po Duc (what was she to call him, or think of her bio-father after meeting him for the first time?) attacked his pancakes with the same precisely squared cuts and deliberate mixing of breakfast elements as she. They both interspersed their sweet and buttery carbs with single bites of bacon and scrambled eggs.

A warm tingle started in her toes, running all the way up to her scalp at the idea she had inherited her penchant for tidiness from him, rather than have developed it as a counter to the chaos of her first two years with Jacquie. Rod on the other hand seemed almost alien in his random messiness, even if he did look so very much like Duc.

"Mom," Liz whined, "aren't we supposed to be discussing a strategy for finding Dad?"

In her reverie at finally finding her bio-dad, Sprite had forgotten their primary mission. She ached in empathy with her friend. The thought of losing her dad, the man who had rescued and raised her and her twin with love, left her aching and anxious.

"Actually, Liz, I have dispatched my old team from my fieldwork days to follow a new lead," Dad said, after checking his phone for the umpteenth time in the half hour since they started eating.

"But I thought we were all going to free him!" Sprite protested.

Dad's face became stern, ready to lecture her, like the first time she'd failed algebra and been demoted back to business math—a much more useful class in her mind.

"Sprite, the kidnappers are armed and ruthless. I will not take you into such a dangerous position when I have a highly trained team of combat veterans ready to jump at my command. They are in position." He held up his phone and wiggled it. "And they will alert me when they have scouted the situation and feel the time is right to move."

"Why aren't we helping if they are still observing?" Rod butted in. He'd cleaned his plates and planted his fists on the table, ready to leverage himself upward and into fighting mode.

"Because we are being observed. I want to lull the enemy's suspicions while presenting a perfectly normal family picture. If we are here, chatting calmly, then they have nothing to worry about. Right?"

A cute woman in her thirties with orange stripes in her ordinary brown hair bounced up behind Tess and draped herself across the right shoulder of the singer."

"Didi Dogooder!" Tess exclaimed even before she turned to kiss the other woman's cheek. "You made it after all. Is Chad with you?"

Sprite looked to make sure Didi's con badge showed her con name rather than her married name.

Didi held out her naked left hand for all to see the absence of the huge flashy diamond and wedding band she used to wear. Then she placed a fake crystal ball on the table where everyone could see it. Encased in the glass were her wedding and engagement ring, complete with the three-carat emerald cut diamond.

Didi's eyes crossed as she gazed deeply into the ball. "I see a brighter future for both Chad and me." Then she blinked rapidly as if coming out of a trance. She'd rehearsed her fortune-telling act a lot.

"Chad's here, sleeping off last night's champagne. We celebrated the divorce becoming final. Now his father can't order me around anymore." She practically danced in place. "Just wanted to say 'Hi' and let you all know you don't have to talk to the dog-do-badder senator. He can't touch me now." She scooped up her crystal ball, twirled, and spotted another table of friends to tackle.

At that moment Tess stiffened her already straight posture and tilted her head as if listening intently.

Dad's phone pinged an instant later.

"They're moving him!" they both said in unison.

"Ellie, please pay for the food and then take Liz back to your room. Don't move outside the con until I come for you. I think Liz is hosting a panel on the pros and cons of genetic manipulation." He slapped his credit card on the table. "Tess, are you available to assist?"

"At your service. I haven't had a decent work out in too long." She motioned to her daughters to come with her. "You two, hang back until I summon you into the situation. You know what to do if anyone tries to escape."

Sprite's eyes widened in wonder as Phonecia's finger elongated and sprouted thorns. Hastily, she tucked her hands into her jeans pockets as she remembered where they were and who was watching. There was a reason her original name had been Blackberry and E.T. had been Salal.

Of course, Sprite knew that both girls had been raised in the forest by a dark elf. They both had second personalities as dangerous plants. But under Tess's loving nurture they'd both learned to control their defensive urges. Mostly. But Sprite had never witnessed their transformation, and she had never shown them hers.

"Sprite and Rod, you are with the girls," Dad ordered. He lifted his cane, activating the sensors. The dragon's eyes blinked slowly red then green and back again.

Sprite had never seen them do that before.

"Dad, Sprite and I have defenses," Rod protested.

"Have you ever tested them against gun fire?" Duc asked.

"No, they haven't," Dad replied for them, bristling with indignation that he would ever risk his children against such an outrageous notion.

"Then don't assume your armor will withstand a projectile. We evolved to protect normals from heat, molten lava, and toxic ash, not modern weapons." Duc stood firm between the twins. His hands flexed and fisted, ready to grab or punch as needed. "Trust me on this!" He eyed the twins with equal intensity.

Sprite's scale heated on her chin. She suspected it turned red with the need to activate in defiance of Duc's pronouncement.

Just as the blob on Tess's shoulder began to turn red and... stretch.

"Trust Duc," Dad ordered in his best drill sergeant voice. "Now stay back and do your best to detain but not confront anyone trying to flee the scene. That is where I need you the most."

Sprite reached for Rod's hand. Dad hadn't excluded them. He'd just given them less active roles than they wanted.

Rod squeezed her hand in reply. They communicated their disappointed acceptance wordlessly.

Chapter Sixteen

Bryce slapped the roof of the big, black SUV (what a cliché) signaling the driver that all of the passengers were inside and belted up. The driver beside him wore desert camo, as would the rest of the team when they met up a half mile away at the next-door hotel back parking lot.

Barely eight o'clock. The con, in both hotels, hadn't begun stirring yet.

"Um... Dad, when did you have time to call your team? I thought they were all in New York," Rod asked from the backseat. He and Duc bookended Sprite.

"While you and your sister changed out of wet swimsuits into people clothes." No wet swimsuits in the house. That was a rule he'd established the first time he sat in a sopping wet kitchen chair. The kids spent so much time in the pool trying to keep their body temperature regulated he'd installed a shower and changing area in the laundry room between the kitchen and pool access. That quickly became an extra full bath and the old office grew into a bedroom, a nice suite for when Lou came to visit.

The basement collected work-out equipment and was otherwise unfinished.

"That doesn't explain how your people got here from the east coast so quickly," Sprite added.

"They weren't in New York. I called the secondary team two minutes after we got the news that Lou had been kidnapped. They've been close but on standby since then." Bryce stretched his legs forward in the big vehicle. His cane hardly seemed necessary with massive amounts of adrenaline pumping through his system. Though the walking stick did provide him with a variety of hidden weapons and tools.

This was what he'd needed for a very long time, to be moving, with a plan of action, accomplishing something important. Damn but he missed fieldwork.

His phone pinged. A blueprint of the hotel came up on the screen with a fat red dot in the top northeast corner, then a series of thin, red dashes indicating the path of retreat. He texted back.

How many?

Half a heartbeat later came the reply.

Two. Heavily armed and masked. Possible six more in waiting.

That hotel housed some of the con overflow. Masks would not be out of place. Nor would obvious wounds. Guests would assume that Lou's bloody and bruised face and any restraints were just great stage make-up.

"Dad?" Sprite asked, leaning forward as far as her seatbelt would allow. "Has anyone found Stella, Uncle Lou's assistant? Liz said that he planned to travel with her so he could get some work done. Something about writing an important paper."

Bryce forced his face into a blank mask. He pulled the brim of his hat a little lower to cast deeper shadows. He sent a rapid text to his second in command and received a picture back in seconds. "Duc, is this the woman you saw at the RV?" He held up his phone to show him a photo.

"I can't be certain. She was not wearing a lab coat but did wear a weirdly shaped silvery hat—more like a hair covering. Frankly the woman I saw more closely resembled the woman the kids refer to as Honor Harrington in size and posture. Do you have a picture of her well-dressed male companion?"

"So far he's stayed away from the proximity of Lou. Though there is a man my team have seen talking on his cell phone a lot. One of my sergeants has traced his calls to and from the hotel room. They are trying to catch a picture of him now."

"What about Honor Harrington?" Rod asked. "If she's as highly placed in HS as she claims, why isn't she here with us?"

"I don't totally trust her motives, even if she does have the proper credentials and security clearance." Bryce didn't have the time to examine the itchy feeling that any mention of the woman left behind. "Sprite, did Liz say anything about the nature of the work Lou needed to do this weekend? He usually leaves that part of his life in the office." Which was why Ellie had married him. He represented safety when Bryce had lived on the edge of danger every moment.

Still, the timing of their separation bothered Bryce. He'd come home from six weeks in central Africa, half of which he'd been in hospital with two gunshot wounds and a deep machete slice across his abdomen, totally exhausted and knowing that Ellie's safety depended on them separating. He'd made serious enemies during the mission, and previous ones, enemies both mundane and paranormal, who wouldn't hesitate to torture and murder his wife as leverage to get to him.

But Ellie had filed for divorce weeks before and moved in with Lou mere days after Bryce kissed her goodbye, his mind already in central Africa assessing supply routes and maps. Bryce came home filled with grim determination to leave Ellie. He'd opened the door into an empty apartment.

"Sir, we have a complication." Colonel Zachariah said the moment Bryce stepped out of the SUV. "Homeland Security is claiming jurisdiction and has ordered us to back off."

"Kidnapping and torturing a U.S. citizen without evidence or a warrant is a crime. Holding them for ransom is another crime. Demanding custody of my teenaged children as that ransom is a worse crime. Stopping that crime is every agency's jurisdiction. We got here first." Bryce set his cane in place beneath his left hand and moved to step around his first officer.

"Sir, there are a dozen armed HS agents assisting one of their own between us and the man we need to rescue."

"Then they have elevated themselves to the top of the most wanted list. I'm taking over this mission. Call the FBI and inform them. Invoke Security Code K&R10-BMalpha." He held out his hand for the remote communications unit and its corresponding headset.

"Yes, sir!"

Bryce affixed the earpiece and spoke quietly into the mic. "I want at least one of the leaders alive for questioning. The object of this mission is to retrieve Louis Metcalf alive and well. Do not endanger him with unrestrained firepower." He checked the app on his phone that showed the red dotted line of the escape route. They were still in the hotel building.

He deployed his mere dozen troops. Then he made certain he had a paranormal in key positions to work with the professionals. He made sure a sharp shooter watched with each of the teams.

Tess and her girls hunkered into the shrubbery on the south side of the hotel, watching service entrances.

Rod and Sprite were too eager to go with Duc to the beach access gates.

He passed off to the Colonel the worst chore of calling Major Arbuthnaught. She might have a high security clearance, but she was involved in the kidnap. He knew it in his gut.

WITH ONE OF DAD'S ARMED troops behind him, Rod scanned the gate in the fence between the clapboard service hut and the north wing of the hotel. In the shade of the main building and back wings, the secluded area was likely too chill for even the hardiest guests at barely eight in the morning. Anyone willing to embrace the early temperatures would choose the open ocean, as he and Sprite had done. The angle of the nearby Coast Range kept the sunrise at bay a little longer than at the con hotel which was already in full sun.

Unlike the con hotel with the pool enclosed on all four sides by building wings, the luxury lodging had an open fourth side facing the beach. Outsiders were discouraged by a chain link fence with redwood slats running through the mesh. A narrow gate opened with a key card allowing guests only onto the steps leading to the ocean waves.

High tide closed in on the headland jutting into the ocean at the curved end of the beach. Frothing spray crashed over the jagged rocks, about ten feet above the low tide mark. Each new wave rose higher and higher. Rod bet there was a storm out there pushing the water harder than usual.

The air smelled of salt and seaweed. Not a hint of diesel from the lone, low-slung fishing boat on the edge of the horizon.

He couldn't see anyone wandering about the beach or around the hotel pool except a single, college-age, blond man who wore a white shirt, green vest, and black slacks—an almost identical uniform in style and cut to the con hotel staff who wore red.

He let a clump of low-growing, coastal pines shield him. The trees encircled a kitchen dumpster.

Nearby, Sprite sprawled on the ground in the shadow of a stack of deck loungers outside the fence. Duc had chosen a different stack of tables to hide beneath. In full armor all three of them blended into the packed dirt and tufts of beach grass.

The employee pulled a pair of binoculars from beneath his vest and squinted through them out beyond the waves.

Rod shifted his attention briefly toward the object of his scrutiny. The same boat he noted earlier, with a low profile and a cabin moved slowly southward. It was really only visible from here when it bobbed upward on an incoming wave. He sliced the air crosswise with a flat palm. Both Sprite and Duc acknowledged his alarm with the same gesture.

The corporal wearing desert camo brought his rifle to bear, peering through the scope. He barked a few words into the communication device clipped to his shoulder. Then he turned his attention back to the pool enclosure. His finger remained loose, outside the trigger guard. He had to wait until the vest man was outside the chain link fence.

Rod doubted even his dad could guarantee a shot at this distance wouldn't hit the metal mesh and wooden slats and then ricochet.

A quick check at the ocean showed him that the low-slung cabin cruiser had moved closer and dispatched a Zodiac inflatable boat that could float in very low water. With an incoming tide it could actually beach and then float away on the next wave. They'd be vulnerable for only a few moments.

The distance from the base of the cliff to the waves had shortened in the last few moments. Ten meters at most remained.

Then the man in the red vest turned toward the north wing of the hotel and beaconed someone forward.

Rod got a good look at his profile. Major A's nameless sidekick. He was supposed to be at the National Guard base with the Russian Mercenaries in custody. One of which was now in the local morgue.

So, where was the Major?

SPRITE SENSED MOVEMENT behind her. More like a change in the shushing sound of the waves playing with the sand. A quick look over her shoulder showed her three armed men, led by Tess and her daughters. Tess twirled over her head with both hands a long staff that stretched and stretched to about a meter and a half while it extruded a curved blade at each end. Fine tines bristled from the outside edge of blades. They looked razor-sharp.

The Celestial Blade!

Tess's books featured a sisterhood in a fantasy setting of women warriors who wielded such weapons against demons or intense evil.

So that's what Duc had meant when he said her books were autobiographical.

Did Dad know?

Of course he did. Dad knew most everything about the real lives of the paranormals they met at cons. In his last years of field work for UN black ops he had dealt with as many demonic terrorists as horrific human warlords.

Duc tapped Sprite's shoulder and pointed to the incoming tide and the Zodiac approaching silently, without the outboard motor running. The pilot used the waves to bring it closer.

The man in the green vest now grabbed a stumbling Uncle Lou by the arms and thrust him toward the locked gate. Uncle Lou blinked rapidly in the morning sun. He still wore his usual khaki shorts and science fiction movie T shirt but no sneakers or flip flops. He hunched over his ribs. His bruised jaw and split lip looked out of alignment. One eye was swollen shut and a scabbed blood trail descended from above one eyebrow and his nose.

His hands were restrained behind him, thus upsetting his balance even more. A black-garbed, blond man—the second Russian mercenary—prodded him from behind with what looked like a semi-automatic handgun.

Dad would know with one glance what brand and size of ammunition.

Using hand gestures, Duc sent her and Rod to the outside edge of the hotel buildings and thus beyond the line of sight for the people within the fence. Their job was to sabotage the zodiac from the water. Their armor would blend in with the sand and keep a bubble of air around them for longer submersion.

This entire operation was a team effort. She swallowed her apprehension of having to depend upon anyone outside her family. And maybe Patrick and Liz. Well, add Ellie to the growing list of people she trusted not to betray her and Rod.

They didn't have to rescue Uncle Lou by themselves. He truly needed rescuing. He wasn't like Dad with his years of fieldwork and experience to deal with bad guys. Louis Metcalf, middle-aged and slightly pudgy, held down a desk and worked with digital photos. Dad on the other hand... well no one but Dad knew how he'd escaped numerous clashes with terrorists.

She and Rod hit the waves simultaneously, about ten meters on either side of the Zodiac and in full view. If the pilot noticed their approach, he gave no indication, keeping his wraparound sunglasses in place and his face toward the fence.

The click and clank of the lock on the gate opening barely reached her through the muffling water. But the pilot stiffened and half-rose from his seat near the stern.

Rod held forth a viciously long knife (how'd he get that past Dad? Or had he borrowed it from the corporal with the big rifle?) and slashed the rubberized hull right beside the motor supports.

Bubbles of air leaked out, a tiny bit at a time. The zodiac lost a bit of buoyancy.

With a nod, Sprite took the blade from his hand.

Pressure built in her chest. Her lungs ached. Her usually good underwater vision narrowed, darkened. Menacing shadows lurked on her periphery.

Her mind shouted *SHARKS!*

The compulsion to open her mouth and draw a deep breath nearly overwhelmed her.

She couldn't.

The boat leaked another stream of inflation.

The bubble of air within her armor begged her to use it before it too succumbed to the lure of the darkness and dissipated like the stuff coming out of the Zodiac.

A moment of concentration and she felt that tiny bubble move inward, granting relief to her lungs.

Not much. Just enough.

Instinct directed her hand to the boat's hull. She slashed downward, twisting the blade right and left, opening the slash further.

She bobbed upward the last meter, the natural buoyancy of her armor speeding her trek. She broke the surface silently and breathed again.

The Zodiac sagged, its rim dangerously close to the water. The pilot still didn't notice the change, even as a wave slopped over the edge onto the plank seat. He held his position, crouched forward, peering at the action on the beach.

Chapter Seventeen

Soft sand tugged at Bryce's aching joints. His balance twisted sideways, making his feet follow in odd directions.

Colonel Zachariah caught his elbow and stopped walking long enough for Bryce to catch his balance.

When his knee stopped wobbling, Bryce planted his cane in the ground, and nodded his thanks to the colonel.

"We can take it from here, sir," Zachariah said quietly.

"Not when my children are in the thick of it and my injured best friend is a hostage."

A few more steps and he caught sight of Tess, the Celestial Blade in full view. That meant close proximity to extreme danger or demonic evil. They crept to the corner of the chain link fence that separated the hotel pool from intrusion by non-paying guests.

"Rod and Sprite are in the water, sir. Right behind a small boat that is wallowing. Close to sinking." Zachariah directed Bryce's attention to the now distressed pilot anxiously trying to bail the boat, still ten meters from the shore.

The click of the lock opening in the gate sounded loudly.

The gate opened.

"Patience," Zachariah whispered into his wireless headset. "Wait until you have a clear shot. We want those terrorists alive for questioning."

"Don't endanger Lou." Bryce added his own warning.

The second Russian mercenary emerged first, a long-barreled revolver in his left hand, Bryce didn't recognize it, a foreign design, possibly a prototype. He scanned the entire beach, even the shadowed corners. A dozen soldiers in desert camo with HS patches on the arms and backs crowded close behind the Russian, pushing forward before he wanted to move.

The merc's eyes widened and his mouth opened in a snarl.

Tess sprang forward in a lunge worthy of a ballet dancer, blade sweeping wildly. The gun flew out of the merc's hand.

Phonecia and E.T. followed their mother, hands and arms extending to vine thinness and length as they partially transformed to their native dark elf forms of forest vines, blackberry and salal. Phonecia's thorns raked the Merc's face and arms. E.T. shoved poisonous berries into their victim's mouth.

Lou took advantage of the distraction and jammed his elbow into his captor's gut.

The still nameless minion of Major A doubled over on a long exhale dropping his gun even as Lou plunged sideways, away from danger.

Duc ran from the shadows, covering Lou with his own body. His armor blended with the sand, making them both invisible.

And then Bryce's troops ran forward. Strong muscles and the stamina of youth and fitness made the powdery sand seem like hard tile beneath their booted feet. The culprits froze in the face of a dozen weapons aimed at their hearts or heads.

Two of the HS soldiers tried to retreat into the hotel. Three of Colonel Zachariah's troops appeared behind them. The HS men dropped their weapons and held their hands high above their heads in surrender.

Their fellows outside the fence did the same.

"That was too easy," Bryce muttered. "Do not drop your guard!" he shouted to one and all.

The words came out a raspy croak as his traitorous lungs stalled and his compromised knees collapsed.

"DAD'S DOWN!" ROD SHOUTED to his sister.

The Zodiac dipped beneath the waves one last time. The pilot needed only a second to survey his situation and dove into the water, now rushing toward shore.

Sprite trod water for two heart beats until she was sure the boatman could swim. As he set off with long and competent strokes, she began her own retreat from the ocean to land on a diagonal.

Rod followed her, angling them so they'd emerge within feet of where Patrick fixed an oxygen mask over Dad's face. The situation must be serious if he chose the mask over the canula.

Movement erupted all around them as they set feet on damp sand above the tide line. Armed soldiers converged on Dad. The two guarding the merc and the minion shifted their attention.

Both of the prisoners wobbled to their feet, hands bound behind their backs with plastic zip ties. The Russian was faster than the man in the green vest. He began running northward and toward the waves on a zig zagging diagonal. The Zodiac pilot aimed his own strokes to intercept him.

Rod could see the long utility blade strapped to the swimmer's thigh. The Russian would be free of his restraints in seconds. "Where are we needed most?" he asked himself and his more decisive twin.

"Dad," she said flatly. "We can't swim much more today. The minion's fresh and rested. Leave him and the pilot to the troops." She took off in a sloppy and slow run as the dry sand made for uneven footing.

Rod followed, trusting her judgement. He had to bite his lip in indecision. With each step, the Russian mercenary got further and further away.

Duc emerged from the sand, lifting Lou with him. He studied the fleeing men and the injured victim in his arms. He scanned the beach back and forth, not knowing where he was needed most at that moment.

"Give me your weapon," Dad said. His words rang to the amassing numbers of people surrounding him, some had taken a steady kneel and aimed long barrels at the pilot and the merc. Everyone seemed frozen in place as the ocean paused in hurtling waves forward. In half a moment it would begin its retreat.

What about green-vest? Where had he gotten to? Did anyone care?

Rod looked to where his father had pulled himself upright and got his knees under him for better balance to shoulder and aim a rifle. The oxygen condenser hummed beside him as he took a deep breath and ripped off the mask.

An explosive shot shattered the moment of silence.

The weapon's kickback threw Dad to the ground. It shouldn't have. Rod knew Dad had had sniper training.

The merc collapsed face down, his hands still behind his back. The pilot who should rescue him stood over him, knife ready to slit his bonds.

Then a second bullet from a smaller weapon disturbed the sand at the boatman's feet. He dropped his knife and held up his hands in surrender.

Colonel Zachariah's troops surrounded him.

A helicopter roared above, its rotors churning a down draft upon them all as it descended to the sand.

A second chopper tracked the low slung boat near the horizon. A rooster tail of water escaped the now roaring jet engines. A spray of bullets added their own enveloping water splashes. Rod dismissed the boat. Authorities had the crew in hand.

Rod and Sprite fell to their knees on either side of Dad while Patrick replaced the oxygen mask on Dad's very pale face. His lips were turning blue.

BRYCE SUCKED IN A SHALLOW hit of oxygen. The mask irritated the burn scar on the left side of his face. But he needed the extra air. Then a brief interruption before a stronger flow relieved his spasming lungs.

A different profile replaced Patrick, behind and to the right.

"Good job, kid." A different voice, half-remembered, older, deeper. "Call me when you finish pre-med. I might be able to help with med school applications with the promise of a military residency afterward." He handed Patrick a card. "Now, General Maxwell, just keep breathing, sir. Long and slow. Your lungs will figure out what to do if you just give them a chance and stop fighting our help."

Had he been fighting medical assistance? Yeah, probably. He hated giving control over to someone else, to equipment rather than his own body.

Sprite and Rod came into his line of sight, kneeling on either side of him, on a level with his hands. They looked wet. What else was new?

Which reminded him, he needed...

"Stop being a general for two minutes, Dad. Be our father and recover."

He released some of the tension in his chest and let the oxygen do its work.

"That's it, Dad. Relax and breathe. We've done this before. Now breathe in, hold, out, hold. Slow and easy." Rod coached him.

"Okay, now let's get you up a bit," the older man behind him said. "Patrick, you take my place, sit with your knees bent almost to your chest and let them support his back. General, sir, we're going to lift you by your shoulders and scoot you backward. Don't try to help, and don't fight us. You'll breathe easier if we can get you up, just a bit."

Bryce shifted his gaze as much as he could to take in more desert camo and a medical caduceus on a collar. Military medic. One of his own team. He'd been new when Bryce retired. He couldn't remember a name. Just a vague introduction as he briefed his team on an operation.

He didn't remember much of anything about the fire except surprise that the hands that lifted a fallen beam from across his chest had been juvenile. Rod. Sprite had rolled him free of debris. Then the armored twins had worked together, dragging him by the ankles into the blessedly cool air of outside. Then nothing for days.

As much as letting others move him and take care of him grated on his nerves, he allowed it to happen for the twins. His children.

The noise of a helicopter revving up and taking off roused Bryce from his extended self-concern.

Propped up, his field of vision widened. Controlled chaos greeted him. Just as the aftermath of a mission should.

He shoved the oxygen mask aside to bark out orders. "Zachariah, report."

His colonel's big hands with an oversized-do-everything-but-breathe-for-you black watch strapped to the wrist pushed the mask back in place. "Louis Metcalf is on his way to the E.R. in Brookings. Once he's stable we will take him to a secure facility. I sent two armed soldiers with him. He's hurt but will survive. Might need surgery to fix a broken jaw."

That would keep the Looney Moose quiet for a bit.

"What about..."

Zachariah shoved the mask back into place. Annoying man, but very good at his job, which meant taking care of his troops as well as executing the mission. Bryce wouldn't have transferred him to the team if he wasn't.

"The Russian mercenary has a bullet wound that missed his spine by millimeters. He'll recover too, but so far is not talking. Adam Mathieson is missing."

"Who?" Bryce asked, not bothering to move the mask but trusting his second in command to understand.

"The nameless minion semi-attached to Major Arbuthnaught," Sprite added. "He wore the hotel employee vest and directed the kidnap as far as we can tell."

"The man in the Zodiac appears to be Homeland Security and won't speak other than name, rank, and serial number until he gets orders from his superior officer," Rod added.

"Major A?" Bryce had to think twice before referring to her with her con nickname of Honor Harrington. Honor was a valiant heroine of her novels. The major was looking more and more like a rogue warrior.

"She's no longer answering her phone. HS—the real and trusted agency—has begun searching."

"And that's enough for now," the medic interrupted. "An ambulance is here to take you to the local urgent care. Your... um bonus warriors have returned to your hotel and the convention. I heard something about panel discussions and 'filk?' practice."

Ah, the con goes on.

Chapter Eighteen

"The Phantom does not return in triumph in a wheelchair," Dad announced as Sprite tucked the condenser beside him where he could adjust the flow on his own.

Early afternoon on Saturday and the con had begun the transition to full-on party mode. More costumes, that grew skimpier by the hour, more booze, obscure jokes that only special cliques got and laughed at uproariously. The Master of Ceremonies pranced about, having added a lei to his loud shirt, a flower behind his ear and an umbrella to his oversized martini glass.

Sprite soaked up the special atmosphere that she'd missed the last three years during the pandemic.

"Your new costume, Dad," she said, tilting his hat to a more rakish angle that shadowed the left side of his face. "Wheelchair, surgical mask, and O2, you look like a refugee from the pandemic."

Dad scowled at her. Then he quirked a silly grin at her and Rod as he showed them a new text on his phone.

Scrap reports no demons harmed in today's kerfuffle.
No one tasted or smelled particularly icky. All mundane.

"No one knows you in this guise," Rod added as he moved to take command of pushing the chair. "You could be anyone."

"Doctor's orders, sir. You have an hour to rest, dinner in the room, and then you can attend parties and concerts until ten." Patrick made a show of checking the condenser and the fit of the canula beneath the yellow medical mask. He practically glowed with pride at the military doctor's approval of his EMT work.

Sprite shared his joy. "You know, if you shift your specialty from studying criminal minds, to keeping PTSD victims from turning violent, a residency with the military makes a lot of sense," she said. On the ride from the hospital back to the con he'd voiced his concerns, needing the financial assistance of the program—basically free medical school and a military commission—but not seeing how the residency applied to his chosen field.

"Something to think about. Can I claim the first dance after the masquerade?" He leaned over and kissed her cheek.

In Sprite's eyes he seemed to have grown another inch or two. Or maybe he just had good reason to stretch his spine with new-found confidence.

"I leave you in good hands," Duc said, finally emerging from the big black SUV that had provided them door to door service. Colonel Zachariah had ordered his troops to take care of their general and his family, whatever they needed.

Duc patted Dad's shoulder. "I have my own life to tend to."

"You aren't staying for the con?" Rod asked. He looked at the newest member of their family, standing nearly eye-to-eye with the tall man.

Sprite shared a bit of her brother's hero worship, as well as a wistful need to learn more about her bio-father.

"Not my scene anymore. I will be in touch. Colonel Zachariah has my full report, and he has promised to address my concerns since Bryce cannot act upon them right now." He shook Rod's hand, bowed to Sprite and Patrick, then crouched in front of the wheelchair. "Let the twins take care of you, sir. Colonel Zach and I are making plans. We will protect the paranormals this rogue segment of HS wants to outlaw." He stood, tall and straight, then shook Dad's hand too.

"What plans?" Sprite demanded. "They concern Rod and me too."

"Later," Duc promised, looking over his shoulder at someone across the lobby. Then he left, with long and rapid strides, without further explanation.

"There you are!" Jacquie shouted, still five meters away. "I know where to find the Looney Moose. He's just down the road in the luxury hotel..."

"Not anymore," Rod said. "You are late. As usual. Who paid you to delay your news?"

"We found him this morning. Now he's in the hospital. No thanks to you," Sprite replied. She felt as if her words dripped the acid churning in her stomach.

"I meant to tell you last night, after the concert. But you all disappeared, and I had a date with the Master of Ceremonies..."

"Your hook ups are legendary. And always more important than your responsibilities," Rod said. "I'm betting your reward for *not* finding Uncle Lou before we found him on our own, must have been worth a half million." He looked down at his bio-mother with disdain.

"Three quarters," she blurted out, then slapped a hand over her mouth at her flub. She quickly recovered, batting her eyelashes and pouting. Her signature flirtation. "Don't be like that. You are my babies and will always be important to me..."

"Don't make yourself even more of an ass than you already are!" Didi Dogooder said, rudely bumping Jacquie aside with her shoulder. "No wonder your life and heart lines on your palm are so muddied." Then she blew Bryce a kiss. "See you later. I owe you a Tarot reading." She sauntered toward a knot of friends that included her newly ex-husband who still stayed with her.

Sprite had to turn away from Jacquie's gasping protests. She'd run away if she could. Right now, Dad needed her, and she made a habit of living up to her responsibilities.

"I think we've all had enough excitement for one day," Dad said on a yawn. "Go find a new rock to crawl under, Jacquie. And don't plan on collecting the other half of your fee for finding Lou. The rogue elements of Homeland Security are on the run or taken down. And watch your back. Your ability to find people borders on the paranormal. You could find yourself outlawed as well."

"But... but... I helped you!"

"Dad, I'll wake you with food in an hour or so," Sprite said, letting her brother wheel their father toward the elevator. "What from the room service menu sounds good?"

"Whatever sounds good to you, Sprite. Light on the fat, heavy on the protein. Wake me before then if Ellie and Liz return with news of Lou. Too bad the Looney Moose has to miss the best party of the year."

Jacquie seemed to shrink within herself as she stared at them gape-mouthed. Then she straightened her back and returned to party mode, looking for her next hook up, the only thing truly important to her.

Both Sprite's and Rod's phones pinged an incoming text.

"Ellie says that Uncle Lou is out of surgery and waking up. His jaw is wired closed but he's already demanding a tablet or pen and paper, anything to write down what he knows and wants us to do," Sprite said. A bit of the tension from this morning slid off her shoulders.

"Liz reports the same," Rod confirmed.

"Then you two can shower and party the rest of the evening. I may drop in on Tess's concert to see if she's turned our adventure into a ballad already," Dad said. "Oh, and Patrick, my daughter may be eighteen, legal *but* still socially naive. I'd be happier with both of you if you wait, probably until you finish your medical residency. But if you can't wait, protection is *required*. The same goes for you and Liz, Rod."

"I'm very aware of consequences, Dad. That's what happened to Jacquie. Remember?" Sprite hugged her boyfriend. They followed her brother and father into the elevator with his arm over her shoulder and hers across his back. She endured a momentary pang as she realized that she was shifting away from being joined at the hip with her twin, to a different kind of closeness with Patrick.

"We have some gaming to finish," Patrick said. "And a late lunch. I'm starved."

"Pizza," Rod added.

"And don't forget, we still have to find and arrest Adam Mathieson and interrogate Major A," Dad said as the elevator doors closed them in. "Finding and arresting him is Colonel Zach's job. You all just be on the lookout and stay out of his way."

That was Sprite's dad. Always thinking and planning his next strategy, even when exhausted and chained to his oxygen condenser.

BRYCE CAREFULLY SAT in one of the straight, and small, banquet chairs two steps into the ballroom. His cane steadied him. He leaned on it far more heavily than he liked while his condenser hummed in its shoulder pack. He pushed his chair back about two inches so that it connected to the wall. That gave him enough room to stretch his legs to ease his overworked and cramping muscles.

One shot. All he'd done this morning was take one shot, and the effort had knocked him flat.

Well, he had traversed about one hundred meters of soft sand to get to the back of the hotel unseen. Pavement would have been no challenge. He'd had to work three times as hard.

Center front of the ballroom, the wooden panels had been cleared to become the stage for the costume contest, and now the dance floor.

He found Sprite and Patrick dominating the crowd of young people and somewhat older con attendees who'd never quite grown up. The music was wild and rhythmically compelling. He'd never liked the current popular mixture of acid rock and rap. But then parents hadn't liked the musical choices of their children for many, many generations.

His mother had told him stories about the hysterics her parents threw when she turned up the stereo to play Motley Crue or Twisted Sister CDs. Now they were considered classics.

Still, he found his feet tapping to the beat. Even the blasted oxygen machine seemed to catch the rhythm and fill his lungs in time with the bass notes.

"I was told that you should be in bed, resting," Ellie said, coming up beside him. She placed her hand on his shoulder and squeezed gently, careful of all his cords and attachments.

He reached up to squeeze her hand and then draw her around him to sit in the empty chair to his side. She moved without protest, stepping gracefully over his extended legs, like she used to do, twenty years ago.

It felt good to have her beside him again, natural, comfortable, and special at the same time.

"How's Lou?"

"Obeying doctors' orders about as well as you do. He can't talk, and he's hooked up to multiple IVs that keep him in place a bit better than your portable air machine does for you. Liz is staying with him and loaned him her tablet. He's typing reports and emails and orders to the medical staff at half the speed of light. He's not shy about making his needs known."

"He must be on pain drugs to move so slowly." Bryce grinned at the image of his oldest friend using the tyranny of the invalid tactic.

"Even on drugs he spells better than I do, and I used to teach spelling to fourth graders."

Another chuckle-worthy image.

"Sounds like he will recover and return to work sooner than the docs want."

She nodded agreement, followed by another silence. "Oh, Bryce, they had to shave his beard to do the surgery on his jaw. It has been a part of him for so long, I almost didn't recognize him." She dropped her face into her hands.

"The Looney Moose without a beard. I don't think even *I* would recognize him. And I introduced you to him." Bryce had to swallow his laughter at the idea of his friend without a neatly trimmed, but lush beard.

"I've never seen him look so vulnerable. So lost."

"That he would be."

"He has a receding chin and buck teeth." She swallowed heavily. "I don't think I'll ever... stop laughing." She burst into quiet chuckles that quickly turned to sobs.

The music blended into a slow ballad, something closer to Bryce's choice of listening, but also an enticement for Patrick to pull Sprite into a close embrace. Too close for Bryce's comfort.

"Be honest with me, Bryce. How are you doing?" Ellie leaned closer to him, allowing their shoulders to touch. She hadn't released his hand from her own yet either.

Glorying in the small intimacies, Bryce took an extra-long breath knowing he had to enjoy Ellie in this moment and no longer.

"That bad, huh," she said flatly at his prolonged silence.

"The local doctor wanted to send me straight back to the med school in Portland and get my name on the list for a lung transplant."

There. The truth was out there.

"Do the twins know?"

"Not yet. I invoked patient privacy before the medics could talk to my children. The locals don't know that the twins, now that they are eighteen, have a Power of Attorney that includes sharing medical stuff." His eyes found Sprite and Rod without effort, marking their joyous celebration of life with the ancient ritual of dance. He wondered how close the modern movements mimicked the freeform religious rites of their tribal ancestors.

"Will you do it?"

"Not sure yet. You and I need to talk."

She stilled but did not move away. "Rod and Sprite need this news..."

"I need to know if last night was a one-night stand, or if you are willing to make some kind of commitment to a scarred, and scared, invalid."

"Or if I'm still tied to Lou beyond our shared child—who is now legally an adult and getting ready to go off to college."

"My kids will be flying free of the nest soon too. But they don't want to go very far and leave me alone."

"What kind of prognosis did they give you?"

"Vague. The doc who checked me out this morning isn't an expert. She suggested that the transplant would put limits on my lifestyle, diet and exercise, life-long anti-rejection drugs and such. But a longer and more comfortable life. I could banish the condenser forever."

"And if you don't?"

"A steady decrease in mobility and comfort. I'll be chained to the machine every minute of the day and night. Gradually reducing all activity until I'm a total invalid."

"Then I suggest you investigate all possibilities so you and I can have at least a couple of decades together. My only condition is that you never, ever, under any circumstances go back into the field again. You can leave those adventures to younger and fitter troops."

"Even though the lives of my children and best friend are at stake?"

"Even then. You have to learn to delegate and let your children learn to stand on their own two legs."

Or swim to a fight where others can't. That scared him more than anything he'd seen them do today.

He kissed her then. "The kids will be up dancing and gaming until after midnight. We can have the suite to ourselves for a couple of hours."

"Sounds good to me."
His phone pinged an incoming text from Po Duc.

Adam Mathieson sighted 50 miles northeast of you. I know where he's headed. It will take him 80 hours or more to reach his destination without a 4X4 and directions. GPS not enough.

Chapter Nineteen

Sprite slipped her hand into Patrick's as they lined up to parade out to the bonfire. Usually the Master of Ceremonies led this ritual on Friday night. The delay probably meant he was too drunk to stand up, let alone wield fire. Tonight, a tall slender man from the pagan community stood at the top of the stairs to the beach. His commanding height looked taller yet with a headdress of deer antlers—a full and rare, five-point white tail buck—and a forest green cloak embroidered with golden yellow Celtic knot work. He held aloft an unlit torch.

At some invisible signal the man began to process forward. The last ray of sunlight sinking below the ocean horizon seemed to jump from the darkening sky onto the torch. It sprang to life, guardian of the blessed sunshine until dawn tomorrow, when once more the world would come to life.

A respectful hush spread through the crowd as they walked solemnly toward the tower of driftwood on the beach.

Sprite marveled at the way this ancient ritual drew together the usually rowdy gaggle of partiers.

She drew Patrick closer so that their shoulders touched, and she sensed her pulse aligning with his.

"I've missed this," Patrick whispered. "Nice to know that three years of lockdown and a murder couldn't diminish the most important part of the con."

"Yeah," she agreed and squeezed his hand. She didn't know if she should mention that in some bronze age cultures similar ceremonies took place across Europe on the summer solstice. In those times the fire on the shortest night of the year also marked a night of fertility and mating. If she mentioned the purpose of the night, would he take her words as a suggestion that she was ready to engage in them?

Not yet. She knew she wasn't ready, even if he was.

For once she kept her mouth shut on her thoughts.

The pagan priest at the front of the procession reached the bonfire and stopped. The crowd fanned out around him, encircling the tall teepee of dried wood. She remembered one thing from chemistry class: sea salt embedded in the drift logs would burn in different colors from ordinary branches gathered from the nearby forests or cut cord wood. She looked forward to the dancing flames.

When all of the people fully encircled the bonfire, the priest thrust his burning torch into the center of the tower to a place prepared with tender kindling.

No one spoke.

Sprite barely breathed, waiting for the dry grass and tiny twigs to catch fire.

Then, with a whoosh, of sound and light and smoke, flames caught and spread to slightly larger branches, wavered and steadied and finally anchored in its new home.

The crowd expelled a group sigh and then a triumphant yell.

Someone produced a flat, circular drum with a double-headed stick and began a bouncing beat. A reed flute picked up the rhythm, adding a lilting descant, an almost tune. The clear baratone of the priest's voice gave undecipherable words and melody to the impromptu music. Individuals and couples broke away from the circle and began free dancing, pounding the sand with bare feet.

Patrick tugged Sprite's hand and twirled in wild gyrations. Sprite mimicked him until she found her own rhythm, feeling the tug of moon and stars as they popped into view as the last afterglow of daylight faded. She spun, arms out, palms up, and caught the energy of life, blending it with herself, and Patrick, and Rod who appeared at her side.

Her twin looked a little lost and alone. Liz had stayed in the city to be close to her dad. Rod had no one to celebrate with.

Guided by the same thought, she and Patrick each grabbed one of Rod's hands, drawing him into their prancing. Her blood sang with the glory of the night.

They broke apart and came together again and again. Gradually Rod drifted away from them, giving her and Patrick an illusion of privacy. He participated in the dancing but was still alone.

A part of Sprite needed to draw him back into the celebration. But she recognized a need to plait together her relationship with Patrick. Just the two of them, as she hoped they would someday be together.

Shadowy couples separated from the community, seeking their own solitude. Rod stayed near the fire while frequently turning his head toward the main building of the hotel, searching, hoping that Liz would appear.

When she didn't, he seemed more alone than ever, needing her and only her.

He drifted outside the widest circle of partiers. Beyond any hope of inclusion in their revelry.

Sprite's scale began to itch and burn. Another shadow approached Rod from the receding waves, like a mermaid freed from her fishtail. Female, definitely. Tall like Liz.

And yet...

"Isn't that Major A?" Patrick whispered into Sprite's ear. "What's with the tin foil helmet?"

"I dunno, but she has a gun."

Without thinking she flashed an image of the approaching shadow to her twin.

Rod reared his head up and around at the same time he lifted his leg in a broad martial arts sweep. His bare foot connected with the major's wrist. The gun flew away, burying itself in the semi-soft sand between the attacker and the waves.

"You have no right to resist arrest!" Major A screamed. "You are an illegal citizen."

"Tell that to my dad!" Rod snarled in reply. "And Uncle Lou Metcalf."

"And the entire U.N. black ops Division," Sprite added.

Patrick said nothing as he dove for the last place they'd seen the gun, barely out of reach of the major.

"I answer only to Homeland Security. My authority tops the U.N. on my own soil." Major A snarled with bared teeth, much more intimidating than Rod.

Sprite edged closer. Three more scales popped into place, overlapping the primary.

The major edged to her right, one foot sweeping the sand in search of the gun.

Patrick rose with the weapon in hand. He held it as if he knew what to do with it.

Sprite's armor snapped into place. All of it, leaving only her eyes and nose clear.

Major A tackled Patrick, grabbing his gun hand. Her tin foil helmet fell into the water and drifted backward, toward deep water, sinking rapidly.

The weapon exploded.

Sprite lost her balance and flailed backward as the bullet ricocheted off her belly and returned in the direction from which it came.

Major A screamed as blood began pouring from her upper right arm. In one smooth movement, she clamped her left hand over the wound to staunch the bleeding and rose to her feet. Her long legs took her to the tide hardened sand and sprinted away, every fourth step sent water spraying outward. "If you all would just shut up I could think clearly," she cried.

Patrick shifted his weight to the balls of his feet in preparation for sprinting after the wounded woman.

Rod grabbed his arm to hold him back. "She's probably got back up and transportation. We'll have Dad call in a report."

Sprite's armor collapsed.

"Are you hurt?" Rod and Patrick asked at the same time, both rushing to her side.

"We can't tell Dad. At least not yet," Sprite said. "He'll spend too much time and energy worrying about me and not focusing on the other problems, like that executive order Uncle Lou is supposed to write, and how to find Mathieson, who might very well be waiting for Major A before setting off into the wilderness."

"Yeah, they are probably hoping she managed to kidnap me, or you," Rod agreed. "Can you walk?" He turned his attention back to his sister.

Sprite lifted her tee and felt across her abdomen. "No blood, but it hurts like I've been kicked by a mule." Her shoulders hunched and her spine wanted to curl into a protective fetal position. "At least we know that our armor will ricochet a bullet but still hurt. We are resistant to arms fire but not impervious."

"Let me see," Patrick said, adding his delicate exploration of her skin to her own.

Warm, soothing, gentle. More than healing spread from his touch. Longing and lust filled her. She bit the inside of her mouth to contain her hormones.

He turned her so the light from the bonfire showed a swelling, red lump. "Looks like you'll have a nasty bruise, but the skin isn't broken. We should get some ice on it."

The revelry around the bonfire continued without interruption.

Then the ping of incoming texts shook Sprite and her twin out of their speculation of what to do next.

"Dad. He needs us *now!*" Rod said. "I'll run up first. You come at whatever speed you can manage."

The urge to linger with Patrick and let his wonderful hands explore her body almost glued her feet in place.

Her phone vibrated again.

ROD STOPPED SPRITE from entering the suite with an arm in front of her. He cocked his head to listen and perhaps learn why Dad had summoned them from the bonfire ritual.

"You are not going!" Ellie shouted. Panic colored every syllable.

"But..." Dad started to protest.

"I agree with her." Was that Duc speaking in the same tone Sprite used to calm testosterone-fueled arguments Rod shared with Dad?

Rod slid his key card into the lock and pushed the door open, almost before the mechanism disengaged.

Sprite followed hot on his heels.

"What did we miss?" Sprite demanded, hands on hips, feet spread, and her chin jutting stubbornly—just like Dad or Rod did when defied.

"You promised, Bryce. That was my only condition to us getting back together. *No more fieldwork*. I mean it. It's why I left you the first time. The condition holds."

"But..."

"Wait a minute." Rod held his hand up. "A moment of clarification. 'Getting *back* together'? 'Left you the first time'?"

"Little known history," Ellie said turning her back on all of them and staring out the window at the glistening waves in the moonlight and the bonfire still burning. "Your dad and I married, right out of college. He'd attended on a ROTC scholarship. We were together two years while he served as a sniper in the U.S. Army Rangers. Military forts and bases often had their own schools for the families. I always had a job as an elementary teacher. We were happy."

She paused long enough to take a deep, fortifying breath. "Then he was recruited for black ops by the U.N. and we moved to New York. I never knew where he was, when he'd come home. *If* he'd come home. They wouldn't even let him call me when he was in the hospital, critically wounded. I hated living in the city and found the school systems more like armed camps than any of the forts he was assigned to. I turned to Lou for comfort and companionship. He gave me more hints about Bryce's whereabouts and condition than your father ever did." She turned back to face him, head hanging in defeat. "I loved you, Bryce. I still do. But I couldn't deal with that lifestyle. And I won't again. You stand down from this mission or I walk out right now, and you will never see me or Liz again."

To Rod, she looked as if ready to start walking at any second. She needed only a word to keep her.

"Why should I worry about not seeing Liz?" Dad croaked out, eyes opening wide.

"I moved in with Lou only days after you left for Central Africa. We'd been close for weeks before that. I honestly don't know which of you is her father. And I don't care to know."

Dad closed his gaping mouth.

"While your history says a lot about both of you, Adam Mathieson is getting closer to my people in a secret sanctuary and putting them in danger," Duc said. He stood up from his perch on the edge of the loveseat. He fingered his car key. "The terrain around Mathieson's destination is rough and isolated, deeply forested. Bryce, if you were to go down again, there is no way we could call for help or get a rescue helicopter in. I need the twins—not an invalid, retired, genius general or not. In a worst-case scenario, Jacquie's finding talent may become necessary." He looked as if he needed to spit a bad taste from his mouth.

Rod itched to tell them about Major A. He looked to Sprite for agreement. Permission?

She shook her head and frowned at him. She was the one who hurt, it had to be her decision unless the bruise stopped her from participating in their adventure.

"I can send Zachariah..." Dad said. He looked more tired than Rod liked.

Patrick must have noticed the grey tinge to his skin as he hurried to turn up the air flow on the condenser.

"No authorities. My people are in hiding for a reason. Now that we've rescued Lou, he can finish writing that Executive Order for the President to announce next week. They plan to classify all paranormals as 'extraterrestrial aliens.' No rights. Subject to 'enhanced interrogation.' We need to gather our families and go deeper into the wilderness."

"What Executive Order?" Rod demanded.

No one in the room would look directly at him, or Sprite.

"Well?" Sprite asked. She moved closer to her father and grabbed his chin, forcing him to look at her.

Duc inched away as if recognizing the real power in their family.

Ellie swallowed a grin.

Rod made a mental note to stay out of the line of fire from either woman. Probably Liz too.

"Some short-sighted big wigs in the Senate, led by Senator Desdaganet—Didi Dogooder's ex father-in-law—have decided that anyone exhibiting paranormal talents are space aliens, and therefore not human, without any rights or citizenship. Your presence on this planet is illegal. Therefore kidnapping, torture, imprisonment, even murder is the new policy for the government," Duc said, evenly, without the emotions churning across his face and along his stiff spine.

"Lou would never..." Ellie gasped, covering her mouth in horror.

"Lou is well known for his fascination with UFOs and he hangs out with us weirdos at the cons. He was asked to write the order," Bryce said flatly.

"He stalled as long as he could," Duc added. "We think he came to this con, not just to spend time with his daughter and ex-wife, but to consult Bryce about it."

"If Lou doesn't write it, they'll just find someone else, less knowledgeable to do it," Dad muttered.

"We need to stop Mathieson and divert Homeland Security away from this rogue faction. But do we have to include Jacquie?" Sprite made a disgusted face.

"She's a finder," Duc said. He didn't look overly happy about that either. "Mathieson is highly trained. He can use the terrain to mask his presence."

"I don't like her either," Rod finally added his opinion. "I hope we won't need her talents."

"She's a sex addict," Ellie spat. "Is there any way you can contain her... enthusiasms?"

"I know some things about her she doesn't want her bosses, the press, or the police to discover. I'll make sure she behaves," Dad said.

"Dad, wait a sec," Rod said. Then he looked straight into Sprite's eyes. "We don't need Jacquie."

"Why?" Duc asked, following Rod's gaze toward Sprite.

She squirmed under the intense scrutiny. One hand pressed against her belly where the bullet had hit her armor.

"What do you mean, Rod?" Dad asked, also turning his attention to his daughter. She dropped her hand lest he sense her deep bruising.

"How many times has Sprite found your car keys? Or my phone, or the lost kitchen gadget that's needed immediately but hasn't been used in a year?" Rod asked, finally looking away from his twin and fished in his right hip jeans pocket to find his phone. It wasn't there of course. It never was even when he knew he tucked it away where it was supposed to be just minutes ago.

Sprite pointedly drew the phone out of his right front pocket and scooped up the car keys from the lamp table where Dad had tossed them the first time they entered this room, yesterday afternoon.

"I think we've concentrated so much thought on managing your overt paranormal talents that we've overlooked the more subtle ones," Dad said, shaking his head.

"If you have evidence, maybe it's time to turn Jacquie over to the police," Sprite said quietly. "I don't know if I can find a man hiding in the woods, but I can try, and I won't require a hefty bribe to do it."

"Are you certain, Sprite? She is your mother."

"No, she's not. She's a chronic abuser. The only time she even thinks about us is when she can't find a man to relieve her boredom." She lifted her chin in defiance.

"You mean her addiction," Rod replied. "She's as bad as someone hooked on cocaine. Remember how we watched that senior science prodigy deteriorate? Only took him six months to go from top of the class to drop out."

Dad leveraged himself upward from his chair and took Ellie's hand. "I'll make the necessary calls. Now, get some sleep, kids. You'll think and act better when you are well rested and fed. In the morning I'll work with Duc to figure out logistics and supply lines. Ellie and I need to talk."

"Finally!" Rod and Sprite gave each other a high five. "I'm calling Liz," they said together.

"I'll be crashing in Ellie's room. She gave me Liz's key. I doubt she'll be using it tonight," Duc said, holding up a key card.

"Ice!" Patrick mouthed to Sprite as he too exited.

"Ice," Rod echoed quietly, heading toward the mini fridge.

"Ice will be welcome," Sprite said, collapsing onto the loveseat.

Chapter Twenty

Sprite stared at the tiny gap in the blackout curtains, watching dawn flirt with the darkness. Every time she started to drift off to sleep her mind fell into an endless loop replaying the events of the last two days.

Her midriff ached.

Horribly.

She'd replenished her ice pack—a zip lock plastic bag filled with six tiny ice cubes from the mini fridge—twice. Rod had gotten up about three and fetched her a cup of ice from the machine down the hall while a new batch of cubes froze in the inefficient refrigerator.

She wondered how fast Dad would whisk her away to the ER if she told him about last night's adventures. Maybe after breakfast.

The con would slowly wind down until closing ceremonies at one this afternoon. By four the place would be nearly empty. Only a few die-hards would linger until tomorrow to begin their trip home.

That had been her family's plan. Dinner with friends followed by an early turn-in. Breakfast on the road and home before noon.

Instead, Dad and Duc would use most of that time planning and organizing the next expedition. They wouldn't see home for several more days. If they survived.

She decided not to think about that as the bruising across her belly finally eased.

She and Rod had the day to game and swim and say good-bye to friends. Tess and her children—*Celestial Vines*—would perform their last concert of the con at noon, then pack up and depart on the long drive back to Portland.

Sprite's phone vibrated on the lamp table beside her fold-out bed. An incoming text from Patrick. She grabbed it before it woke Rod. He merely rolled over and grunted. Typical. He wouldn't wake until the sun was fully up. Then he'd want a swim before breakfast. Ocean or pool? She couldn't predict.

R u up?

She scooted into the small bath and closed the door firmly.

Yes. Y r u?

The phone rang within seconds of hitting send.

"Can you meet me on the pool deck in ten minutes?" Patrick asked without preamble or even waiting for her to say "hello."

"Yes. Will you have time for breakfast in the café before you have to leave?"

"Skinny dipping?" His voice sounded bright and hopeful.

"No." Though if the mission went south, this might be her last chance ever...

"Oh well. I'm halfway there."

She surveyed her sleep shorts and chemise. They covered as much of her as her swimsuit—especially her burn scars.

"I'll be there in five minutes."

"Make it two. Please."

The secondary elevator bypassed the hotel lobby and deposited Sprite one level below. The door slid to her left, opening onto a tiny, tiled square and a push door that emptied onto the pool deck. No half-naked swimmers need traipse through the sedate and civilized lobby.

One step and the marbleized tiles chilled her bare feet. A long arm, tanned with red-gold hair, snaked around her throat from the back.

She grabbed it with both hands prepared to bite and flip him over her shoulder.

"You are thirty-seven seconds late, my love."

"Patrick," she breathed, turning her bite into a kiss.

"Thirty-seven seconds without you."

"I wish you were going with us. I have this awful feeling we're going to need a medic." She turned to face him.

His restraining hands became a circle of his arms resting on her hips.

"First, please let me check your bruise?"

"It's better," she said, raising her chemise to just below the swell of her breasts. While her lizard brain yelled at her to pull the skimpy bit of cloth all the way off, her logic demanded that she keep at least part of her modesty intact.

"No swelling, but it's still red. Going to be technicolor blue, purple, green and yellow in a few days." Patrick explored the edges with his fingertips before tugging her garment back into place. "It's up to you to assess your pain level and decide when to tell your dad. But he does need to know about Major A."

"Okay." She shifted her chemise a little to make sure it remained in place, no matter how much she—and probably he—wanted to rip it off. "Eat or swim?" she diverted his attention.

"I can't linger more than a half hour or so. I start training at the fire academy tomorrow morning. This is not something I can postpone. I need to get hired by a fire house near the University if I'm going to have any income at all going into med school." He dropped his head until their foreheads touched.

"Even if the army pays your way?" She shuffled closer until their chests began to mold together.

"No guarantees. I've got a whole lot of classes to pass and tests to ace before I can even apply. Recommendations help, but I still have to prove myself. Becoming an EMT is only the first step."

She had no rejoinder to that, so she rose up on tip toe and kissed him.

He pulled her closer and deepened the pressure, his soul blending with hers.

Languid warmth flowed from her fingers inward. She tangled her hands with his slightly shaggy hair.

He pulled her hips closer yet.

Her pulse sped and throbbed.

Their hearts began to beat together, a single drumbeat in the full symphony of joy.

And then he pulled away, gasping for breath.

Cold filled the nanometer between them.

"What?" she gasped.

Another centimeter crept between them.

"Sex education in school only teaches us about consequences, not commitment, the ultimate in communication, and respect. Your dad talked to me about respect."

"I got the same lecture." She dropped her hands from his face to his chest, granting her a bit of leverage to push him away. If she chose.

If *she* chose.

She needed a few more deep breaths to regain control of her thoughts and her body.

"As much as I want you, want us to be together, I have to respect you and the fact that we are both young and have a long way to go before we can... commit to each other." Slowly he too regained control of his breathing. "Besides, your dad is *really* scary when he's in his protective mode."

"Yeah, he is."

"And after what I saw him do on the beach yesterday, he's earned the right to be scary."

"That was some shot he took. And it wasn't even his own weapon with the grip molded to his hand and the trigger tuned to his touch."

"What's scarier is that you know that. Like you've handled a few weapons yourself."

"Only on the target range. And I'm better with a handgun than a long barrel."

"On that note, I think I should dive into the pool and cool off."

Sprite giggled. "Me too. But just a quick lap or three. Then breakfast. You need fuel before the long drive home."

"Wish you were coming with me."

"So do I. But I've got a mission. Arbuthnaught and Mathieson need to be brought under control. From what Duc tells me, they're close to the top of the renegade faction of Homeland Security that wants to enslave the paranormal community."

"Be careful, Sprite. Please. I still think you should tell your dad about the bruise."

"I'll do my best. I want a raincheck on more kisses like that."

"Then think about university in Seattle. I'm hoping for Med School there so I can live at home and save money." He took her hand and led her out onto the pool deck.

"I've been worried about leaving Dad. But now it looks like he and Ellie might get together, I don't have to be afraid for him so much."

"We'll talk."

Together they jumped into the deep end of the pool.

"SUNDAY MORNING, THE success of the con can be gauged by the number of comatose bodies in the lobby," Bryce said to no one in particular, gazing at several lumpish people sprawled on padded armchairs and sofas, snoring.

Only seven in the morning. Ellie still slept. Sprite had slipped out to swim with Patrick. Rod had gone to the gaming room. Po Duc had yet to make contact with him. He was probably swimming.

And Bryce was hungry. The extensive breakfast buffet in the dining room wouldn't open for another hour. If he wanted to eat now, his only option was the limited-menu café. Sprite and Patrick occupied a corner booth, sitting much too close, kissing more than they ate.

He didn't want to interrupt.

A long-fingered, feminine hand clamped tightly onto Bryce's forearm. He contained his startlement and searched for the owner of that nicely manicured hand. Purple nail polish with golden glitter told him who with a minimum of thought.

"Didi. I see you, too, are an early riser," he said. Then he lifted her arm and kissed the tips of her fingers.

"The time has come, Bryce Maxwell." She giggled and patted his cheek. "We can pick up our flirtation later."

A frown settled in his gut. "You may be single again, but we are both semi-attached elsewhere," he replied, admiring her lushly curved body. Another time, another place he might be tempted. Not now. Not when he and Ellie were just moving toward getting back together.

"I mean for me to read the cards for you," Didi said, fingering the lump in her A-line denim skirt pocket.

"I thought you wanted to poke around into the reactions of the whole family." Bryce couldn't think of a better way to stall. His chest tightened at the thought of revealing anything to this woman. Bright and bubbly she might be. A fluffy scatterbrain at first glance. Something about her offer set his teeth on edge.

A quick glance at Sprite showed his daughter and her boyfriend standing beside their table and indulging in one last body molding kiss before Patrick broke away from her and headed for the exit while he pulled his car keys out of his front jeans pocket.

Sprite seemed to slump and fold in on herself.

Bryce's parental instincts kicked in and he walked away from Didi to offer comfort to his child.

Didi followed him. "Good, you've found a private booth." She smoothed her skirt behind her and slid onto the faux leather bench and swept the empty plates, cutlery, glasses, and coffee mugs to the edge of the table. "Sprite, please summon your brother. This needs to be a family reading."

Bryce's jaw dropped. "How do you know..."

Didi tapped her temple and smiled. "Take a seat, Bryce, here beside me. Sprite, you and Rod need to sit together. You are psychically two halves of one whole."

Sprite obeyed even as she closed her eyes and tipped her chin downward. Seconds later she lifted her face toward Didi. "He's coming."

Bryce dismissed a waitress as she approached with menus. "We'll eat in a few minutes," he told her. The woman stacked the detritus and took it away.

She was on her way back with a damp rag when Rod entered. He took the cleaning cloth away from her and continued on to join them. He gave the table top a quick swipe and threw the rag into the next booth over. "What?" he demanded. "I'm waiting for a call from Liz. She's signing papers to transfer her dad to a care facility."

"If the hospital is releasing him, then he must be on the road to recovery," Didi said. She placed a stack of cards in front of her—the Wildwood set filled with forest symbols—closed her eyes, and tilted her face upward in the direction of the rising sun.

Strangely, Sprite and Rod remained silent, watching her intently rather than pepper her with questions. Bryce felt constrained to respect the moment of meditation.

"I'm going to shuffle the cards then pass them to each of you to cut them. When you touch the cards, think carefully about the outcome of the next few days. Think of the best possible scenario and how you wish it to transpire." Didi suited actions to words. The mirrored tree of life, above and below, on the backs of the cards nearly mesmerized Bryce. All weekend he'd been forced to think in terms of past and present and the unknown future. His actions and the consequences wrapped his heart in chains. He had more than a few regrets, but the best, most positive thing he'd ever done was to adopt his children.

For the first time since Bryce and his children had first met her, Didi appeared deadly serious. No smiles, no giggles, no sunshine sparkling in her eyes.

"I'm not certain why I brought this deck to the con," Didi said. "At the last minute, it just seemed that I would need it." Her long fingers deftly handled the oversized deck. She'd chosen the set with Celtic symbolism, druids and standing stones and creatures of the wild. Bryce didn't question her choice.

As she slid the deck in front of him, he pictured in his mind his family, extended to include Ellie and Liz, sitting in front of the fire at his home, laughing and singing Christmas carols while they strung popcorn and cranberries to decorate the tree. Happy. Peaceful. Loving.

Well, it wasn't what he expected to happen over the next few days, but what happened during their coming adventures would determine if his daydream would ever be possible. Then he grabbed half the deck of cards and placed the stack facedown on the table and the other half atop it. Then he tapped the entire deck together, hiding the place where he'd cut them.

Didi slid the cards across to Rod. He repeated his father's actions, but only taking a third of the deck off the top.

Sprite removed a single card and placed it on the bottom of the pile.

Didi raised her eyebrows at that.

Chapter Twenty-One

Sprite wondered at the choice of decks. She didn't know much about the Tarot but thought the traditional style so popular at fairs and for sale in the dealers' room at the con might work better for her mixed and blended family. She'd watched Didi wield that deck many times over the years. It had begun to fade and fray. This stack of cards looked fresh, barely touched by human hands.

Not that she believed in this mystical nonsense. Logic did not enter into the idea of psychic guides and spirits and stuff.

And yet... normal logic did not explain why she and Rod could change their exterior when threatened or those around them needed protection. Or that Tess carried an imp on her shoulder that morphed into the Celestial Blade, and her adopted daughters carried the defenses of poisonous berries that extrude from E.T.'s fingertips, and Phonecia's arms became thorned vines.

Duc had called them guardians.

Didi fanned the cards out on the table, separating the tops from each other but keeping the bottom corners tightly meshed. "Bryce, please pick a card. You may look at it, but do not show it to me or the twins yet."

"This one will do," he said, taking a random one from the far left of the deck. He placed it face down on the table without glancing at it.

Rod chose one at the center. He studied it long and hard then held it against his chest.

Sprite fought a compulsion to take the card next to the gap left by her brother's selection. No other card pulled at her. It was the companion of Rod's card or nothing. She couldn't look at it. Not at all. Yet she knew it was somehow connected to her twin. *Two halves of one whole*, Didi had said.

That summed it up.

Or did it?

"There are four people missing in this moment. They are important to you but not immediately needed for this reading. Still..." Didi selected four cards, seemingly at random. As she slid them off to the side she whispered each name in turn. "Ellie, Patrick, Duc, and Liz."

"Why that order in the naming?" Sprite asked. She looked at her own card and felt a hole opening in her gut.

"That is the way the cards presented themselves in my mind." Didi tapped Dad's card.

He flipped it over. A wide-eyed faun peered out from beneath a standing stone configuration. Three rough-hewn uprights, capped by a fourth. Grass, trees that echoed the tree of life on the back and a long horizon across an open plain that stretched to a soft sunset.

"The Four of Stones. Protection," Didi said on a smile. "That sums you up to a tee, Bryce. You are the anchor and the shelter of your family as you approach your sunset years. No longer the active warrior and defender. You are a shield and a hiding place. Stout and authoritative."

"Is that what the symbols carved into the stones represent?"

"Only you can interpret those ideals. Think about it. Now for you, Rod." She turned over the card. "The Woodward, reversed."

A solid warrior wearing leather and a crown of a mountain lion's head and holding a vessel and a spear with an oddly carved top. Beside him crouched a lynx.

"Part of the Major Arcana," Didi murmured. "Fitting as you approach your mental and physical prime. You are the defender of those who are lost and alone, striding forward with confidence in a wild landscape that seeks to ensnare you with throned vines."

Didi dropped her head as if exhausted. She breathed shallowly for a moment, as if it took great effort.

Sprite had seen Dad do that often enough to know that this reading taxed Didi's strength.

"I have not forgotten you, Sprite," Didi said, head still bowed. "I have saved you for last because you could be the most important person in this lot. If you let yourself be." She lifted her head and fixed Sprite with a stern stare.

Her blue eyes seemed to shift toward hazel, then green, and settled into violet as her smile returned. She held her palm flat, waiting for Sprite to place her card there, face up.

Didi gasped.

No one spoke.

The sounds of the café faded, became distant. A grey mist seemed to isolate the family from reality.

"The Wanderer. First of the Arcana."

Sprite glanced at the images: A girl in a ragged green top and layered skirt in shades of brown, tripping from foothold to path atop a stream. Lush as well as withered trees surrounded her. And a rainbow sprang forward from her feet. A static picture that seemed to move forward within her mind.

"You leap ahead of your companions on a path of your own choosing, and yet you keep those you love close. You are the first line of defense in a changing world."

Didi slumped, beyond exhausted.

"Waitress!" Dad called. "Coffee all around, bacon and eggs all around."

"I'd rather have a Denver omelet with sausage and whole wheat toast, lightly buttered," Sprite said, loud enough for the waitress to hear, halfway across the now crowded and noisy eatery. She'd eaten lightly with Patrick, thinking she didn't need anything more than oatmeal with fruit. Now she knew she'd need more to fuel her day. A lot more. "I choose for myself," she said.

BRYCE'S GUT GREW HOLLOW with anxiety. At the same time his muscles relaxed and filled his head with a sense of peace. He was doing the right thing.

Schedules had been coordinated, supplies arranged, maps consulted, and backups set in place. All was ready.

I'm doing the right thing, he told himself.

He marched through the lobby, his shield prominently displayed on his belt, oxygen condenser gratefully left behind. His combat boots made enough noise that all of the lingerers, and malingerers, noticed him.

His three team members, now in civilian clothes and discreetly armed, lifted their chins and nodded acknowledgement of his presence as well as their readiness to guard the exits from the dining room. Three more soldiers waited on the other side of the French doors that led to the patio.

He searched for two upright but red-eyed con-goers in particular. The Master of Ceremonies, still wearing a loud shirt and khaki cargo shorts, was easy to spot. As usual, he was meticulously groomed with freshly trimmed beard and his clean, long blond hair pulled back into a ponytail.

Jacquie, in her ubiquitous garb of oversized blouse, leggings, and white pumps with a spike heel, clung to the MOC as if her life depended upon it. At least five different ropes of beads draped her neck in varied lengths from choker to a chain of metal beads that nearly hit her waist.

That longest chain was as much weapon as decoration. In the right hands, it could become a garrot. The bruises on the throat of the dead Russian mercenary came to mind. Fingers had crushed the man's windpipe, but those beads in the hands of an expert could have restrained the man first.

At this point, Bryce wouldn't put anything past Jacquie. Or her *amour du jour*.

Years ago, Bryce had done a surface internet check of the MOC. It revealed very little. He might act as host of five or six different cons a year, but he had almost no web presence of his own. Yesterday, while supposedly resting after the trip to the ER, Bryce had hacked into con records—notoriously insecure—to find a legal name for the man. All he got was the initials JEL.

That was enough.

The information led him to FBI databases that put his prey on the periphery of organized crime activity. No one had any evidence to implicate him more than just being sighted among the bigwigs of the syndicate more than ten years ago.

Bad copies of blurry photos showed a man, clean-shaven, short-haired and wearing a bespoke suit that would cost the first year of college tuition for the twins. At the time he appeared barrel chested but not the portly, borderline obese man currently acting as Master of Ceremonies. The profile held a lot of coincidences.

The next photo in the collection showed Senator Desdaganet at the funeral of his long-time aide and chief of staff. Directly behind the politician's left shoulder stood a shadowy figure of the same proportions as the MOC. His beard was short and neatly trimmed. His hair had grown long, but not long enough to secure into a ponytail.

Bryce pulled up software from his external hard drive that was illegal for him to possess after his retirement. With three clicks he engaged facial recognition that pinpointed distance between the eyes, the length and shape of the nose, cheek points, and six other features that did not change even with plastic surgery.

Because of the blurriness of the photos the software confirmed only four points of absolute match.

Enough to go to court.

That placed JEL deep within the inner circle of the Teflon-coated senator.

The man who led the faction to declare paranormals as space aliens and illegal citizens.

Bryce didn't trust the transition from Mob hanger-on to politically powerful Congressional mover and shaker. Nor did he trust the way Jacquie clung to him. Her life might very well depend upon staying in JEL's good graces. This weekend had too many loose ends. One of them at least he could tie up, right here and right now. He'd deal with Marjorie Arbuthnaught later. Bad enough that she photographed numerous costumed people who might or might not be paranormals in hiding, but she'd shot at his children!

Oh yes, Sprite had showed him her bruise. Already healing but bad enough that the bullet would have killed her had she not engaged her armor.

He ground his teeth together one more time before moving. His anger had neared the boiling point all morning. Now it was time to do something about it.

Didi's Tarot reading didn't mean anything. He wasn't just a passive shelter. He was, as he always had been, a warrior needing to defend his family. And seek revenge.

He'd let the FBI worry about JEL, especially if he threatened anyone at the con.

General (retired) Bryce Maxwell intended to take down Marjorie Arbuthnaught himself. With his bare hands if necessary.

Later. When he'd dealt with Jacquelyn Johnstone at the bottom of the chain of miscreants.

"Jacquie, it's time you take responsibility for your actions," Bryce said to anyone who happened to be listening. He marched toward the brunch buffet, raising his shield, making his authority obvious to anyone who cared to look. A federal warrant rustled in his inside jacket pocket.

Two o'clock on Sunday everything was sparsely populated. Officially, the con had ended an hour ago. Jacquie and the MOC picked among the last remnants of the buffet. They'd eaten earlier with a large and loud crowd of organizers and fans while Bryce waited anxiously for the warrant. Now they gleaned the last little bit of privilege the MOC could manage with his comped membership, room, and food.

Jacquie sat with her back to the French doors, making sure she was in a place where everyone would notice her when they looked out onto the patio and the open ocean. She spotted Bryce's prominently displayed badge almost immediately.

Bryce knew she'd noticed his approach the instant her smile of satisfaction froze. She frantically began seeking an escape, face and gaze moving rapidly in one direction after another.

JEL pushed his chair back, away from the table, giving him enough leg room to flee.

Bryce gestured for him to stay put and pointed his cane as if a rapier.

"I won't go easily so you can accuse me falsely, General Bryce Maxwell!" Jacquie screamed.

The MOC jerked his head in surprise. They didn't run in the same circles at cons and he apparently hadn't made the connection between Bryce and his black ops history.

"I'll let everyone in the con community know that you are just out to get me because you had to steal my babies to get custody of them!" Jacquie stood, hands on hips and feet braced to give her leverage to run at the first opportunity.

"Don't make a scene, Ms. Johnstone," he said through gritted teeth. "You'll just make it worse." He retrieved the warrant and shook the folded paper open. "I hereby arrest you on federal charges of blackmail, misuse of authority, influence peddling, aid in a kidnap, and attempted murder. You have the right to remain silent, and I suggest you do so. You have the right to an attorney. If you cannot afford one, you will be provided one."

"I suggest you go with him," JEL said quietly. He subtly moved his chair a few more inches away from her, already separating himself from *her* crimes.

"Don't worry. We are closing in on the evidence to finally convict you of similar crimes," Bryce replied. A shot in the dark but entirely plausible.

JEL paled and pulled out his phone. He punched the first name on his speed dial. Senator Desdaganet?

"But... but... what will my babies think?" Jacquie stuttered.

"Don't worry. They are the ones who pushed for your arrest when I hesitated. Now do you come quietly, or do I cuff you here and now in front of everyone whose opinion you value?" He touched the metal restraints in his back pocket.

Chapter Twenty-Two

R od waited beside the family SUV in the hotel's back parking lot while Duc hugged a tall blond woman with long legs shown off by cut-offs—his wife Mimi. She hefted her rolling suitcase and two miniature backpacks—one pink and one lavender—from the back of their 4X4 pickup.

Rod tried hard to hide his grin. The big Dodge Ram had a front winch and a back tow hitch, plus a spotlight bar across the roof and oversized tires. The hulking vehicle shouted masculine power. But it had been painted an absurd dark purple.

"No giggles. The color was a family decision," Duc grunted.

"Of course, Duc wanted a red truck. We special ordered it for all the extra forest fire equipment, so we got to choose a color other than white, silver, grey, or black. But he made the mistake of asking the girls their opinion. Lili said pink, Monique demanded blue, and I said white. So we compromised. I can find it in any parking lot! Hi, I'm Mimi, and you must be Rod." She held out her hand.

"And the two monsters racing around the family coach and four—they love Cinderella and her coach in the movie, so we decided the description was logical—are Lili and Monique," Duc replied.

Sprite giggled. "I love the pun!" Then she introduced herself and held out a hand in greeting to... to their stepmother?

Rod had to stop and wonder a moment. What was their relationship to Mimi, the wife of their bio-father? And the little girls with their dark curls bouncing with their antics at being freed from their confinement within the vehicle, what was their relationship with them.

"Daddy, Daddy, Daddy." The younger of the two girls tugged on her father's con t-shirt.

"Yes, Munchkin. What do you need?" Duc crouched down to put him at eye level with his daughter while keeping one hand clasping Mimi's waist.

"Mama said that you found my sticker book. Did you find it? Please, say you found it." She pleaded with tears in her eyes.

"As a matter of fact, I did find your sticker book, sweetheart. It was under the driver's seat of the teacup car. But I had to borrow one of the little yellow duckies. I'm sorry but I had no choice. I know you were saving it for something special. It's just... it's just that I needed your ducky for my badge." He fished his con badge still on its lanyard from beneath his shirt and showed her the cute, yellow, baby duck stuck to the laminated cardboard. "See? The name they gave me is Ducky, so I had to have the sticker." He traced the letters with his finger as he pronounced the name slowly and carefully.

"That's okay, Daddy. As long as you found my sticker book. I think the ducky looks great on you. Duck—d. u. c. k." She lifted her big, luminous green eyes to his in pride. "I can spell it. I've been practicing."

"Good, now the sticker book is in the car. You can have it when Mama drives you home. Just remember to take it to your room and put it someplace safe." He kissed her forehead, then stood up. The whole time he'd never stopped touching his wife. "Now go play with your sister."

I want that life! Rod told himself. *I want that with Liz.* His heart swelled as his mind swirled away from the con, away from politics and Homeland Security and the mess of his own family and genetics. The relationship he was building with Liz felt better than the rest of the crap in front of him.

He didn't care that Didi had never revealed Liz's Tarot card or that she had named her last in the pool of aligned people.

Liz was the woman he wanted. Not just for now while his hormones jumped at the thought of her, but forever, like Duc and Mimi.

The parking lot was crowded, so Duc moved to corral the girls and shift their circle of play to the grassy verge at the side of the hotel.

Many of the con goers, now in civilian clothing, packed their own vehicles. They were by nature a curious lot and kept an eye on the people they didn't know. This back lot was as public as an auditorium just before a basketball game. And the truck was an eye-catcher, earning many pointing fingers and laughs. The perfect mix of practical and absurd, like most cons.

Then came the complex ritual of moving the child seats from the truck to the little hybrid sedan, the teacup. Duc and Mimi handled it easily, like an often practiced and well-choreographed dance.

Rod couldn't get over how much the two daughters looked like Sprite; half-Asian and half-Caucasian, they had the same soft dark hair that curled around their ears, big green eyes, and delicate bone structure.

"Beach, Daddy?" the littlest one, Monique, paused in her impromptu game of chase.

"Mama will take you to the public beach, with a lifeguard, up the road a bit on the way home," Duc said. He draped an arm around his wife's shoulders as he snagged the older girl in her next running loop. "You can burn off some of that excess energy playing in the waves. But you have to promise me you won't go deeper than water at your knees. You are a good swimmer, but the tide is a tricky monster." He rubbed noses with her before setting her back on the pavement.

"I'll stay with them," Mimi promised and kissed his cheek. "Oh, and take the Sanctuary spreadsheets and update them," Mimi said as she twisted to retrieve a clipboard from the Ram's center console. "People come and go so quickly we don't always know how many and which noses to count."

Duc unclipped the few pages, folded them in half, and tucked them into the side pocket of his duffel. Throughout the movement he never let go of his wife.

"Drive safe, sweetheart," he said and kissed her briefly. Their gazes lingered on each other, hungrily, though a passionate embrace among this crowd might be a bit embarrassing.

Then Duc swung his own luggage and camping gear into the back of the truck next to a huge pack Mimi had brought. His wife checked the clasps and belts for the girls and transferred their luggage into the back hatch of the teacup sedan.

Duc seemed to deflate a moment as he waved good-bye to his family.

Rod opened the hatch of his SUV with the remote and hefted his father's luggage into the cargo space. Then he swung his own into the back of Duc's truck, letting it fall wherever it wanted.

Duc shook his head with a frown and set his gear on the ground. With two swift movements he straightened Rod's duffel and shoved it neatly up against the side of the space, along with two empty packs they'd need at the end of their journey. His pack lined up beside it. Instinctively he reached a hand back and grabbed Sprite's rolling suitcase just as she tried to lift it over the tailgate. Duc settled it beside the other luggage and secured it all with a bungy cord.

"Where's Dad?" Rod asked his sister—his real sister not the two half-siblings he'd barely been introduced to. Duc had promised an official family get-together later, when they'd all had a chance to get used to the idea of extended members—maybe a Fourth of July picnic.

Sprite scanned the exit from the hotel. "He was right behind me..."

The door opened and Dad emerged, one hand firmly on Jacquie's arm, practically dragging her in his wake. But in a different direction. Two State Police officers followed—one male, one female. Members of his own team spread out around the parking lot, covering all angles of escape.

They did allow a big limo to leave. Rod caught a glimpse of flowing blond hair on broad, masculine shoulders. The MOC deserting the sinking ship like a rat?

A State Police cruiser sat, idling a few meters away. Colonel Zachariah stood outside the sedan with a clipboard in his hand.

Duc's scale began to redden and pulse. He scanned Jacquie's body, her leggings and blousy top, and fixed on her high heels and multiple necklaces that varied from choker to a loop of filigree metal that dipped to her waist. "I think you two made the right decision about turning her in. She'd be more trouble than she's worth finding our targets. And she's not trustworthy."

"Now wait a moment, Po Duc, I'm damned good at what I do. I'll find who you are looking for." Jacquie dug in her flimsy spike heels.

SPRITE TOOK A DEEP steadying breath and faced her bio-mother full on, for the first time since Bryce Maxwell had rescued her and her twin from this insane woman.

"As long as there's no man distracting you, from your real job of finding and rescuing people," she snarled.

"Or a fat wad of cash that is more interesting," Rod added.

"I found your precious Looney Moose," Jacquie retorted.

"By the time you told us where to find him, we'd already rescued him and medevac had taken him to the hospital," Rod jumped into the fray.

Sprite was glad for his sense of protection, not wanting her to have to bear the brunt of Jacquie's displeasure.

After Didi's Tarot reading, she had found a growing sense of confidence buried deep within her. She needed to lead, not meekly accept whatever malice others dished out.

"I was busy." Jacquie harumphed, crossed her arms in indignation and half turned her body away.

"With a man. Another one-night stand?" Duc added.

"And if you know Duc's name, why didn't you put it on the twins' birth certificates?" Dad shifted himself to face Jacquie and stare her down. "It would have made the legalities of the adoption a lot easier if we had a name to track him down and *ask* him how he wanted his children cared for."

"I didn't want to ruin his life and plans for the future," she mumbled.

"If I had known, I'd have made certain that you never had custody," Duc replied. "Sure, I couldn't afford to take the children at the time, but I have family who would have gladly welcomed them into their homes and lives. I'd have stayed in contact with them, made certain they got training in their talent and learned our history and lineage."

"That's all water under the bridge," Jacquie dismissed the conversation with a shrug and a wave of her hands. As she always did. "Now, where are we going, and what do I need to bring?" She whirled around to inspect the contents of the pickup.

Her face lost all traces of color and animation. "When you said camping, I thought you meant an RV at a trailhead and branching out in a different direction each day... Not bushwacking for a week!"

"You aren't coming with us. The police have a different destination in mind for you." Sprite closed the conversation and moved to stand by the absurd but oddly comforting Ram.

"I can keep you warm and comfortable in the tent, Duc," Jacquie purred, running her long nails down the man's chest. She might have intended flirtation, but on her the gesture seemed more feline and predatory.

"Not interested." Duc turned his back and began fussing with the luggage in the back of the vehicle even though it was all secure and not wiggling at all.

Colonel Zachariah stepped up and handed his clipboard to Dad. "Sign on the bottom line and initial in the three places highlighted in yellow," he said with a flat voice, barely looking at Jacquie.

"I officially transfer custody of my prisoner to you, Colonel. Please read her rights again and get her out of my sight. I'll testify if and when this comes to court," Dad replied. "With her connections she might not survive long enough to go to trial."

The female state police officer stepped up and neatly cuffed Jacquie's hands behind her back.

Sprite felt a moment of deep satisfaction. She need never fear this woman again.

"Just a minute. I haven't done anything wrong!" Jacquie twisted and squirmed, trying to avoid being guided into the back seat of the cruiser.

"Jacquelyn Johnstone, you are under arrest for coercion, blackmail, aiding a kidnap, attempted murder, and interfering with a federal investigation. You have the right to remain silent."

"I want a deal! I have a lot of valuable information. I've got ledgers and receipts signed by the MOC!" Her shrill voice was cut off by the slamming of car doors.

"Turn her over to the FBI. They might cut a deal. Then again, maybe they won't," Dad said.

Colonel Zachariah nodded and retreated to his own vehicle, waving the extra troops to join him.

The state police officer flipped on his lights and siren as he revved the engine and sped out of the parking lot, onto the highway headed north.

The few lingering con goers applauded and hooted.

"Are we loaded and ready to go?" Dad asked. "Sprite and Rod, you'd best ride with Duc so he can brief you. Ellie is with me. We'll rendezvous at her house for dinner. Liz will meet us at the house after she gets Lou situated at the care facility. I'll talk to Lou later and get as much info as I can from him. You three can head out toward the sanctuary at dawn after a good night's sleep."

Sprite breathed a big sigh of relief. And suddenly, the bruise on her belly didn't ache quite so badly. "I'm looking forward to learning as much as I can about you and our heritage, Duc, while we search for some bad guys."

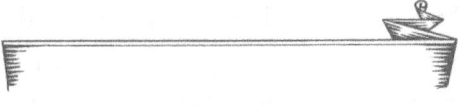

Chapter Twenty-Three

Duc automatically checked that the twins had their seat belts latched before putting the Ram into gear. He had to bite his cheek. His passengers were adults, not four and six. But they were still his children. His blood. Part of his heritage if not immediate family. He needed to watch out for them on this adventure.

Time to start preparing them. Facts first.

"As a first responder, my DNA is on file, complete with the junk factors that I know contain the paranormal tendancy. With your Dad's resources, he can compare it to yours any time he likes," he said after he'd merged into traffic headed for the exit off the Redwood Hwy onto Caves Rd.

Bryce's pearl-white SUV followed him, only a car length behind.

"I think he already has," Sprite said. "Otherwise, he wouldn't have agreed to us going with you on this mission."

"I still don't like the idea of Dad driving as far as Ellie's house," Rod added. He had the shotgun seat and kept checking behind him. "And I *really* don't like the idea of her driving *my* car."

Duc pointed to his phone on the dash mount. "I'm tracking him. If he gets into any kind of trouble, we'll know. He's tracking me too. Instant communication between us with a touch of that button." He kept one hand on the wheel and his attention on the road as he pointed to the * button at the bottom left on the keypad.

Sprite twisted the phone so that she could see the screen. She and her twin nodded approval in unison.

Duc *really* wanted to know just how telepathic they were. That was a talent that could have evolved naturally out of their Guardian heritage or might be limited to the twin "thing."

"I have a theory that paranormals evolved out of need," he mused aloud. "About 65,000 years ago during a volcanic winter that lasted decades, humanity nearly starved to death. Worldwide populations decreased dramatically from about two million to two hundred thousand. Scientists figured that out because of dramatic narrowing of our DNA profiles. We in the Guardian class of paranormals believe that a few of the best hunters in each tribal unit changed into the form of the apex predator of the region to bring in meat for their people," Duc said. He tried to sound friendly rather than like his Anthropology 101 professor.

"Like werewolves?" Sprite gasped.

"They're real!" Rod echoed.

"Yes. Also werecougars, and eagles, and sharks—though they've mostly died out now. Hasn't been a verified sighting in a hundred years."

"Cool," the kids said together.

"The sharks aren't extinct. They are hanging out at cons winning costume awards," Sprite mumbled under breath.

"Or they became lawyers."

She and her twin high fived, then sank back into their seats, smiling.

"One of the men taking shelter at the Sanctuary may be the last of his kind. He carries fire within him. He can bring flames to any fuel—even saturated wood—instantly. He can be a source of light and warmth in the darkest cave. He can also draw heat out of burn wounds. He saved my life once and prevented scarring."

"Wish we'd known about him when Dad was caught in the big fire," Sprite said, sadly.

A moment of silence filled the truck cabin.

"So where do we fit in?" Sprite asked, breaking the somber mood.

"About the same time the volcanic islands of southeast Asia went through a very active period—part of that volcanic winter problem. But during long years of dormancy, the islands had become heavily populated. Good farmland at the base of the mountains, fishing in the ocean, and the waters provided protection from enemies. Then the volcanos turned on them and their havens became roaring monsters."

"Someone needed to help them escape and protect them from ash and flame." Rod said.

"We read an article about it. Tess's husband, Gollum, shared it with us," Sprite explained. "He's an anthropologist, among other things."

Duc nodded. If he took the time to explain the multiple degrees Guilford Van der Hoyden-Smythe had collected the conversation would wander way off track.

"We have no way of knowing if our armor was an overnight development or something that took place slowly over many generations. A child born with tough skin, his children born with tougher skin that looked like scales, then the next generation born with the ability to hide the scales. As the menace grew, so did the ability."

"But those aren't the only volcanoes in the world," Sprite said. She was definitely the detail-oriented one of the two.

"I have met an Italian and a Turkish family with our skill. Our heritage tends to push us into fire related jobs or law enforcement. My older brother is a police detective, headed for chief. I'm a firefighter and arson investigator. I'm also on the call list to augment the Hot Shots when wildfires overwhelm available resources. I met our distant relatives at a conference for first responders in New York, dealing with large scale disasters."

"911 happened before we were born," Rod said quietly. "Still we see and feel the aftershocks." Ah, he was the intuitive and empathic one. He'd reach similar conclusions to those of his sister but by a different route of logic.

"Most of the Guardians tend to stay close to their genetic origins. The Turk talked about a magnetic pull from his mountains taking him home whenever he strayed too far."

"So, how did we end up here?" Sprite asked. "We're Asian."

"My grandparents got caught up in the Viet Nam War and had to flee along with thousands of other boat people."

"So which volcano calls to you?" Rod asked, needing to know why he hadn't felt the pull of any one mountain in the Cascade Range.

"An island in the China Sea or something local?" Sprite added her own query.

"The Three Sisters," Duc said while rummaging in the console to come up with a flashlight. "South Sister, Charity, has a growing bulge. She's going to blow, probably not this year, but within the next decade or two."

Rod spotted a holstered handgun at the bottom of the storage unit.

"What about the other two?" Sprite's eyes widened as she leaned forward, between the two seats. Her gaze moved northward and slightly to the east. "I can almost feel a magnetic tug…"

"Faith and Hope, they're the north and middle sisters in the cluster, are tied geologically to their big sister. Scientists don't know if they will drain some of the pressure off of Charity or are building something dangerous deep within them."

Rod held up his hand palm out, trying to feel… something… in the direction of the looming menace of a mountain. Instinctively, his head turned further north. "Mt. Hood is warming up but venting nicely through hot springs," he said flatly. Somehow he knew the truth behind his statement, though he'd never paid much attention to the dormant volcano in his back yard.

"So, when did your… instincts switch from the China Sea to the Cascades?" Sprite brought the conversation back to the original track.

"My family settled in Eugene. Both my parents, their siblings, and the rest of the extended family were born in the area. The Sisters are our closest hot spots and we identify with them. My grandparents' generation, the ones with the armor gene, still feel half empty and continually turn westward toward *their* home mountains. My parents and aunts and uncles tended to establish their own families with other boat people and feel torn between their past homes and the current one, where they were born. Only my generation has branched out and found mates among other ethnic groups. But the Guardian gene remains strong in most of us."

"Is Mimi French?" Rod asked. "I'm guessing from the names. Though she looks more… Teutonic."

"Her family originated in the Alsace area, close to the French/German border. But that was many generations ago. We only found that out by doing an online genealogy test."

Rod squirmed in his seat as if uncomfortable. Sprite checked the screen to make sure Bryce was still close behind them. He was. She rubbed her abdomen as if in pain.

Bryce had told him about the bullet bruise. That was good to know that a handgun bullet would ricochet. Who knew what damage a high-powered rifle would inflict?

Duc figured Bryce was monitoring their conversation as well. He had access to devices most people never knew existed. He'd wait for a bit of privacy to ask Sprite how she really felt. First rule of backpacking: don't take anyone sick or badly wounded into the wilderness.

"So, what is this Sanctuary we are headed for?" Rod asked, but only after Sprite had jabbed him with her elbow and they had exchanged another one of their silent communications.

"One of the reasons the rogue element of Homeland Security has been able to push their agenda as far as a Presidential Executive Order is that paranormals can't hide as well as we used to. People are uneasy about them because they are unknown and therefore a potential enemy."

"That's hardwired into our brains. Never trust the 'other'. I read it in a book," Rod said.

"I didn't like the book," Sprite said. "The author didn't prove his thesis that charismatic leaders revving up their followers to go to war is akin to faith. What he did prove was that charismatic leaders are still revving up their followers to go to war against any *outsiders*, whether they are separated by religion, language, geography, or race. It has little if anything to do with faith."

"Exactly. You have both been bullied in high school. I've seen bullying go beyond teens throwing insults and setting up pranks. Telepaths, shape changers, witches and their familiars, are threatened, every day, with violence, maiming, even murder. All of it is justified by the concept of imminent threat. Courts are allowing people to get away with it on the grounds of self-defense," Duc said, mourning every life lost to prejudice.

He had to swallow hard before he could speak again. "My grandparents and parents followed the example of some European witch families and have set up sanctuaries for persecuted paranormals. We choose isolated areas, some with caves, others with abandoned buildings. Only recently have we run underground utilities into ours so we can communicate with the outside world if necessary. Adam Mathieson, with some help from Jacquie, has found our cave. We think he's headed there. The one reported sighting of him, in Florence, was at a National Guard Armory, gathering troops and weapons. Enough to blow up the cave and kill three hundred fifty people."

"Major A probably joined him," Rod mused. "She could get medical aid and join the expedition."

"We have to stop them!" the twins said in unison with fists clenched tight.

Duc agreed. Grateful they hadn't asked the next logical question with open communications between his phone and Bryce. The telephone ether was too easily hacked.

"ROD, WHY DON'T YOU take Liz to the diner across the street for a coffee or something," Bryce said handing his son a couple of twenties. He barely looked at the money, instead he stared at the wasted and bruised figure of his oldest friend. Even the clownish beard patches looked more pathetic than funny. The medical people had moved Lou from the high-tech, expensive hospital to a nursing home only a mile from Ellie's house. That procedure had taken most of Sunday and left Lou exhausted and in pain.

Setting up Duc's expedition had taken the same amount of time. Backpacking permits during fire season had taken the longest—though Duc had assured him they'd likely not have to hike far from the end of an abandoned Forest Service Road terminus. Bryce had little fear for his children. They, and Duc, had armor evolved to withstand lava. A forest firestorm wouldn't even singe them around the edges.

Mathieson's and Arbuthnaught's high-powered weapons and their loyalty to a fanatical xenophobic policy scared him more. Bryce ached all the way to his core at the thought of losing his children.

That aside, he now had the difficult chore of telling Lou that Bryce and Ellie were getting back together.

Lou tapped his tablet with a stylus to gain Bryce's attention. Then he turned the screen for him to see.

Good luck with Ellie. She's a handful. But you knew that already.

"How did you know?" Bryce plopped into the guest chair—a not very comfortable fake leather and steel square thing with a seat too short for his long legs. He had to bend his artificial knee at an awkward angle.

Well, in this situation he didn't deserve comfort.

Liz.

"We didn't intend to hurt you, Lou."

I'm the Looney Moose. I've seen it coming since she and I decided to split. You belong together. We don't. Good Luck with her temper.

He scratched at his stitches as soon as he finished. Then he drew a frowny face on the tablet.

"I'm now truly retired. My work was always the biggest barrier between us. Even after the fire, I still worked from home. In the back of my mind, I somehow figured I'd be back in the field someday."

Not realistic.

"I know. I know. But the possibility kept me going. The possibility kept me from believing I'm old enough to retire. I'm not old enough according to Social Security, but I'm tired and still trying to come to terms with my disabilities."

We both are.

Bryce leaned back and counted up the years. Four years living with Ellie part time during his years in the ROTC program while she finished her teaching degree. Then two years of marriage while they jaunted around the world from military base to army fort. Always, just behind his left shoulder, recruiters for the black ops team waited for him to reach the top of his field as a sniper. Then another three years working for them taking down warlords and arms dealers. About that point his work shifted toward paranormal ops. More and more the warlords and arms dealers had become puppets of predatory demons.

But he couldn't tell Ellie any of that, so she left him, screaming charges of neglect.

Two years later he'd adopted the twins.

They'd lived with his sister in New Jersey while he transitioned to mostly coordination work from an office. When he did go into the field—short term projects that took him to a surprising number of cons where predatory paranormals prowled—he had built-in babysitting.

Then the fire happened four years later.

Two years of rehab, plastic surgery, medications, physical therapy.

Psychiatric therapy.

The move to Portland for the better air, and proximity to the medical school and experimental treatments, should have made the act of retirement a reality.

But it hadn't.

Yesterday's adventure had felt like a nail in his coffin. Another one came with the recommendation to investigate lung transplant. While he and Duc had waited for permits, and the kids had swum and gamed, Bryce had made phone calls, sent emails, and read internet sites. He didn't like his options or his odds and nothing would happen until tomorrow, Monday, when offices opened.

But Ellie had come back into his life again.

Because now she knew he'd stay home where he belonged?

They needed to talk about that. He didn't want a relationship based upon pity.

Enough. He had more important things on his mind than reliving his disastrous past emotional life.

"Lou, I need to know everything you know about this crazy Executive Order to make my children illegal citizens." A whole lot of peaceful and benign paranormals were likely to be caught up in this widespread net of paranoia as well.

Laptop. Draft wording.

"Sorry, chum, your laptop disappeared with Mathieson. We found your flash drive in the shaving cream can with the photo of Po Duc and Jacquie. I haven't been able to hack beyond that to the final layer of encryption."

If Lou could move his jaw enough to grind his teeth, he would have. His attempt at moving made the bruising around his eyes and down his cheeks to his neck stand out against his pallor. Even the patches of beard starting to grow back in looked more grey than brown.

Bryce leaned over to the bedside table and retrieved the water glass with a straw. Carefully he placed the straw into Lou's mouth and ordered him to suck. How often had someone else done this for himself over the years?

Lou took a moment to type a string of twenty alphanumeric symbols.

Bryce made a note of them on his phone before Lou could erase them. Wow, that was complex. How did Lou remember it all?

No one with even the most sophisticated software would be able to put together that password. Lou really wanted that information protected.

Moving on before his friend tired beyond helping, he'd start with something simple. "Where's Stella? I thought she was coming to the con with you."

Lou typed something on the tablet and showed Bryce the screen. A silly grin touched the corners of his mouth. He couldn't smile more than that.

Bahamas. Getting married to Mikey, the nerd from accounting.

"She finally did it! Wondered how long it would take her to commit to anyone but her work."

No fuss. No prep. He hustled her onto an airplane before she could think twice and back out of it.

His typing slowed, as if he grew tired. Time to get to the heart of the current problem.

"Who is behind this, Lou? It's not enough that I'm sending my kids and Po Duc after Mathieson and Arbuthnaught. I am no longer physically able to go with them. But I still have contacts and means to fight this all the way to the Supreme Court if necessary."

Fanatical people with too much power. One a senator. So right wing they are off the grid. Invoking religion and xenophobia.

Lou took a deep breath through his O2 cannula. Bryce did the same in sympathetic reaction. He realized he'd needed to do that for some time.

Then Lou wrote three names on the tablet.

Bryce whistled through his teeth. "I don't think even a pedophilia scandal will bring down these people."

Arbuthnaught and her tin hat fanatics hold the puppet strings, while Desdaganet directs. Got a bug up his ass about telepaths and psychics. Feeds A's paranoia.

"I thought so. Any ideas where she might have disappeared to?"

Lou pushed aside the tablet and closed his eyes.

Bryce suspected that his old friend was faking sleep. But he needed the rest and an orderly hovered near the door. Time to get back to his kids. They'd all spend the night at Ellie's house before Duc took them deep into the mountains at dawn.

Chapter Twenty-Four

"Liz, how are you handling our folks getting together?" Rod asked. He held her hands across the table of the all-night diner. They felt like ice.

"I can't think beyond my *dad* getting well. He endured so much at the hands of those *terrorists!*" A tear slid down her cheek. "He won't admit it, but he's in a lot of pain." She stared into her half-empty coffee cup while they waited for their fish and chip dinners to be delivered. She'd missed the family meal at her mother's house while sitting with Uncle Lou, and Rod was always hungry.

"I know. My dad is the same way. It's really hard watching him endure and knowing there is nothing I can do except be close by." He gripped her hands a little tighter, urging her to look up.

"I'd planned to spend the summer looking at housing options in Corvallis. I've decided to go to Oregon State University in the fall. Now I don't know. I need to be close to Dad, but I want Mom and Bryce to be happy. She and my dad were comfortable together, but never truly happy. They've remained friends even after the divorce."

"You're expecting our folks to move in together in Portland." Rod's voice sounded flat to his own ears. Part of him wished Sprite were here to add her opinion. But she was doing what she did best, organizing their backpacks and video chatting with Patrick every time he stopped for gas or to stretch his legs at a rest stop.

Rod was happy to let his sister do her thing while he spent time with Liz. At least he'd be able to find what he needed in his pack, for their first day out. By the second day on the trail, he'd have messed everything up.

Duc had been studying maps and talking to people on his cell phone in a foreign language that had some Asian lilt. Rod suddenly felt an empty spot beneath his ribs that he'd never learned the language of his ancestors. Time enough for that later, in community college. Right now, he needed to concentrate on Liz.

"I kind of wish, now, I'd accepted Portland State for classes in the fall. Dad will need to find a care facility closer to Mom and to Bryce. But that's only for a few weeks. Then he'll need in-home care. I want to be there too." Liz dropped her hands and moved to sit straighter while a young man their age deposited their plates in front of them. An older woman supervised his every move. Likely the kid was just learning the ropes of his summer job.

"Our house is kind of small. Ellie, I presume, will share my dad's room. Uncle Lou has always stayed in the guest apartment beside the pool. When Dad decided we needed a shower near the pool—no wet swimsuits in the house!—" he tried to imitate his father's deep tones in a stern dictatorial manner.

Ellie giggled.

"We converted the family room into the apartment."

She lifted her face and appeared interested enough to really listen to him describe the house and the room limitations.

"Of course, the basement is just a workout room and junk storage with plumbing but no fixtures for a bath. If I cleaned that out, I could make it into a bedroom for me. You could have my room."

"It sounds like your family does everything together." Liz looked away.

Rod couldn't decipher her expression, so he plunged on with his own daydreams. "If we merge our families, I suppose you and Sprite could share her room and I wouldn't have to finish off the basement. That is if you come to Portland." Rod looked up at her hopefully.

She studiously applied malt vinegar and salt to her fish. "No. No matter where I go, I'll get a place of my own. Dad promised to help pay rent as long as it's not too extravagant. I didn't grow up with a sister at my side twenty-four seven, and a parent including me in their work and hobbies. I'm an only child and I need space and alone time. I need privacy in my head. Even a dorm will be better than living cheek by jowl with family in my face all the time. You and Sprite and Bryce thrive on a special kind of closeness. I don't know that I would."

"Meaning your mom questioning every class you take and wanting to check every line of your homework?" Rod looked up with a grin.

"Not just Mom. The Looney Moose is worse. He's been trying to keep on top of my schoolwork long distance from New York forever. I can't imagine him being in the same town, let alone the same house."

"Sometimes I think about living on my own," Rod mused. "Maybe moving into the guest apartment by myself." He made a production of dipping his thick home-fries in ketchup while he thought the idea through. "Sprite and I have a telepathic bond. We don't know if it's just a twin thing, having to rely on each other so much during the chaos of our early life, or part of being paranormal." He couldn't engage her gaze while sharing this very intimate part of his life.

"How far does it stretch?" Liz asked, her own bite of fish paused half-way to her mouth.

"Don't know for sure. It was active all during the con, even when I was alone with you, and she was with Patrick."

She looked up, eyes wide and mouth agape in horror. "E... even when we... were you know... making out?"

He almost laughed. "No. No. We don't share *everything*. It's just sort of an awareness in the back of our heads. We know where the other one is and their overall mood. One time she tripped in the locker room at school. I knew she'd scraped her knee pretty badly and needed first aid, but I also knew she didn't need, or *want,* me to come help. I also know to tune her out when she and Patrick are together. I'd know if he over-stepped her boundaries and wanted me to interfere. Otherwise I just ignore her."

"Did... she say anything after the aborted bonfire Friday night?" Liz blushed and a special warmth blossomed in his belly. He took a long swig of water to cover that special memory.

"Nope. She was so wound up in her own thoughts about what she and Patrick had, or had not done, that she avoided talking to me. We'll talk when the time is right. If the time is ever right."

"So, in the meantime, I take some time on my own to search out housing in Corvallis. I might look for work/study at one of the wineries or vineyards through the Ag department. I've already decided my major will be in biogenetics, finding ways to offset grape diseases triggered by climate change."

"My grades weren't good enough for work/study. I'm going to bust my butt in just study the first year," Rod grumbled. "I'm leaning toward sociology among minority populations. Maybe incorporating paranormals..."

"But for the summer...?" she asked quirking up an eyebrow while sensuously sucking ketchup off one of her fries.

Did she know how much that turned him on?

"We'll see if you find your own apartment..."

SPRITE GRABBED HER phone on the first ring, hoping Patrick called to say he'd reached home safely. She feared, though, that Dad was calling with horrible news about Uncle Lou.

She quickly excused herself from the living room with some inane sitcom on the TV that neither she, nor Duc, were really interested in. Ellie made noises in the kitchen that sounded more like stalling than producing anything edible.

"Hi, Patrick. Are you home?" she asked brightly, relieved that so far, no news about Uncle Lou was not bad news. She stepped out onto the back patio of the tidy little bungalow and pulled the sliding glass doors closed behind her. Breathing deeply of the cool night air eased some of the ache in her too-tight shoulders.

"Not quite home. I stopped in Olympia for gas and a stretch. Then one more hour to home." He yawned.

A special tingly feeling blossomed from her heart outward. He'd called her on the road home again just because he could.

"I'm glad you are safe. Anything interesting on the trip?" What did one say on a check-in call?

"Long and boring. Miles and miles and miles of forest and farmland with an occasional rest stop or cluster of travel businesses." He yawned again. "Did you tell your dad about your bruise?" He sounded a bit more alert with a purposeful question.

"Yes. I told both him and Duc right after breakfast. I know that we have to find Major A as part of this puzzle. That's more important than my pride."

"What did they say?"

"Dad arrested Jacquie and the state police hauled her off."

"That's good to know but not what I asked."

"Well, Dad was all angry and ready to haul me off to the urgent care clinic, but Duc calmed him down. He's had a lot of EMT training and confirmed your diagnosis that it's just a deep bruise. It should heal on its own, given time. But it's going to be very uncomfortable, especially driving on the abandoned Forest Service road we have to travel tomorrow."

"Ouch." Patrick said in sympathy. "Did he have any suggestions to make you more comfortable?"

"Well, he said the ice treatment did as much as anything could other than pain pills, which I don't want."

"And...?"

"What makes you think there's an 'and' in that statement?"

"I know you, Sprite. You are all about hiding your emotions and controlling that scale on your chin."

"Agreed." She sighed, knowing she had to finish relating her conversation with Duc. Driving on freeways and paved roads was not easy today. She wasn't looking forward to tomorrow. "Duc suggested I try transforming, going full armor for half an hour or so. That engaging both of my forms might put right some of the bruised tissue."

"Sort of like the old tales of werewolves changing and changing back to reattach limbs and heal dangerous wounds." Patrick had grown up on comic book versions of superheroes and ancient monsters.

"Yeah, that sounds like what he was trying to say without bringing up the forbidden topic of werewolves and other kinda-sorta-maybe real monsters in front of my father."

"Have you tried it?"

"Not yet. I haven't had a moment of privacy all day until now. And... and I'm kind of scared."

"You've never been hesitant before. I've seen you change in an eye blink. Yesterday, when we rescued your Uncle Lou, you and your brother were only seconds slower than Duc. What's wrong now?"

"What if I get stuck..."

"You've never gotten stuck."

"I did the first time." She shuddered with the all too vivid memory of the need to plow through smoke and falling roof supports just to help the man who had rescued her and her twin from the perpetual nightmare of Jacquie.

"You were, what, six? It was your first time, and you were scared out of your mind about the fire and your father being hauled off in an ambulance. I'm right here. Put the phone on speaker and you can talk me through everything you feel. If you get into trouble, I'll hang up and call Rod to help you."

"But he's off with Liz while Dad visits Uncle Lou. He might not want to come."

"Why didn't you go with them?"

"Visitors are limited to one at a time. I'd be the third wheel."

"Is that third wheel with Rod and Liz a problem?"

"Maybe. It's just that everything is changing so quickly. Too quickly. Armoring up is another change."

"My feelings for you aren't changing. If anything I'm more committed to you... to us, than before. I'm there to back you up. I've got Duc's number to call if you have a problem. Or maybe, if he's there at the house with you, you should have him guide you."

"No." No that would be too embarrassing. She didn't like changing in front of strangers. And Duc really was still a stranger even if they shared blood and talents. She just hadn't spent enough time with him to feel comfortable with something so personal and... and intimate. Yesterday, before the rescue, she'd gone off to the shelter of some trees and shadows to change, with her back turned to both Duc and Rod.

Her scale began to itch. It wanted her to change, right now.

"Then talk to me. Tell me how you do it," Patrick coaxed her. He made it sound seductive, almost like asking her to strip before they made love.

She could do this for him. She'd done it for him once—the armoring up, not the stripping or love making. If she thought of this as a precursor to the next stage of their relationship....

Good thing they were just talking, not video chatting. That would come later when he reached home.

"Ooo...okay." The itching and burning of her scale intensified. She desperately wanted to scratch her chin, wishing she didn't keep her nails longer so she could scratch herself until she bled and release the building *need* with oozing blood.

"What's the first step, Sprite? Tell me what happens and how it feels."

"Heat. I can only protect myself from the intensifying heat by releasing my scales."

"Then do it. Shield yourself with pumice. Keep the lava flows away with your armor."

She took a deep breath and let her stone plates burst forth, snapping into place in a cascade of relief.

They covered and protected the angry bruise on her abdomen. The persistent ache receded like the tide. Bit by bit, surging forward a bit, only to be pulled back. Back and away.

Her knees buckled and she sat heavily on the redwood decking.

"I didn't realize how tense I was from the constant pain," she whispered into the phone, aware that neighbors might be listening in.

"How does the bruise feel?" Patrick asked. He dropped his seductive tones to more clinical and objective, like he was already a medical professional.

"Still a bit tender." She touched the area of the bruise with hesitant fingertips. Her armored hand wasn't as sensitive as skin, and pressed harder than she expected. No wincing, just an awareness of something delicate beneath the layer of stone protection.

"Okay, I'm going to have to go in a minute. My battery is fading and my gas tank is full. There's a line behind my car."

"It's working," she said breathlessly, amazed at the immediate relief of the acute pain. "I think I should hold the armor for a while. Duc said ten to fifteen minutes."

"Go for the ten. It's not like you are reattaching a limb or healing burn damage. How about I chat with you again when I get home? I'll use my laptop and you can show me the progress on the bruise."

She heard the closing of his car door and the rev of him starting the engine. "It's a plan," she replied, knowing her voice was muffled by the stone scales that covered her head and face, leaving only her eyes, nostrils, and a tiny slit of a mouth opening.

"I love you, Sprite. Take care of yourself. We'll check back in an hour."

"I love you too, Patrick. Drive safe."

Chapter Twenty-Five

Duc winced as his truck bounced through the first of the washboard ruts on the service road off the main highway. He slowed from his break-axle speed of 25 MPH to 10. Then he glanced over his shoulder to where Sprite stretched out on the back bench seat.

"She's sleeping," Rod said as he eased forward to peer through the mud-spattered windshield. "I think she spent most of the night on one of the lounge chairs on the back deck. She does that when she's really upset and has swum for about three hours without stop."

Duc had to think about that. "What upset her that much? Besides having been shot at?" He ached in sympathy and wondered how she could sleep while being bounced about by the ruts in the road.

"Don't know. I was with Liz." He shrugged and continued peering at the landscape as they transitioned from coastal forest to high elevation scrawny vegetation. Spindly and sprawling madrone trees dominated.

"I heard you come in. It wasn't that late." Duc eased through another deep rut. He didn't want to trust any other vehicle on this road, even official Forest Service rigs. But his coach-in-four with the extra equipment handled the variable surfaces better than most.

"Liz snores," Sprite grumbled. "I chose to sleep on the deck, just like you chose to sleep in the truck, and Rod didn't even bother opening the sofa bed in the living room." She tried to roll over but had to fight the seat belt that nominally held her in place.

"Why are you awake now?" Duc asked. He'd hoped to spare her the worst pain of the seat belt crossing her bruised abdomen.

"I armored up last night for ten minutes. The bruise is healed. But the exercise left me jazzed, so I swam. It's a miniscule pool by the way, barely three strokes long."

"I didn't know we could do that!" Rod exclaimed. "Why didn't you tell us? I might have tried out for football if I'd known we can heal ourselves so easily."

"We didn't know Duc four years ago. We didn't know anything about who we are or our heritage," Sprite protested. "Both of us should have tried out for swim team, but our grades didn't support extracurricular activities. Besides, it wasn't that easy. It took all my concentration to hold the armor that long. My instincts wanted to come back to human at two minutes. I wanted to run and run and run."

"But it worked?" Duc asked. Then he had to grab the steering wheel harder to drive over a fallen tree that had lost most of its branches, but not all.

"It worked," Sprite confirmed. "But now I'm exhausted from only a few hours sleep and this godawful drive."

"Look, look, look," Rod demanded. "Over there." He pointed to the metallic gleam of a black SUV canted onto the downhill side of the road, one wheel in the air, its opposite hard up against the trunk of a coastal pine—one of the few remaining at this elevation.

Sprite sat up. "The back hatch and one door are open. It looks abandoned."

"The engine is hard up against a house-sized boulder," Rod added.

Duc stopped his truck and set the emergency brake. "Question is: who does it belong to?"

"And how long ago did they abandon it?" Sprite added as she unfastened her seatbelt and moved to open her door.

"I'd almost bet that it's Homeland Security and it slid off the road about maybe an hour ago," Rod surmised, also disengaging his restraints.

"Both of you stay here!" Duc said emphatically. "I'm the trained arson investigator. If Mathieson or Arbuthnaught was driving, they may have booby-trapped it when they left or be lurking in the woods. I know what to look for and where."

Rod looked like he'd protest. Duc fixed him with a stern stare, the one he reserved for mob bosses who ordered buildings burned for the insurance and urban re-zoning.

The boy backed down, anchoring his butt in the padded bucket seat—chosen by Mimi for comfort.

Sprite cringed backward into the seat behind her brother.

Both of them planted their feet flat on the floor.

Damn! that stare worked on these two very curious and intelligent teens. He'd have to remember that when his girls hit their rebellious years. And the new baby too. Mimi had decided to test this coming Friday, but she was pretty sure she had a baby incubating inside her.

He pulled himself out of his happy reverie. The two rogue agents were still a problem. He grabbed his holstered gun and buckled it around his waist, just in case.

Reassured of their compliance, Duc began circling the crashed vehicle. He murmured comments into a digital recorder. No plates. Likely removed by the occupants. Tire tracks slightly distorted by moisture left over from a passing drizzle last night. Hatch open and cargo space empty—not even a fast-food wrapper. Hood twisted and up. Front bumper ripped off and tangled with a tree that used to grow beside the boulder. Extent of front-end damage suggested speed coming down the hill from the road, a distance of ten meters, not far enough to generate the speed needed for this extent of damage, if they had been traveling at a safe speed before losing control and careening off the road.

And then he spotted the dents and scraping on the rear bumper.

ROD WATCHED DUC TURN away from the crashed vehicle and pelt uphill through crushed underbrush and torn earth. Anyone else would struggle in that landscape. Not Duc. He made short work of the trip with physical strength and familiarity with wilderness terrain.

Just like a movie hero.

"Fire up the shortwave radio!" Duc called as he crested the hill and jerked the truck door open.

Rod fumbled with a control panel mounted beneath the console between the two bucket seats. One knob/button, whatever, had a red dot in the middle. He pushed it and was rewarded with a loud hiss and crackle of static.

"What?" Sprite asked, peering out the window toward the crash scene.

Rod knew the moment she spotted something suspicious. She sat back and fastened her seat belt before Duc turned the key in the ignition. He rolled forward fifty meters at a painstaking pace then stopped again.

He grabbed the mic for the radio from its mount on the dash and began twisting a knob until the static solidified into a steady beep. Breathlessly, he began barking his ID and location into the machine.

Rod found the GPS coordinates in one corner of the dash. Now this was starting to feel like the adventure he craved.

Duc repeated them. "Looks like a jerry-rigged incendiary device below the rear bumper, dead center where a towing hook would attach. Conditions are very dry despite some light rain last night. One spark will set off one hundred acres in seconds. Over." He released the talk switch on the mic and took a deep breath.

Rod released the air he hadn't realized he'd been holding.

His scale throbbed warning of impending danger.

Sprite's scale turned bright red and pulsed.

Duc's was two steps ahead and beginning to spread.

A scratchy voice came back, clear and clean. "Repeat coordinates. Over."

Duc did so and his scale calmed enough to hold its current condition.

Rod's wanted to explode. He forced himself to breathe deeply, evenly, trying for a meditation trance. He checked on Sprite. She too took steady and even breaths, maintaining control.

"I have two civilians with me. Moving forward, out of immediate danger. Repeat, two civilians. I cannot stay and disarm. I do not have proper protection or tools with me to disarm. Over."

"Acknowledged. Suggest minimum one mile separation from device. Will have a skeleton crew at your current location within the hour. Lousy timing. Everyone we can spare is fighting the KL Creek fire. It's 50% contained. That little bit of drizzle overnight and a calm wind is really helping. But it can explode any minute if conditions change. Can you get your civilians to safety and return to disarm? Over."

"No. I do not have protective gear or tools. Removing to a safer location. Keeping this frequency open for further reports. Over." Duc holstered the mic and put the rig in gear. Then he turned off the radio.

"Um… didn't you say you'd keep that frequency open?" Rod asked. He sat on his trembling hands rather than reach to scratch his scale.

"Yep. That's what I said."

"But you aren't," Sprite said. No hesitancy in her voice.

What had she noticed that Rod hadn't? Tingling prickles raced up and down his spine. Not chills. More like his scale had found a different place to begin snapping into place but stopped just before breaking free of his skin.

"Would Arbuthnaught and Mathieson really set a new wildfire just to complete their mission?" Rod asked. He kept looking at the slopes up and down from the overgrown track, that might once have been a forest road, for any sign of a dry creek bed or game trail that would facilitate an escape.

Suddenly the danger felt real, not just a script with actors who wouldn't truly get hurt or die. They had to stage the stunts so the actors could come back in the next blockbuster.

"*Never* underestimate a fanatic," Duc barked. "I don't think they care what kind of damage they'll cause as long as they can find the Sanctuary and wipe out their enemy."

"But we, meaning paranormals, aren't the enemy. Their own fear and prejudice is," Sprite protested.

"But you are sane," Duc said flatly. "Your dad referred to Arbuthnaught's troops as 'Tin foil hat fanatics.' That tells me more than a psychiatric evaluation."

"Problem is, they think they are sane and that we are not."

"Precisely. Fanaticism has its own rules. Trouble is, no one else is allowed to know the rules and they change in a heartbeat. Just like the predatory demons from another dimension that your dad used to fight."

Rod wanted to cry at the thought that a rogue faction of a federal agency, dedicated to protecting the country and *all* its citizens, would wipe out this beautiful wilderness to destroy a few people with special talents.

Fear of "the other" drove them beyond reason.

Sprite was right. That's what the author of that strange book had proved. Fear was a much stranger, and stronger, motivator than faith.

"I CAN'T BELIEVE I LET my children go away with Po Duc," Bryce said, slamming his fist into an open palm. The view from Ellie's back deck showed him a few suburban roofs rising toward the nearest mountain, and beyond that more mountains. Embedded deep in one of them was the labyrinth of the Oregon Caves, a protected National Monument.

Where one mountain was riddled with limestone caves, the entire region must have supported cave systems. One of them now held Duc's Sanctuary for paranormal refugees.

"They aren't children anymore. At eighteen they can make their own decisions. *And* you conducted a very thorough background check on him. He's an upstanding part of his community, a family man, educated, earning a decent living," Ellie reminded him. "You even double-checked his DNA. He is the father of your twins, right down to the same 'junk' anomaly which we now know to be their paranormal origins." She came up behind him and placed a hesitant hand on his shoulder.

He grabbed it before she could pull away and wrapped her in a tight embrace. His fingers dug into her back a little too fiercely. He eased his grip before she winced or cringed.

"Sorry if I hurt you." He dropped his hands back to his side.

"Don't pull away now, Bryce Maxwell. We are in this together."

"Are we, Ellie? What happens next?"

"Today? You do a bunch of laundry for you and your children. Then we have lunch. I've a nice chicken salad with fresh strawberries. Then we go visit Lou for an hour, no more, because he's still weak and needs his rest."

"And after that?" Bryce pulled her close again but without the fierceness of desperation.

"After that, I need to go to my office and take care of a mountain and a half of paperwork." Her head came to rest on his shoulder.

"Skip it. Quit your job and move in with me." Not a hard decision. A warmth spread outward from his belly. She felt so *right* in his arms, like she belonged there, now and forever. "Now that we've found each other again, I don't want to let you go,"

"That's a big decision, Bryce. A huge change in the entire family dynamic."

"Is it really? All three of our kids are heading off to college. Are you ready to live alone?"

"Correction, your two are going to community college for at least a year. They'll still be at home. I'll be the intruder."

"Never." Bryce dismissed her objection.

His gaze continued to inspect the mountains. Worry had inserted a pellet of ice in his heart, and he couldn't banish it. What if something happened to one or both of his children?

"Rod and Sprite have made you the center of their lives, taking care of you, nursing you. *Protecting* you. That's a hard role to give up."

He had no answer for that.

"How about we postpone this discussion until the twins get back?"

"A wise decision. We should ask their opinion of adding you and Liz to the family."

"In some ways I think Liz will be more of a problem than Rod and Sprite. She and Lou are incredibly close. They video chat at least once a week and she visits him in New York every chance she gets. Or he comes here and gets a motel room nearby. One of the reasons Lou came to BeachCon was to spend this week with Liz in Corvallis finding student housing and applying for work/study. If I move in with you, it won't disrupt her relationship with her father."

"Damn. This all comes back to Lou. Your marriage and divorce. Liz fighting to maintain contact with Lou. Lou's mysterious mission for Homeland Security..."

"That's what doesn't make sense," she replied, breaking the embrace and beginning to pace the compact deck.

"Nothing about The Looney Moose makes sense. The Executive Order, the rogue element of HS. The extreme chances and risks that Arbuthnaught and Mathieson are taking..."

"Fear of telepaths invading our privacy, it's a trope in SF media and literature."

"Not just that... it's... the government has taken extreme measures to deny any evidence that we have had visitors from outer space. They arrest anyone with evidence that aliens walk among us. Why completely reverse their long-held stance and accuse paranormals of being space aliens and therefore illegal residents? What has spooked them about paranormals now? If they just kept their mouths shut there wouldn't be a problem. They could continue to harass, arrest, and deport Mexicans, blame them for everything that's wrong with this country."

"We need to talk to Lou," Ellie said.

Bryce fiddled with the car key in his pocket.

"After lunch." She grabbed his arm and led him toward the kitchen.

"Wait!" He turned back toward the mountain. "Is that a puff of smoke?" He pointed to a spot halfway up the first visible slope.

"Can't tell for sure. Let me get the binoculars."

"That's... that's the direction Duc was headed with my kids!"

Chapter Twenty-Six

Another severe jounce as Duc navigated the latest of a series of axle-busting potholes. Sprite had to cross her arms over the site of her bruise and press hard. She felt as if she hadn't healed any part of her with her transformation routine last night.

Nausea burned in the back of her throat.

To distract herself she half-turned to see if anything was happening at the crash site. Nope. They'd traversed three sharp bends in the road/game trail in the last half mile.

"Brace yourself, the next one is bad," Duc said. His knuckles looked pure white where he gripped the steering wheel.

"You know this road well?" Rod asked before Sprite could. He gritted his teeth until his scale pulsed.

A brief touch to her own chin confirmed that her instincts recognized danger but not imminent.

"I helped dig some of these holes and fell small trees across the track to discourage intruders. When I'm not avoiding pursuit, I take a *slightly* easier route." He took a deep breath as he guided his truck into and out of the wide hole at about 2 MPH. At this speed the springs barely engaged.

"Walking would be faster," Sprite muttered. Her stomach settled but the bruise ached as if she'd... been struck by a bullet while wearing Kevlar.

Well, she had been struck by a bullet and it had ricocheted off her armor.

If Major A was walking this trail, she'd be hurting too. Maybe suffering from blood loss.

That made Sprite feel a little better.

"Trust me, this portion of the road may look flat, but we are climbing. Very shortly it will steepen to a 10% grade—paved highways are required to install truck runaway ramps if a 6% grade is longer than a half kilometer. That's a stiff pull if you are walking. Worse if you are carrying a pack." Duc clenched his teeth and depressed the accelerator.

Another log crossed their path. The engine revved. They were over the obstacle quickly.

The path ahead looked clear, two ruts with a weedy median. Sprite identified huge bull thistles and predatory blackberry vines everywhere except the ruts. That gave her proof that other vehicles negotiated this road often enough to suppress weed growth.

"Are those nettles?" Rod asked on a gulp.

"Yeah. And they burn bare skin with the briefest touch. Throw them on a fire and the smoke is toxic. Believe me we are safer in my truck than walking."

"But are we faster than Major A and her minion?" Sprite asked. The ache in her gut eased as the trail smoothed out but became narrower. They were above the big evergreens on the foothills. More light filtered through the smaller trees. She felt less claustrophobic but more exposed.

If Major A and her troops spotted them, a high-powered rifle could kill them. Her hand lingered over the window control. A closed window might protect her. She had few doubts that Duc had installed bullet-proof glass. But the lack of fresh air would build heat inside. Her armor was ready to spring into life as it was.

BANG!

She cringed and ducked, arms over her head as something crashed into the windshield.

"Just a low hanging branch, Sis," Rod said. "I saw it coming."

Still shaking she pulled herself upright. "We've added another obstacle to the road," she said, peering out the back toward the red-gold bark and dusty green leaves of a madrone branch.

"Something like that happens every trip up," Duc chuckled.

"Wait!" Rod cried. "Do I smell smoke?"

"Damn!" Duc floored the gas pedal. "We need to get out of here."

"But I didn't hear an explosion," Sprite protested. "It wouldn't be from the bomb on the crashed car."

"You're right." Duc's breathing eased. The speedometer dropped from 15 to 10 MPH. "I thought, perhaps, Arbuthnaught could have emptied their extra ammo of gunpowder into the device beneath the bumper. It would have flashed and spread sparks. Even at this distance we'd have heard something."

They'd covered about a mile. Maybe two. Duc's comrades in the Forest Service had barely had time to get to the crash, let alone set off the makeshift bomb beneath it.

The breeze coming through the open window shifted. She detected a very faint whiff of smoke. Then it was gone.

"That's not woodsmoke. Or not much of it. There's an overlay of tobacco," Duc confirmed Sprite's suspicions. "One of the idiots lit a cigarette! I certainly hope one of them is smart enough to stomp out any embers blowing about."

Sprite kept her face close to the window, sniffing for any further hint of fire in this very dry landscape.

"I'VE NEVER NOTICED before that tobacco smoke is so much stronger than wood smoke. Is that a learned skill or just something we do?" Rod asked.

"I can tell the difference between the charcoal in the grill and the propane in the fire pit," Sprite added.

"Yes and yes," Duc replied. "I've always been able to tell the difference between Grandpa Po's cigarettes and Mom's burned pancakes. Didn't know what lava smelled like until Mimi and I went to Hawaii for our honeymoon. I knew instantly that the volcano dominates the air as well as the landscape. Even all the lush tropical flowers can't cover it up."

"We went up Mt. St. Helens for a class field trip," Rod mused. "I could tell that it smelled different from the foothills but didn't think about why."

"I remember that trip," Sprite added. "I spent most of it sifting ash through my fingers, wondering why it felt so familiar, and why it reminded me of my armor. My logic skills were not well developed yet, and I couldn't make the connection until now."

Duc shrugged as he swung the truck around the next bend and emerged onto... a perfect circle of flat. A dead end.

Three deer, a doe and two fawns, who had been grazing on the new grass at the verge, started at their intrusion and bounded off, uphill.

"Is this a trailhead parking area?" Rod asked, scanning the area for traces of other humans who might have been here recently. The dirt was too dry and hard packed to reveal footprints or tire tracks. Even all traces of the deer had disappeared, except for a faint, dry, musky scent that had nothing to do with his own testosterone. No. Not musk. Something dusty, unique to the deer, but not musky. That scent belonged to a... predator.

Coyote. Bear. Cougar. Something he wanted to shy away from.

"This is a trailhead, but you won't find it on any maps." Duc grunted as he hauled his large backpack out of the back of the truck. "Grab your gear. We've got a bit of a hike from here, only a kilometer, but a lot of it is uphill. And do keep an eye out for cougars. They've got kits this time of year. Hungry kits." He set his pack with a sleeping bag roll strapped to the top to make a nice neck brace upright on the tailgate and backed into it. That meant he only had to lift the monstrous thing a short distance before settling into the straps and fastening it across his chest and around his waist.

"If we do encounter a predator, stand still and hold your arms out to the sides so you look bigger than you are. Sprite, you need to be between your brother and me since you are the smallest and look the most vulnerable."

Rod decided to copy his technique. Then set up Sprite's the same way. But he had to help her. Her short legs didn't give her the height and leverage she needed. In the end, her pack, the smallest and lightest of the three, had to settle down from the truck rather than up.

"You are carrying a lot of gear for a short hike," Sprite said. Her own sleeping bag rested more on top of her head than nestled into her neck.

"We're spending the night in the cave. I've also got supplies for the people you need to meet." Duc set off up the same trail the deer had used. "And paperwork to keep track of who is in residence and who has left. It's a mobile group."

"Don't you run the risk of those spreadsheets falling into the hands of the authorities? I'd think an encrypted computer database would be safer," Sprite said. She tried to think up ways to put firewalls and layered passwords around the records. Like Dad used on his work records.

"Ever tried to read an ancient Asian language with only about a dozen native speakers and almost no written records?" Duc laughed. "Grandpa Po is one of those native speakers. I can decipher it, but only because I helped invent the written version based on proto-Mandarin characters."

"Like that book about the secret language in the Chinese harems and the tight sisterhood that embraced it?" Sprite asked.

"Exactly. The discovery of those journals, political commentary, and poetry is what inspired me." Duc's steps took on a new lightness and spring as he approached the broken underbrush where the deer had disappeared.

"What about Major A and Mathieson? They possess the kind of cunning and insanity to figure out something like that," Rod mused, wishing he'd thought to ask his dad for a gun. He thought they might very well encounter predators. Whether human or animal remained to be seen.

BRYCE PACED OUTSIDE of Lou Metcalf's room at the care center. The place smelled of bleach and other chemical cleaners and stewed prunes. Better than unwashed bodies and stale urine so common in many of these facilities.

Smells he didn't want to live with as he had so many times since the fire. If he had to undergo a lung transplant to regain a measure of health and longevity he'd likely have to endure another hospital and rehab center.

Would it be worth it?

He peeked through the crack between the partially closed door and the jamb. Ellie, his Ellie, sat on the side of her ex's bed. She laughed heartily, throwing her head back as she placed her hand atop Lou's. His face lost some of its frozen quality as his eyes crinkled with mirth. But his wired jaw wouldn't allow him to smile or laugh out loud.

The staff had shaved his entire beard so he didn't look too much like he'd lost a fight with a lawn mower. But he couldn't hide his receding chin and slightly buck teeth anymore. His beard regrowth didn't show beneath the bandages. Chances were, the scar tissue wouldn't support facial hair. Lou was in for creases there.

Ellie was doing a good job of keeping his mind on other things and his hands away from scratching his stitches. He caressed her face tenderly though.

A surge of jealousy rampaged through Bryce's gut and mind. His field of vision narrowed and took on shades of red.

Then Ellie turned her head and caught his gaze with her own. She smiled. That special smile, he liked to think she reserved just for him.

"Come on in, Bryce. I think I've tired him enough that he shouldn't resist your questions too much," she called, holding out her free hand.

Bryce closed the door behind him, waiting for the latch to click. He didn't want to have to worry about eavesdroppers.

Lou freed his hand from Ellie's grasp and picked up the tablet and stylus.

Bryce pulled up a visitor's chair and plopped down into it, grateful to rest his knees.

"Excuse me, boys, I need a restroom, and you two need privacy. I'll wait for you in the courtyard." Ellie gestured toward the wide window that revealed a garden in the center of the complex. Paved paths wandered through rose beds and around a fountain that sparkled in the sunlight. The place invited patients and guests alike to partake of fresh air and find a measure of ease in the natural setting.

Bryce breathed a little easier just knowing that such a place brightened the lives of people recovering here. He didn't want to think about those who'd been sent here to die.

"Nice digs, Lou," he said by way of introduction.

Food's awful. Everything through a straw. Itches like poison ivy.

"Been there, done that." Bryce remembered the days after his first plastic surgery to repair some of the scar tissue on his face. He hadn't been able to open his mouth or move those muscles for days. He hadn't been allowed to shave for a week or more afterward. He'd itched and wasn't allowed to scratch. His own beard now grew in patches, bald under the skin grafts, so he made sure to stay clean shaven. Twice a day.

He squirmed uncomfortably. The best way to take his mind away from awful memories was to get down to business.

The business of UFOs and visitors from outer space.

"Why, Lou? Why would the government do a 180 and now admit that UFOs are real and aliens walk among us? They have spent decades denying and covering up anything related to the subject."

Not gov't. Rogue HS wanting psychics as weapons.

"That's old news. The CIA and the Russians tried it in the '50s. Results, if any, are still classified."

New evidence. Paranoid. Easier to deal with public outcry against little green men when half already believe. Psychics still a myth they need to hide.

"You know that my kids may be caught up in the hysteria."
Lou nodded rather than go to the effort of writing a response. His eyes squinted with the effort of keeping them open.
"How do we counter it, Lou?"

Take down Major A. Get her to talk.

Then he wrote down 'Desdaganet,' the prominent senator, a man who'd been re-elected five times despite sex scandals, money laundering scandals, back door arms deals in Eastern Europe and Africa. A man Bryce had been chasing since his early days in black ops.
"Where's the evidence? He's slippery and hidden behind too many firewalls. My best hackers and undercover investigators can't touch him."

Flashdrive. 6 layers of encryption.

Bryce had only found five layers and then stopped when he found the picture of Duc and Jacquie with Duc's armor scale highlighted.

Deeper. Find numbers hidden in the photo.

Lou dropped back against his pillows, letting the tablet slide from his slack fingers.
Then he roused a moment and typed one more phrase.

Didi a teep. She knows things.

"Didi Dogooder. The senator's ex daughter-in-law?" Bryce gasped. The happy-go-lucky pixie who flitted about cons up and down the coast was a telepath?

Maybe reading crystal balls, Tarot cards, and palms weren't tricks but the real thing. The reading she'd done for him and the twins certainly felt real.

He should have looked at the extra cards she'd sealed in an envelope and promised to mail to him after... after this mission finished and the relationships settled.

He was willing to bet big bucks Didi knew things about the senator that no one wanted made public.

Lou closed his eyes and didn't stir when Bryce lifted the tablet from his friend's hand.

Quietly, he leveraged himself out of the chair and left the room to find Ellie. He needed some time with his computer and his secure cell phone—the one the twins weren't supposed to know about (like that would ever happen)—to call in favors.

Didi needed protection and Colonel Zachariah was the man to get it for her.

Chapter Twenty-Seven

"The trail is clearly marked from here," Duc said quietly. By mutual agreement, they hiked silently, not betraying their presence to anyone who might follow.

He'd paused often on the trek up this latest slope, making sure the twins didn't labor too hard. Though strong and fit, their athleticism had been limited to swimming and walks through curated forest paths in parks. Wearing athletic shoes that had more to do with fashion than durability, support, and stability, he suspected they had blisters forming on their heels.

Rod had lagged often, more from curiosity at strange rock formations and new-to-him plants than fatigue.

Sprite, the one Duc truly worried about, kept plodding along at a steady pace, settling in to a comfortable rhythm. Her gaze shifted often between where to place her feet and what might be lurking in the forest.

Now Duc dropped back so he could truly observe how they handled this difficult trail.

Rod surged ahead, still keeping Sprite in the middle. He touched tree bark and rock moss, learning their textures, marking them in his memory. Not all the trees he examined held only the essence of tree. Some were human at heart. Good thing they tolerated human touch. Some cherished the silent communication.

At the next outcropping he hesitated for about three heartbeats. The boulder at the base of an upward surging cliff supported no moss. Rod did not touch it, merely pointed it out to his sister.

Sprite hesitated the same amount of time, studying it, nodding, and then moving on.

As Duc came abreast of the rock a human figure uncurled from its guard post. The woman shed her armor. "Hola," she said, her voice heavily accented from South American Andean tribes. She wore faded jeans and a long-sleeved T that might once have been chocolate brown but now resembled the local dirt, as did her skin. Her dark eyes and hair from a distance looked similar to the black moss hanging from some tree branches.

Duc folded his hands together and bowed to her in greeting.

Ahead of him, the twins halted abruptly and whirled around to face the sentry, eyes wide and mouth agape.

"Soldiers may follow us. I wish to interrogate the leaders. Though armed, the soldiers may be innocent. Or not. Please detain with as little harm as possible." He used hand signals to give more information. His people were used to communicating silently and staying hidden. At times like this he wished he could share telepathically with his own people as the twins did with each other.

The woman touched her right hand to her heart and bowed her head. She pulled an old flip phone from her jeans pocket and texted an extensive message. Then she knelt down and covered herself in armor, blending into the granite boulders.

Rod looked like he wanted to speak.

Duc held up his hand, palm out. "Later," he mouthed. He'd heard strange rustlings in the underbrush behind him. Someone followed. But they were clumsy and had not yet found the true trail.

He smiled, figuring whoever was behind them was trying to follow a GPS device and not succeeding. The family foundation had selected this area for the Sanctuary partly because satellite signals bounced strangely among the native volcanic rocks and gave false data to devices. One had to have been here before to find this place.

Another quarter mile uphill and Duc spotted the double tree that sprouted on either side of a boulder. The trunks leaned toward each other about a foot above his head and merged into one, encasing the big rock in an arch. He always thought the two trees looked like lovers stealing a kiss.

"Almost there," he whispered. This was the most vulnerable spot. Arbuthnaught and Mathieson weren't stupid. If they had survived this far, they could find the Sanctuary with little effort.

"ARE YOU SURE YOU WANT to hide Didi and Chad *here*?" Colonel Zachariah asked Bryce. He stood in front of an aging Mom-and-Pop motel in Cave Junction with his hands on his hips and feet spread as if ready to plunge into action at first glimpse of an enemy presence.

"Looks like almost every other small town in the U.S.A.," Bryce replied. "It's tourist season. All they need is matching flowered shirts and khaki shorts to blend into the background. If she'd put away her Tarot deck and stop consulting a card drawn randomly from the deck every five minutes."

Colonel Zach chuckled. "She doesn't look Romany, so the gimmick does stand out in a crowd." He shook his head. "I still don't like it. I'd prefer an authorized safe house in a big city. With back up. Lots and lots of back up. And state of the art listening and recording devices." Zachariah turned his focus to the giggling couple who unloaded a single rolling suitcase each from the black SUV that screamed law enforcement.

"You'd be spotted in five seconds. However, the mini satellite dish in this rusty old pickup looks like I'm on my way to the metal recycling center." Bryce patted the trusty dashboard of the near antique truck—one of three dozen visible on the street, different only in the locations of the rust on the frame.

A tech in western shirt, jeans, and boots, kept his eyes glued to the screen of a large laptop resting on the center console.

"We'll be better off as soon as you get your vehicle out of sight," Bryce replied. He meant the shiny black monster SUV beloved of all covert ops.

Another series of giggles followed by a guffaw of laughter erupted from the now open doorway of an upper-level motel room. The tech held his headphones away from his ears and grimaced.

Zachariah and Bryce shook their heads in dismay as they departed to their own vehicles parked behind the hardware store. "They act more like newlyweds than recently divorced," Zachariah said.

"If you had to move into the senator's mansion the day you returned from your honeymoon and live there under constant observation for ten years, wouldn't you be giggling with joy at release from the constraints?" Bryce had to smile. With the twins on a backpack trip with their bio-father and Liz taking off for Corvallis to look for student housing, he and Ellie felt almost like honeymooners. Ellie did have to go to work Wednesday through Sunday, and they both had to visit Lou at least once a day, but other than that they spent most of their time together, without anyone else to notice how often they retired to the bedroom.

"About the senator," Zachariah said, dragging Bryce's attention back to their current problem.

"What about the senator?" Bryce tried to wipe the silly smile off his face and deal with reality.

"Didi gave me a bunch of leads to follow, but eavesdropping telepathically isn't evidence."

"She's kept her talent well hidden. I think Tess is the only talented person who knew about it. Makes me wonder what changed to make the senator go after all psychics just to get rid of her. His normal procedure would be to arrange an accident that left her dead and Chad a grieving widower in need of his daddy's guidance."

"Doesn't Chad have some teaching credentials or something? Usually men in power try to keep their sons close and involve them in the family business. Chad's a more likely candidate to be chief-of-staff with a fancy office in D.C. than Joseph Elijah Levinson."

"Can you follow up on JEL a bit more, see what kind of hold he has on the senator to keep his job?" That bothered Bryce. That tentative connection to organized crime from ten years ago was one of those things that just didn't go away. Once the mob got their hooks into a person, they didn't let go easily.

"I did notice that JEL burst onto the con scene about the time Didi came into Chad's life and he fully embraced the Science Fiction culture. Is the Master of Ceremonies spying on her? And what were his credentials to becoming the MOC of the con circuit other than a flamboyant personality?"

"My questions exactly. I need a spreadsheet to compare his appearances to Didi's con memberships. She often takes a spot in the vendor's room with her cards, crystals, and palm reading. She bills herself as a spiritual consultant. Her track record of being right is around 90%. Random guesses, even with good body language and psychology skills should be only 50% or less."

Above the parking lot, the motel room door slammed shut, and the blinds closed in the one window looking out onto the balcony.

"Looks like the kids are settling in quite nicely. I'll go back to my computer and spreadsheets. You can return to your team," Bryce said, gaze still glued to the corner room.

"I have undercover troops in the rooms either side of Didi and Chad. And back up hanging out at the nearby diner and coffee shop. No uniforms or display of weapons," Zachariah mumbled. "Time for me to return to base and get some sack time. I'd forgotten that working with you means next to no sleep for days on end." Scratching his three-day-old stubble, he climbed into the black SUV and headed south on the highway.

Bryce gave the red door of the motel room a last look and departed in his own vehicle. Ellie awaited him for lunch at the winery where she worked. She insisted on keeping her job until they made a final decision on moving in together.

As for his own work, he'd really like to pry into Didi's mind, or at least get her talking in a casual atmosphere rather than a cold and official interview by the authorities.

Hmmm. "I think, I need to fire up the grill," he mumbled. A trip to the grocery store and produce market seemed the best place to start.

After lunch with Ellie. He had to remember that Ellie came first now. Always Ellie first and not his work.

SPRITE WATCHED A PERFECTLY ordinary western red cedar, thirty-five meters tall, and at least, a meter in diameter... dissolve. Pull in on itself and shrink might be a better description. *Transform* into a tall man with flowing dark hair and copperish toned skin. He wore nothing. Not even a breech clout and didn't seem embarrassed. His chiseled features and toned body could have been etched by the landscape into the classic portrait of a native American.

Wow, that was one beautiful man. Long, lean muscles and flat chest made Patrick look scrawny by comparison.

She would not look at the enticing groin area. She wouldn't. No matter what her hormones wanted her to do.

She jerked her gaze away from the man/tree to fix on her brother, the one safe entity she could trust in either of his forms.

"Wow, this is better than a con," Rod said quietly. "Nothing is what it seems and yet it's almost familiar. Kind of tickling the back of my mind with ancient memories suddenly awakening."

ROD HALTED, ONE FOOT in the air, as he approached the tree man. He extended his right hand, ready to greet him in the normal American and western European manner.

The light changed, became muted by vast quantities of ash in the air.

It smelled different too, of salt, and water, and... something burning. Not wood.

"No. The test is not necessary," Duc said. He sounded very far away.

Automatically, Rod checked his twin sister. She stood right beside him, also frozen in this odd place between here and there, now and then...

"Your rules. No exceptions," the tree man said in a deep, sonorous voice.

With the words came the knowledge that the natural form of this man was a sequoia, a native of the region. He took his name from his parent form.

Duc bowed his head in acceptance and stepped back.

But he didn't move. The distance between them increased.

Rod and Sprite hadn't moved either, other than their armor snapping into place.

"You are who you are meant to be, in the place of your origins," the deep voice chanted as the man's hands wove an intricate pattern. Language and yet not language. A different form of communication.

The air exploded as the volcano behind them shot a new fountain of sparks and lava skyward.

Rod searched the sandy beach at his feet for... There off to his left, he heard a small child cry. She'd become separated from her family and stood trapped between two rivers of flaming rock.

He did not think, did not plan. His feet moved across the hot sand and the molten lava. While aware of the tremendous heat, Rod did not feel pain. Only the need to rescue the child.

Behind him, he knew that Sprite—she had a different name now, but it meant Sprite, just he had a different name that meant strong spear shaft, a rod—helped a heavily pregnant neighbor into a dugout. A tribal leader raised a mast and fixed a sail.

Escape. They must all escape the angry gods of the mountain. The sea, with its treacherous waves and hungry giant fish, was their only refuge.

Rod had to hurry to help the child or be left behind. Still running he scooped up the girl into his arms and perched her on his shoulders, her tiny legs crossed around his neck and her toddler arms grabbing him around his forehead, like a living crown. He plunged into the waves. His armor kept him afloat and the little, so very vulnerable child, above the water.

He stretched and stretched his arms in long even strokes. His legs pumped in rhythm with his arms. The armor around his feet spread into broad paddles.

His muscles grew heavy with fatigue. So easy to give up and just let the water take him.

But he had to keep going. For the child on his back. For his twin who did not yet know how to live without him at her side.

He passed the surf line and continued to race ahead of the lava and the steaming water, toward the boat, the last boat off the island. His sister reached a hand down to take the burden of the child from him. Other hands assisted him aboard the crowded boat.

I've had this dream before. It's only a dream.

Was it merely a dream, or a memory?

The light changed again.

With a jerk Rod came back to the land of his birth, not the land of his origins. The time... caught up with him and he knew his name, his age, his family, and the place of his birth.

"Did you see what I saw," he asked Sprite breathlessly.

"I think so," she murmured. "It felt so real. So hot and humid. The water temperature rising dangerously. I think I had to jump out of the boat and swim beside it to keep it from overturning with so many people aboard."

"I can still feel the rope made of palm bark in my hands as I swam on the other side of the boat," Rod replied.

"You are true guardians. You may pass on to the Sanctuary," Sequoia intoned, making a ritual bow and blessing gesture.

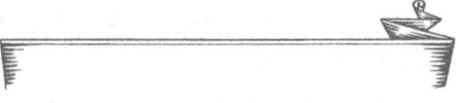

Chapter Twenty-Eight

Sprite shook herself free of the lingering sensation of being in the wrong time and wrong place. Part of her needed to go back to that island and make certain that all of her people had escaped the wrath of the mountain gods that rained fire and lava.

As her eyes became used to the shift of light from a smokey yellow to a dusty green full of life she shifted her feet and found a new balance at the edge of a large clearing.

Duc was occupied with hand language and exchanged bows of greeting and information. Almost a dance. Perhaps he and the tree man conversed in the ancient sign language of the original tribes. More likely they used signals developed by all of the inhabitants of the sanctuary.

More and more people emerged from the concealing underbrush. Humans from six continents dominated the two dozen figures peering at her as curiously as she examined them. Then she spotted some differences: excessive hair on predatory shape-changers, a total lack of body hair on people with big eyes and small mouths, outsized feet and hands, and a woman with eyes nearly blind from opaque cataracts but fingering a deck of Tarot cards as if she read the intricate designs with her fingertips. She'd seen Didi do that, her meditative trance replacing actual blindness.

What had Didi said when she read Sprite's card?

You leap ahead of your companions on a path of your own choosing, and yet you keep those you love close. You are the first line of defense in a changing world.

The strangeness of the vision world piled on top of this new reality. She may need to leap forward later. For now she needed to observe and learn so she could lead them all to safety.

Sprite felt as if she'd stepped into another world. A third world to negotiate. This was the world that con costumers tried to recreate and succeeded for the most part.

This was the world where she and her twin belonged, among shape-changers, psychics, and... and a teenaged boy with flame-red hair that moved and crackled like a real fire. Paranormals, one and all.

A wave of vertigo washed through her. Her peripheral vision started closing in on her. The light faded....

"Easy Sprite. Sit a moment until you get used to this," Duc said. He clasped her shoulder and guided her to a sawn-off stump.

"Will I be sitting on someone?" she murmured, not certain if she actually spoke or only thought the words.

"No. It's just a stump. We smoothed and shaped the top of a broken tree, that really was just a tree, so that the weary might find a bit of rest."

"I hope you thanked the spirit of the tree for this donation to your community," Rod said. He supported Sprite with a hand behind her back and another at her elbow. "I know this isn't what we are used to, but somehow it feels like home. And family."

"Because it is," Duc replied. He offered Sprite a sip of water from her own canteen dangling from the bottom of her pack.

She took it gratefully, finding an anchor in the familiar act of just taking a drink, even though the water tasted warm and flat. It was water. One of the four elements of life. She, Rod, and Duc represented Earth. The young woman with white feathers for hair had to embody Air. The boy with flames for a headdress represented Fire. And the bald family with bulging eyes and puckered mouths probably found Water as their natural habitat.

"The telepaths evolved to communicate with and bind all the elementals together," Rod said.

"And the shape-changers sprang from the best hunters of their tribes with the need to feed their people during the decades long volcanic winter," Duc said, completing his theory of where they all came from.

"We can't stay here," the woman with the Tarot deck whispered. She turned a tight circle in place, her hands opening and closing as if she trapped information in her palms. "We are too exposed, and I sense lurkers in the woods."

"Armed predators," added a small, ordinary boy. He pressed his index fingers against his temples so tightly his knuckles turned white.

"How many?" Duc asked. He pulled Sprite to her feet and urged her and her twin beyond the little clearing to a tumble of boulders the size of houses.

A small round shadow between the rocks turned into a crevice. One by one, the people slipped into the short, narrow doorway. Duc and the hairy man with sharp canine features and mottled gray and beige skin waited to be the last to enter.

Sprite shed her pack and passed it to waiting hands just inside the crevice. Rod did the same. Then she turned sideways, mimicking the others who entered the hiding place. She had to crouch down a bit to fit. Two meters, then three, she sidled between suffocating rocks.

How did larger people get through if she at five feet, two inches and barely one hundred pounds had to squeeze her body to fit these tight confines?

Behind her, Rod found it easier to crawl, then slither along, pulling himself forward with hand grips carved into the rock. The men ahead of them had to push the packs ahead of them to keep the frames from snagging on outcroppings.

"You look more like a snake than a rock," Sprite whispered. She giggled, relieving the tension of their flight to safety.

She had to hold her breath to squeeze around the next bend in this too-narrow crack.

The passageway grew so that both she and Rod could stand and replace their packs on their backs.

They walked easily along a broad path of hard-packed dirt. The people ahead of her relaxed their shoulders and began conversing again in their communal sign language.

Sprite absorbed their mood, and her steps became lighter. Rod, too, ceased to trudge and walked easier.

Suddenly a world of light and space opened before her. A natural cave right out of the Ali Baba stories greeted her. Bright blankets or tapestries covered rock walls, a creek emerged from beneath an outcropping to her right, ran through the dirt floor and disappeared again on the far left. She heard the joyful murmur of the clear water as it moved over rocks and clean sand. People, men and women, wearing normal clothes of jeans and camp shirts, but barefoot, hovered over a hearth with a huge cauldron balanced on a steel tripod. Children ran about in unorganized play. The bigger ones made a game of jumping the creek. One of the men dipped a ladle into the depths of the cooking pot and sipped from the broth he retrieved.

"Lunch is ready," he announced.

The woman beside him dribbled a handful of crushed plants into the mix.

Sprite's tummy growled. She realized she hadn't eaten since breakfast with Dad very early this morning. Whatever they cooked smelled wonderful.

The tree man gestured toward rocks that had been shaped to form seats with backs to lean against. Sprite set her pack beside one and shrugged her shoulders free of the strain. How many miles had she hiked today?

She didn't know how far, only that most of it had been uphill and her thighs and calves needed rest.

Rod stood beside her, studying their surroundings, pack firmly on his back. "Are you sure we're safe?" he whispered to her.

A quick look around assured her they were among their own and out of reach of their pursuers. Temporarily.

The woman who had presided over the cauldron handed Sprite a wood bowl and spoon filled with the fragrant soup. Lots of carrots and potatoes, along with spinach and kale and other veggies she didn't recognize, until she smelled mild wild onion and garlic. She ran the spoon through the broth to release more of the aroma and caught a chunk of white meat.

"Ordinary chicken," the woman laughed at Sprite's look of puzzlement.

The woman's partner came along behind her with a wooden platter strewn with thin slices of dense, brown bread filled with seeds and smelling of olive oil and more garlic. Sprite's mouth watered.

Finally, Rod sat down on the boulder beside her. "I'll have some of that, too, please," he said, flashing his most endearing smile, the one he used to wheedle teachers into giving him more time to finish his homework.

Always a flirt, her brother could sell used cars to a used car salesman.

Other matters took on some urgency. She looked to the Tarot card reader, trying to capture her attention.

With a slight nod, the woman pointed to a dark corner of the cave with a red curtain in front. Sprite investigated and found a clean and odorless latrine. Sprigs of sage and other aromatic plants she couldn't name filled tiny crevices in the rock wall. She didn't care to know the depth of the hole, just that it served its function and the crudely carved, but sanded seat would prevent all but the tiniest of babies from falling into it. A stack of broad and soft leaves completed the essential supplies.

Returning to the main living space gave her the opportunity to scan more of the sanctuary without being obvious in her scrutiny. She needed to know another escape route. Just in case.

"Where's Duc?" Sprite whispered to her twin. His oversized pack had managed to come into the living cavern, but not their bio-dad.

Rod looked around warily as he swallowed the last of his soup/stew. She'd become so used to Duc being just behind them she hadn't noticed when their bio-dad had dropped out of sight.

"He's mimicking a rock, blocking the entrance," Sequoia said. "Now keep your voice down. Sound carries strangely inside and out." Then he removed the folded papers Duc had given him from a fold of skin that acted much like a pocket, perched a pair of reading glasses on his nose and began reading the spreadsheets.

DUC BREATHED DEEPLY and slowly, managing a state of meditation that left him hyper-alert while his body remained unmoving, doing a good imitation of volcanic rock. Just one among many.

Adam Mathison crept into the clearing; side arm drawn. He swept the clearing with his squinting gaze and the muzzle of his weapon.

Behind him Major Arbuthnaught stumbled over her own feet. She looked like she hadn't slept much, and she cradled her left arm in her right. The black sling didn't appear to do much good in supporting or comforting her wound. Did blood loss account for the paleness of her face and the wrinkled paper texture of her skin?

Her gun remained holstered on her left hip. The weight of it tilted her balance to that side.

If a squad of National Guard troops had followed them, they remained far enough back in the tree line that Duc could not see them or hear their feet shuffling in the undergrowth.

Arbuthnaught had the Homeland Security credentials to commandeer support troops. Duc had to wonder if they followed orders blindly or truly believed the spiel of anti-paranormal venom these two fanatics preached.

"Come out, come out, wherever you are," Mathieson chanted in a childish sing-song. "Oh Android Spartacus, you can come out now. We won't hurt you. Your father sent us to protect you."

Duc's brain grew heavy with the need to stop thinking and blindly obey the mesmerizing voice. An unacknowledged paranormal talent for hypnosis?

"Sarsaparilla Aphrodite, come out and play with me." Again the light tones that fell into the rhythm of children's games.

A raven croaked disagreement as it circled the clearing. Its raucous call severed Mathieson's delicate and lulling voice with a sharp and clashing tone.

Thank you, my friend, Duc thought. He wished he could shake his head free of Mathieson's spell. But safety lay in absolute stillness.

Did the man know he used psychic tricks even though he fanatically fought paranormals? Either that or he'd been trained as a hypnotherapist.

"Aphrodite, show yourself," Major A barked like a drill sergeant. "Android, your father sent us to bring you home. You have no business hanging out with these dangerous outlaws!"

In that moment, Duc knew the woman failed in her self-appointed task. Neither of the twins would respond to the names their mother had given them. Bryce might hold the honorary rank of general, used to keeping secrets tight against his chest, but his family worked on shared information and co-operation. Sprite and Rod knew why they were here and what their dad's ultimate goal was.

These two rogue agents needed to be taken down now.

Major A drew her weapon, aimed, and fired in one smooth motion. The bullet—a honking, huge, monster of a hollow point—exploded against the granite cliff wall two meters to Duc's left. Sharp shards of rock flew in every direction.

He had to get out of here, now! Taking a huge risk, he freed his legs of their natural armor and scooted backward into the crevice.

Another bullet slammed into the hardpacked dirt where he'd been lying not five seconds ago.

A third bullet fired.

Chapter Twenty-Nine

Bryce plugged in his headphones and microphone to his work laptop. Two in the afternoon on a Monday in late June was a bold time for an op to go down. Here in the U.S. the weekend was almost sacred for clandestine missions. The work week was reserved for... work.

Ellie had taken off for her office and would likely stay there until early evening. Then she'd come home for a late supper.

Bryce had privacy to observe and offer advice to Colonel Zachariah and his men who guarded Didi and Chad. If all transpired as planned, he needn't worry about feeding the young couple tonight while he pumped them for information about Senator Desdaganet's activities in the past and his plans for the future.

"We have activity," the colonel's voice came through the headphones.

Bryce adjusted his screen to avoid reflection through the window.

Yes! The bright red door of the small two-story motel came into focus. He had dozens of questions about the set up that had taken place without his supervision. He took three deep breaths and forced his shoulders to drop below the level of his ears. More controlled breathing exercises while he clenched and relaxed his hands, and he found he could focus on Zach's helmet cam without interrupting him.

"I'm retired," he reminded himself, over and over. "I no longer do fieldwork."

But if he didn't concentrate on this operation he'd pace and fuss about the twins climbing that damned mountain where he'd seen that single puff of smoke. In his head, he knew they had achieved adulthood and needed to explore their roots and get to know their bio-dad.

His heart ached that he could no longer hold them close and surround them with protective cotton wool.

He wished he could have implanted GPS chips in them. All he had was data indicating Po Duc's ridiculous purple truck had parked about three quarters of the way to their destination and not moved for several hours.

"Stay safe, kids," he said to himself.

Then his attention riveted upon his computer screen where a flashy red vintage convertible pulled into the motel parking lot. The driver backed it into a narrow space not meant for parking, right next to the staircase. Wearing black slacks and tailored black shirt, with his long blond ponytail stuffed under a billed cap, the MOC stood from the driver's seat. He stepped onto the seat and from there onto the third step of the iron staircase that wound up to the second story. He had an easy exit when he completed his task.

SPRITE SANK ONTO THE cave floor, back against the wall beside the exit crevice. Knees pulled to her chest and elbows resting atop them, she hid her face in her arms. A whimper gathered in her throat. The pressure of fear hindered her breathing.

She counted the bullets. Memories of the night of the bonfire when Major A had shot directly at her and of the bullet that had pushed three of her armor scales into her abdomen... Searing stabs radiating outward from the point of contact. Her head had spun with dizziness. Remembered pain roared to life inside her mind.

The third bullet thudded against something softer than granite.

"Duc!" she whispered, mindful of the prohibition against betraying the others with voices that carried.

A man's booted foot reached through the crevice, swinging to find a brace. When it encountered nothing it rested briefly on the ground, then the toe dug in and the ankle wiggled until the calf appeared.

A second foot appeared and repeated the flailing dance for a purchase in the open space.

"Duc?" Sprite asked.

A mumbled reply.

Rod sprang to her side. He too sat awkwardly, bracing his feet against the wall on either side of the opening. With both hands he grasped the flailing foot and pulled.

"Come on, Pop, you've got to wiggle those shoulders free," he grunted.

Not knowing what else to do, Sprite shifted to sit beside her brother and pulled the other foot.

"We must leave, now," the tree man touched her shoulder. His anxiety traveled through his hands to where he grasped her.

"Not without... Pop." Suddenly the affectionate sobriquet seemed natural. He wasn't their dad. That term belonged to Bryce Maxwell, the man who had rescued and adopted them. But she and Rod could no longer deny the blood connection between them and the big, Asian, rock of man they hoped to rescue.

Duc's legs and butt came free!

He bent his knees and heaved until his shoulders scraped either side of the opening. Moments later his head and arms followed.

Sprite sighed deeply, not aware that she'd been holding her breath—the worst thing she could do according to a martial arts instructor. She needed to keep oxygen flowing through her blood to strengthen her muscles.

"Pop?" Rod clutched at Duc's shoulder while he knelt, head hanging, and he too fought to fill his lungs.

"We can't stay here," he gasped. One hand came up and massaged his left shoulder. "Major A is hurt bad, but she still has a sharpshooter's aim." He rubbed a bruise forming on his cheek bone, just beside and below his left eye. "Nothing serious, just a rock shard bouncing against my armor."

"Where do we go? And how?" Sprite looked around and saw only the empty cavern draped in shadows. A small ray of light came from an unnoticed opening in the ceiling. The two dozen inhabitants had disappeared, along with the cauldron and the bright wall hangings. The fire had been covered with dirt.

A flicker of movement to their far right caught her attention. Tree man held aside a plain mud brown drape. On the other side of the drape, the youth with fiery hair waited, giving light to both the tunnel and the cave. He beckoned them to hurry.

"We have got to widen that back door," Duc muttered as he scrambled to his feet.

Sprite relaxed her shoulders, breathed deeply, and followed him, loping across the cavern floor to the flickering shadows behind Sequoia. They each grabbed their packs and shouldered them as they passed the curtain into a wide tunnel.

Duc whipped an industrial sized mag light from his pack that Sequoia held out for him and shone it all around. He aimed the light toward the ground for a moment while he dug into an outside pocket of his huge pack until he retrieved two energy bars. Chewing quickly he found the packed dirt of their path and began walking.

Sequoia surged ahead of the twins along with flame-boy. "Stay close, try not to trip."

His words sounded more in Sprite's head than her ears.

So, she and her twin weren't the only ones capable of silent communication when in danger.

"COME ON, ZACH," BRYCE said, even though he knew his successor and friend couldn't hear him. He'd turned off his mic via protocol. The only sounds available were those picked up from the surrounds by the camera. "I need to see what JEL is doing."

As if he knew Bryce's anxiety and frustration, Colonel Zachariah inched along the underside of the balcony until he stood at the trunk of the flashy red convertible. The camera showed the colonel's gloved hand turning off the ignition and removing the keys. Their quarry would have a delay in his escape if he made it past their trap.

Then Zach stepped out of the shadows just enough to give him a clear view of their black-clad quarry approaching the room registered to Chad and Didi. He ducked beneath the wide window and crab-walked to the door. Then he stood and drew a compact gun from a shoulder holster, also black and mostly unnoticeable from a distance and the modest resolution of the helmet cam.

From his hip pocket, JEL pulled an extension for the gun barrel and screwed it on. An illegal silencer.

His other pocket produced twin thin metal blades, which he inserted in the lock. A quick twist of the pick and he was able to open the door.

This man was a pro.

Zack didn't move. *Blast him!*

Bryce had to bite his lip in frustration. He *knew* his friend had to stay back, out of the action. His job was to direct his men. Presumably they were all in place.

But Bryce needed to be there. He sucked in a long draft of oxygen through the cannula and remembered why he wasn't storming up the metal staircase, weapon leveled at the heart of the assassin.

Pop, pop, pop! came the tell-tale firing of a muffled pistol.

"No!" JEL yelled.

Seconds later, two fully armed soldiers, with U.N. stenciled to their Kevlar, frog-marched the hand-cuffed hit man out of the motel room, followed by two more uniformed troops.

Bryce sagged in relief.

His phone beeped an incoming text.

> *C&D safe in winery B&B outside of town. Only casualties: a pair of down pillows. Feathers everywhere.*

A chuckle erupted from Bryce's mid-section. He sympathized with the squad members assigned the task of cleaning the room.

> *C&D talking non-stop with details and proof.*

Now Bryce could go back to worrying about his kids.

Chapter Thirty

R od felt for each step with his toes before placing a foot down.

The flame man walked slowly at the head of the procession, giving off a faint glow that barely reached Rod and Sprite. They had only an impression of the vague space around them.

Keeping his left hand on the wall, Rod negotiated a path along the dark tunnel. He heard Sprite breathing rapidly behind him. Other than that, the escape route remained silent.

His heart pounded so hard and loudly, he didn't know if he could hear anything else.

He'd longed for adventure since he became aware of the life his dad lived. His mind replayed the thrills of adrenaline rushes and satisfaction of a job well done. Action movies gave him glimpses of what he might be able to do.

But now? Now he escaped capture and imprisonment, or death, and wasn't so sure what he wanted for his future.

His next step he had to angle slightly to his right to maintain half an armlength distance from the left side wall.

And the next. And the next.

The route curved in a long sweep.

This was all he could do. But he had to keep his ears tuned to the smallest whisper of sound. He had to make sure his sister didn't fall behind. He was responsible for alerting the others if an enemy followed them.

He wasn't certain he wanted this kind of life.

Ahead, he heard a small child whimper.

"Hush," a female voice replied.

Rod came closer and discerned the figures of a tall man carrying a toddler and a slight woman with an infant in her arms. Between them slumped a small child, bigger than a toddler but still very young. Perhaps four or five. It rubbed its eyes with tight fists.

"Tired," it whispered.

Silence and safety must have been part of its training since infancy.

"Let me help," Rod whispered. His heart twisted in sympathy with the child. A girl, he guessed from the shoulder length braids that whipped back and forth as the child shook her head, not willing to accept help or being ignored any longer. A temper tantrum built within her, inches from exploding and betraying them all.

Rod lifted her into his arms and hugged her close, letting her droop across his shoulder, thumb creeping toward her mouth.

Then Sprite stepped beside him and gently rubbed the child's back.

"It's just so unfair," the mother said on a deep sniff. She sounded as tired and frustrated as her child.

Fortunately, the infant and toddler seemed asleep.

"Why do we have to keep running? Every time we think we've found a home, someone who hates us finds us and threatens us with fire, or guns, or arrest for crimes that have never been committed..." She broke off on a sob.

Her husband tried to gather her in a hug, but the babies got in the way.

"Not far now," Duc said, coming up behind them. He gestured an offer to take the small child from Rod. "You okay?" he whispered so softly the communication might as well have been telepathic. Like Sequoia. Danger heightened all of their latent abilities.

Rod could only shaking his head. Moving her might wake her and set off that dreaded temper tantrum.

"I've got her," he replied to Duc.

And suddenly, like a lightning bolt inside his brain, he knew his life's purpose. He needed to help the poor and persecuted, refugees, and homeless. He and his twin had been ever so lucky that Dad had found and adopted them. He'd sheltered them and educated them in ways to protect themselves. He had enough money and political contacts to keep their paranormal abilities off the public radar.

These people had nothing, except what Duc and his family foundation could scrape together for them.

Rod kept walking.

A little more light, watery in nature, flowed around them, giving definition to shapes, relieving the depth of darkness they'd plodded through.

The warm weight of the child comforted him, anchored him during this trek. The minute vibrations in the dirt and limestone beneath his feet told him that they'd come around nearly three quarters of a circle from their starting place. Five kilometers maybe.

No wonder the children were tired. He was too after the trek uphill from the trailhead and then barely a rest before starting off through this tunnel. At least they'd had time for that hearty soup and bread.

"Pop, what can I do to help your foundation maintain a sanctuary? These people need assistance integrating back into society as much as shelter while nursing their hurts. I want... no, I need to help them do that."

The light had grown enough to reveal Duc's grin. "You could become a social worker and learn the ins and outs of the system created to help people but fails miserably. And make it work. Every tiny bit helps." He strode ahead to the front of the line of refugees and held up a hand while he scouted an exit.

"He's right about little bits helping." Sprite said. "I want to do more. People who are persecuted by society need legal help too. I'm going to work toward law school and study the refugee angle, international law, legal aid, and such. Minority populations, including paranormals, are often refugees in their own land. We need to be at the front of those battles."

Rod grinned. Together, he and his twin could fight for these people... their people. He hugged the child in his arms a little closer. She snuggled into his neck and released the fist stuffed into her mouth.

"We'll take care of you, baby."

BRYCE THUMBED OFF HIS phone and rested it gently on the edge of Ellie's kitchen table, precisely aligned as if he'd used a compass and square to find its proper position. Late afternoon light streaming through the kitchen window banished any hint of a shadow on the polished blond wood.

"I should feel something," he murmured. "Anything."

He'd talked to all the right people this morning. He'd even broken through the last layer of encryption on Lou's flash drive to find a crude draft of the dreaded Executive Order. Not Lou's level of vocabulary, grammar, or phrasing. The order of the sentences and paragraphs had no logic either and strayed off topic three times in a single page. The same person had drafted an order from the director of Homeland Security for all personnel to line their helmets with tin foil while in the field. The wording sounded as if Marjorie Arbuthnaught spoke into his head. Random thoughts to be included in the EO.

She sounded loonier than the Looney Moose.

Before he could follow that to any conclusion, the phone rang again. Colonial Zachariah's name and number showed on the screen.

"Yeah, Zach, what you got?" Bryce said, relieved that he didn't need to analyze his reaction to the previous call.

"Federal Justice wants to cut a deal with both of our prisoners." He was careful not to name Jacquie or JEL. Cell phones were never totally secure.

"Damn. I hate to see either of them get less than they deserve. But I have no authority in this matter."

"Your opinion is still valued," Zach replied.

"How valuable is their information?" Bryce scrubbed his face with his free hand. No way was he putting this call on speaker. In fact, he was surprised Zach used a nonsecure line instead of his encrypted laptop.

"JEL *might* help us take down three middle grade crime lords."

"He's a little fish in a very big pond filled with piranhas."

"Yeah, but if we can take down the right piranha, we've canceled a bigger piece of the network."

"I'd say give him a not ideal deal. Some time behind bars and long probation, no contact with criminal associates kind of thing. What about Jacquie?"

"Her intel is more interesting. Goes higher and deeper. She's got pillow talk down to a science. JEL knows drugs, gambling, prostitutes, the usual organized crime fare. Jacquie knows which federal prosecutors those crime lords are paying off. And she's got contacts in Homeland. We can trace that horrible Executive Order outlawing citizens with paranormal talents. Seems there is a secret committee of legislators who created a witch hunt in order to draw attention away from their own attempt at a coup to replace the entire government with their committee."

Bryce bit his lip in a moment of indecision. Remove the vicious trollop from the future lives of his kids, or save those kids from persecution?

"Give her whatever she wants. Just find out who's behind the EO. Even if it goes above and beyond Senator Desdaganet."

"Thought that's what you'd say." Zach chuckled. "I'll pass your opinion along to appropriate Justice System officials."

"Sorry, Zach, I have to run. Ellie's home." He ended the call and went to greet the lady at her kitchen door. "You're home early?" he said.

She threw her arms around his neck and attacked his mouth with her own. Sweet, warm, plump with desire. She back-kicked the door closed so hard the diamond-shaped glass panes rattled in their lattice frame.

He pulled her close, wondering if he could drag her into the bedroom and rip off both their clothes. His hands found her shapely and tight backside, draped in dress slacks. Far too many clothes separated them.

Abruptly she turned her face away.

"What?" he asked, suddenly confused.

"Bryce, will you marry me?"

"Before I jump up and down and shout 'Yes!' like I really want to, what brought this on?" Gently he loosened his grip on her waist to guide her to the curved banquette around the table in the bay window. She scooted in far enough to give him room to sit beside her. With one arm along the back of the padded seat, he tucked her up beside him, with her head on his shoulder.

Idly, she drew doodles on his thigh with one seductive finger.

"What happened at work that brought you home an hour early with this wonderful proposal?" He gritted his teeth against his normal reaction to that all-too-enticing pattern she drew, much too close to his too-long-deprived groin.

"You really want to marry me, just not before we talk through the logistics?"

"I do, and it's more the emotional logic I'm interested in at the moment. We married quickly for lust more than twenty years ago, and I screwed it up mightily. Now I need to know the strength of our love, and truth about what we are letting ourselves in for, before we go crazy. Again."

She took a deep breath and turned his face to hers so they could see each other's eyes. "All morning long as I restocked inventory in the gift shop and sent groups of tourists off with compatible language guides, all I could really think about was you, and our weekend together."

"It was a traumatic weekend. Lou is still in need of full-time care."

"And he's getting it. At least until his beard grows back and he feels comfortable with himself again. But all the time he was held captive and... being beaten, I worried about him, but nowhere near as much as I was thinking about you."

She kissed his chin. He almost lost control. He only had to reach eighteen inches to close the blinds on the window and then lift her onto the table...

"I have been honest about my health. If we marry, I don't want to tie you to nursing me for the rest of my life. I'm not a good patient. I'd wear you down in no time."

"I know that, and it doesn't bother me."

He raised an eyebrow in question.

"I've nursed you through bullet wounds and a ruptured spleen and an exotic, tropical version of pneumonia when we were in our twenties. I know what I'm getting into. It's just... The winery owner sold the business over the weekend. I know he and his wife are overdue for retirement. But out of the blue a small craft business from the valley decided to expand. They made the right offer with the promise of keeping the same family-run, small, old-world business, and Antonio grabbed it. He's keeping his house and a few acres, but the vast tracks of vines and the winery will go to the new people. There are going to be staff changes. Antonio said that he'd recommend they keep me on to manage the gift shop and run the tours."

"He knows you depend upon the job to pay your bills and put Liz through college. Part of a family business is taking care of employees who have become like family."

"I know. And I appreciate that. But all of a sudden, I realized that the winery is not my life. It's not a career for me. It's just a job that pays better than teaching. And then I thought about you and the twins coming into my family, how Liz will always be my baby, but she's grown up and about to fly the nest. You are what I want for the rest of my life."

Then she kissed him again, fully, soundly, a sealing of the deal rather than just a prelude to sex, which was coming. Soon.

One more thing to set on the table.

"What would you say if I told you that you may not have to be my nurse for the rest of my life?"

"What?" She pulled away, her brow wrinkling with concern.

He smoothed her skin with a gentle touch.

"I just got off the phone with my doctor in Portland." Ellie didn't need to know about the call from Zack that had followed right on the heels of the first conversation.

"And...?" The frown was back. They had talked about the possibility of a lung transplant.

"And it is Dr. Crawford's informed opinion that the doctors in the E.R. in Brookings overreacted to the amount of scar tissue in my left lung. It's been there a long time and not going away. But as long as I have regular check-ups and X-rays, keep my O2 condenser handy and moderate my activity, I don't need a transplant. He does want to see me as soon as I get back to town but doesn't expect anything different from my last check up three months ago."

The smile spreading across her face rivaled the outdoor sunshine.

"As soon as we tell our kids, I'm calling a realtor and selling this dumpy cottage. I can't wait to marry you."

Our kids. That sounded so wonderful.

As long as Po Duc hadn't led the twins into a life-threatening situation.

Chapter Thirty-One

Maintaining the rule of silence, Duc stood close to the arched opening of the cave, basking in the cool mist. Two meters ahead of him, a waterfall obscured him from outside view. Thousands of gallons of water plunged from a ledge thirty meters above him, into a pool another ten meters below him.

He had no idea how deep the pool delved before spreading out and drifting away into a creek that carved its way through a narrow canyon to join with other waterways, until they all became part of the Rogue River.

How many thousands of years had the water needed to create this steep-sided-bowl surrounding the pool? Ferns, ground cover, and unique wildflowers clung precariously to the steep walls of this oasis. Only the faintest of game trails led the way out.

An idyllic place that needed protection from human incursions as much as a beautiful mask to the cave system access point.

Above the ridge to the west and south lay an arm of the mountain on top of him. It only stretched a short distance separating this exit point from the clearing where he'd had to crawl through the tight crevice to the main cavern of the refuge. One could walk here, inside or outside the layers of rock. A matter of about two kilometers either way.

If Arbuthnaught and Mathieson knew the area....

He sharpened his gaze to focus on the game trails leading from the picnic grounds to this pocket park. Some had been trampled by people into easier paths. But no longer. The foundation had worked hard with both the Forestry and Parks department to keep this place isolated and less accessible than many wanted it to be. A few neglected park benches and picnic tables rotted in peace on the ridge across the pool from him. Earlier this spring,

Duc's brother, Luc, had placed "Trail Closed for Maintenance" signs back at the road, a kilometer away.

Sprite came up beside him, clinging to the shadows, and idly scratching at the scale on her chin. Her eyes, however, searched the ridge, and she cocked her head as if listening for anything beyond the roar of the water.

Duc's scale itched. A sympathetic reaction to her scratches or a warning?

Subtly, Sprite lifted one hand to her waist level and pointed to the right, where one of the game trails began.

And then he heard the voice that sent cold chills down his spine.

His scales began snapping into place of their own volition.

SPRITE'S WORLD DIMMED, like a cloud had suddenly blocked the sun. She bit her lip to maintain control of her body and instincts.

A woman's voice carried through the noisy waterfall.

"They're here! I know it," Major Marjorie Arbuthnaught shouted. She raised a long weapon above her head as a banner to rally her troops. But her right arm hung limply in a make-shift sling cobbled together with a belt. If she'd sought medical care after her own ricocheted bullet ripped through her shoulder, it had been rudimentary.

Mathieson stepped beside her.

Something light and fluffy blossomed in Sprite's mind. Satisfaction. She'd spent so much time today concentrating on "finding" Mathieson that his appearance fulfilled her quest—a major accomplishment akin to her smugness when she "found" missing car keys and phones.

Maybe she truly was a finder.

Mathieson beckoned forward whatever warriors they'd gathered on the journey here, probably green National Guard troops who thought this merely another training exercise.

The ridge remained empty of all but the two Homeland Security officers.

"I see no signs of occupation," came a voice that Sprite felt she should know but couldn't place.

"Of course, they are here," the major returned. "Can't you hear them. They are in my head. Voices, insidious voices telling me what to do, demanding I succumb to their will." She tried to rub her temples, but her only working hand was occupied with a heavy weapon.

Duc waved forward a few of the paranormals who had gathered in the cave behind them. Three stone people, like she and Rod and Duc, Sequoia whose skin had begun to thicken and darken toward bark, and four others without overt characteristics that could identify them. The man who had flames for hair remained deep withing the cave shadows. A glow around his entire body showed where he stood. Instinctively, Sprite knew that his talents were a last resort. The forest on the ridge was already too dry to risk setting it ablaze. Only the bowl around the pool remained green, moistened by the waterfall.

"They are in there! Can't you see them using the waterfall mist to cloak their presence?" Major A shouted. She pointed directly at Duc with her rifle.

He moved backward, behind the arched opening.

Sprite wished she could see the woman's face. The distance was too great to detail her emotions.

Mathieson took one small step away from her, toward the center of the circular rim.

Rod returned the sleeping toddler to her parents. They all sat with their backs to the cave wall, a scattering of large rocks between them and the entrance.

An intruder, blinded by sun-dazzle, would trip several times before finding them, giving them plenty of time to fade into one of the smaller caves.

Rod made the universal signal of "Crazy" by circling one finger around his temple.

Sprite and Duc nodded agreement.

Latent telepath. No training. Voices partially heard driving her insane, Sprite sent to her brother.

His agreement with her came back as a remote hug. She wished Patrick had been able to join them. Maybe his insights into human behavior would help them.

"Are we supposed to line our helmets with tin foil now?" came the almost recognizable voice from the unseen plateau.

Where do I know that voice?

"I already ordered our field agents and troops to do so," Major A replied flatly. "Didn't you get the order?"

Even from this distance, Sprite could see that the Major opened her eyes wide in dismay.

"I read the memo," Mathieson replied. He sidestepped again, putting another meter of space between them.

Duc, now in full armor, dark basalt colored where locals tended to a paler granite, led his people along a narrow ledge on the western side of the bowl. The afternoon sun highlighted the opposite side, giving them increasing shadows to hide within.

"Look, look, look!" Major A commanded. "They are moving. We have to stop them!" She fired off a spray of bullets that chipped cliff walls and ricocheted at odd angles.

Sprite cringed backward, dragging her brother with her even as her armor snapped into place. She'd experienced the bruising from one bouncing round and didn't want to again. Yellow and green bruises still marred her rib cage and ached—more a memory of pain than physical hurt.

The crucial moment came. The ledge merged into the game trail, directly below the major. Duc and his troops were clearly visible.

Major A pointed her weapon straight down on Duc's head.

"No! We just found you!" Sprite needed to run out there and drag Pop back into the shelter of the shadowy cave entrance.

Rod's fingers dug into her upper arm, as he kept her from running into the line of fire. "You're the logical one," he said through his teeth. "Think it through. Don't just react. Do you think we're the only ones who have noticed she's off the rails?"

"Mathieson is still up there beside her. He drank the Kool-Aid and orchestrated the kidnap of Uncle Lou."

"Maybe someone gave him the antidote." Rod pointed toward Major A.

Six camouflaged armed troops converged on the woman, weapons loosely aimed at her.

"Stand down, Major Arbuthnaught," Colonel Zachariah demanded in a booming voice that echoed around the bowl.

Zachariah. Of course, that was the voice she almost recognized. Zach always had Dad's back, and now he'd transferred that loyalty to her and Rod, and tangentially to Duc.

Major A whirled around, the muzzle of her weapon waving wildly. "Who the fuck are you?" she snarled.

Four military troops, trained by Dad, sharpened their focus and their aim on the rogue agent. The fifth guarded Mathieson.

"Stand down, Major. You have overstepped your authority. You have committed serious federal crimes without proper warrants, you have fabricated an Executive Order for the President's signature that would guarantee the incarceration, torture, and death of hundreds of U.S. citizens, men, women, and children."

"They're fucking aliens from outer space, you asshole. And you are their slave, just like all the other military commanders. Just like the world leadership. They are all alien mind-slaves! Just look at your own U.N. Secretary General, the man who signs your paycheck, as well as your fucking idol Bryce Maxwell. They are all idiots who can't tell the difference between day and night." She pressed her fist to her temple while still clutching her high-powered rifle. "We need a new, clear-sighted government, not the puppets who pretend to rule us."

The barrel now pointed skyward.

"If they'd just shut up, so I can think! That's what's so insidious about aliens. They flood you with strange thoughts and ideas so you can't think, can't find a way to override their influence..."

New blood leaked from her shoulder wound to stain her dark blouse.

While their enemy ranted Duc and his three stone-people had crept up the slope.

"None of us are aliens," Duc said. He clasped her wrist with one hand and the long barrel of her weapon with the other.

Major A fought him, trying to wrest back control of her gun, the situation, her life.

"Look out!" Sprite screamed even as the woman pulled her arm out of the make-shift sling and drew a knife from a sheath on her right hip.

Both she and Rod sprinted forward to the ledge. No time to appreciate the cool mist from the water. No time to assess the danger. No time for anything but to help Pop.

The major's face blanched as she raised the knife over her head, ready to plunge it into Duc's chest.

His armor resisted the blade.

Her desperation overrode her weakness from blood loss and pain.

Duc flung himself sideways to avoid the wicked serrated blade. Still he kept his hands on her weapon.

His feet slipped on the loose soil. He dangled a moment over the deep bowl carved into the landscape. Nothing stood between him and the deep plunge pool of the waterfall.

Where were the three stone people who should have been behind him, bracing him?

They'd crept upward and sideways, planting themselves around Mathieson, a circle of boulders pressing against his legs as high as his waist. He was caught between rocks and a hard decision. He threw down his weapon.

Major A's knife crept between two of Duc's scales, finding vulnerable skin right over his heart.

Almost there. Sprite's legs pumped hard in her mad dash to help her Pop, Rod right behind her, his hand on her lower back, bracing her while she sprinted up the steep slope, clinging to tiny plants and shrubs as handholds.

As she came abreast of the ridge, she dropped into a fetal crouch. Rod did the same. Stone barriers between their Pop and a deadly fall.

Duc's waving feet landed on their backs.

Sprite gratefully took his weight.

Above them, Colonel Zachariah intervened. The stalwart soldier wrapped an arm around Major A's throat and yanked her backward. He grunted with the effort of managing the off-balance enemy and the man blocking her use of her weapon.

The major still had her finger on the trigger. Ten more bullets erupted from the gun.

Duc's feet bounced from the backs of his children and found purchase on the ledge.

His weight sent the major further off balance.

Zach kept pulling her backward.

She dropped the weapon and clawed at his choking grip.

Sprite scrambled to her feet as soon as Duc's weight left her back. Rod grabbed her hand and followed until they both stood safely on the ridge.

A dozen troops in camouflage uniforms with U.N. badges, quietly and efficiently cuffed both Arbuthnaught and Mathieson. Colonel Zach rubbed absently at his bleeding hand where the major's dirty fingernails had scratched him.

Duc's people had melted into the landscape and disappeared.

"You know Ms. Arbuthnaught," Sprite said, facing the woman who had threatened so many. "We aren't space aliens. Most of us can trace our family heritage back sixty-five thousand years. We evolved here as Guardians of Humanity."

"And we will continue to be Guardians, not evil influences," Rod added.

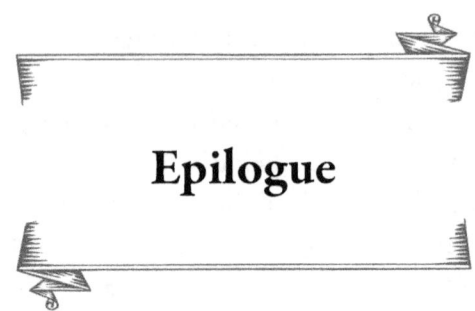

Epilogue

Bryce fussed with the fancy red and gold waistcoat of his Phantom costume. It was too loose since he'd bought it a month ago. Ellie's good cooking and the lack of junk food the twins craved, and a new attack on his physical therapy had reduced his paunch just enough that he had abs again.

Now his face itched where the red sequins outlining his mask touched his skin. The ruffles on his new, silk, poet shirt just got in the way. He wasn't ready for this.

Well, he was ready for marriage to Ellie and all the baggage they both brought to the union. It was the wedding that scared him. Scared him more than facing down a demon inspired, African warlord with automatic weapons and tanks backing him up.

Or a ravenous demon without Tess's Celestial Blade beside him.

"Stop fussing, Dad. You look splendid," Rod said. "Ellie has done wonders for you. I hid your O2 condenser beneath the chair next to the aisle in the first row. Any one of the wedding party can grab it if you need it. But I don't think you will."

"Who are you?" Bryce asked eyeing his son's almost costume of ill-fitting off-the-rack pale grey suit and horn-rimmed glasses. His shirt needed washing and his red tie with gold flecks was off center and at half-mast. "I thought I taught you to knot a tie properly?"

"You did. But you didn't teach Clark Kent." Rod adjusted the glasses so they sat squarely on his nose.

They exchanged a nervous chuckle and headed out the door of the small conference room toward the grand ballroom of the con hotel. This con, however, was not the small beach venue where Bryce and Ellie had fallen in love again last June, but a much larger World Con hosted in a huge hotel by the Seattle fans, in early September.

"Rod, are you okay with Lou being my best man? By family protocol I should have considered you first." Bryce's cheeks warmed and he found it difficult to meet his son's gaze.

"You have got to be kidding. Of course, I'm okay with it. Uncle Lou has been your best friend since, well since forever. By rights he should be giving Ellie away, seeing they used to be married."

"I used to be married to her too."

"Soap opera script writers couldn't match the convoluted relationships of our family," Rod laughed. "So, you did invite Pop and his family?"

"I put his name on the list. Only Ellie and Liz know every person who agreed to show." Bryce gave his waistcoat a final tug.

"Stand up straight, Dad, it will fit better." Rod smoothed out the fabric across Bryce's shoulders as he stiffened his spine and stretched his neck.

"Is it time?" he asked nervously.

"About twenty years past time," Lou Metcalf replied from the doorway. "Can we get this show on the road? I'm strangling in this monkey suit." He ran a finger around the inside collar of his freshly laundered and starched white shirt. His red and gold paisley tie looked as sloppy as Rod's, but his charcoal grey suit was new and bespoke.

"I see you are disguised for your new job as a consultant to the CIA on the UFO problem." Bryce raised an eyebrow.

"Love the job and the paycheck. Hate the duds," Lou demurred. "For this wedding, however, and the esteemed guest list, it's as good as a costume."

Sprite poked her head in the door. "Get your asses in gear guys, the clock is ticking, and Tess's band has warmed up." She'd covered her dark bob with a Princess Leia wig with a crown of thick braids. At least she wasn't wearing white druid robes to someone else's wedding. She looked like a mercenary pilot in red and black leather.

"Is Patrick here?" he asked, suddenly needing the last element of the family nearby.

"Of course. He and Pop are ushering people to their seats," Sprite reassured him. "They aren't really in costume, just con shirts and jeans."

Secretly, Bryce was glad she'd chosen not to wear her armor, which robbed her of her femininity, ethnicity, and individuality.

Lou held the side door open for the party to exit, right across from the matching entry to the ballroom.

"Bryce, please, let me see my babies," Jacquie called from the near distance.

Stunned that she'd dared to appear *today* of all days, he paused mid-step and almost lost his balance.

Lou and Rod were right there offering their physical as well as emotional support. Like they always were.

"I got this, General," Colonel Zach replied. The military man for once was out of uniform wearing a con T shirt and crisp, new blue jeans. He whipped a pair of handcuffs from his back pocket, slapped half around Jacquie's wrist and the other restraint around a ubiquitous Ficus tree twenty yards away.

"A restraining order to keep you away from the Maxwell family was part of your plea deal, ma'am. Do you *really* want to go back to prison for such a minor infraction?"

"But they're my babies!" she wailed.

Rod shrugged and set his dad back on the path toward the wedding.

A bass guitar sounded the deep opening chords for the *Phantom of the Opera.*

"That's my cue," Bryce muttered. He stepped forward in a swirl of his cape, with his cane brandished as a weapon to clear his way.

On the dais to his right stood Tess Noncoiré, showing the early signs of pregnancy with a slight swell of her belly, and her children, instruments and mics in hand. The teenaged boy with the bass guitar sang the lyrics to the popular musical in tones so deep it sounded like he'd dragged them out of the depths of the deepest, darkest, most dangerous forest of his dark elf origins.

A pagan bard wearing leather, braids, and a crown of stag antlers stepped forward to his own mic. "He's a licensed minister," Bryce reminded himself. The pagan bard, too, was part of the con music scene and had performed weddings, memorial services, and even baby naming ceremonies at cons for years.

And then the music changed to the lighter and more joyful tune of *We're off to see the Wizard* with Tess and her daughters singing the lyrics.

The wide double doors at the formal entry of the grand ballroom flew open. Sprite stood framed by the majestic arch. In her black and red space jockey outfit with a coronet of black braids, she strode forward, sort of in time with the music like the confident young woman she had become. Her light saber rested firmly in a scabbard on her hip—the required con peace bond attached to the grip. In direct contrast to her costume, she carried a bridesmaid's bouquet of autumnal flowers in gold and red.

Behind her, Liz stepped into the limelight. She wore the red, short-skirted uniform, with black boots, of Lieutenant Uhura, the iconic character that had given women a place of authority in life as well as on the bridge of a spaceship. She too carried gold and red flowers within sprays of seasonal leaves. As she approached the dais, her mouth lifted into a bright smile, and she skipped a few steps along the road to Oz.

The girls took their places in front of the dais facing Bryce and his groomsmen.

A pause in the music lasted five heartbeats too long.

Panic welled inside Bryce. Had Ellie fled at the last minute? Was he about to lose her again?

Tess crooned, slow and sultry, the opening notes a popular tune from a few decades ago.

> *Wise men say*
> *Only fools rush in*
> *But I can't help*
> *falling in love with you.*

And there she was, his Ellie. Her long gown of red gingham seemed to float. She carried a golden basket, covered in the same red and white checked cotton. A yellow furred cairn terrier—stuffed, he hoped—with black button eyes poked its head out of the folds of cloth.

His bride lifted her gaze to his and she smiled. Her eyes shone with joy as she glided to his side.

"I didn't quite expect this kind of circus," he muttered as he offered his arm to her to finish the last step before the minister.

"All you asked was that it be legal," she replied on a soft whisper.

IRENE RADFORD

"We are all family now, anchored in true bedrock."

About the Author

Irene Radford is a founding member of Book View Café[1]. You can find many of her books, both reprints and original titles, at the café, including her earliest books being released throughout 2023 to 2025. She has been writing stories ever since she figured out what a pencil was for. Editing, as Phyllis Irene Radford, grew out of her love of the craft of writing. History has been a part of her life from earliest childhood and led to her BA from Lewis and Clark College.

Mostly she writes fantasy and historical fantasy including the best-selling Dragon Nimbus Series and the masterwork Merlin's Descendants series. Look for her writing new historical fantasy tales as Rachel Atwood, a different take on the Robin Hood mythology in *Walk the Wild with Me*, from DAW/Astra Books and the sequel *Outcasts of the Wildwood*. In other lifetimes she writes urban fantasy as P.R. Frost or Phyllis Ames, and space opera as C.F. Bentley. Lately she ventured into Steampunk as Julia Verne St. John.

If you wish information on the latest releases from Ms Radford, under any of her pen names, you can follow her on Facebook as Phyllis Irene Radford.

---

1. https://bookviewcafe.com/bookstore/v

Other Book View Café Titles by Irene Radford

Http://bookviewcafe.com/bookstore/bvc-author/
phyllis-irene-radford/[1]

Merlin's Descendants Series *by Irene Radford*

Guardian of the Balance

Guardian of the Trust

Guardian of the Vision

Guardian of the Promise

Guardian of the Freedom

Confederated Star System by: Irene Radford writing as C.F. Bentley

Harmony

Enigma

Mourner

Trance Dancer

Trickster's Dance

Artistic Demons

Confessions of a Ballroom Diva

Confessions of a Piano Demon

Confessions of a Siren Singer

Confessions of a Changeling Dancer

Pixie Chronicles

Thistle Down

Chicory Up

Dandelion Twist

WHISTLING RIVER LODGE MYSTERIES

FAMILY BEDROCK

Whistling Down the Wind
Whistle While You Plow
Whistling Bagpipes
Ghostly Whistles

THE DRAGON NIMBUS NOVELS

The Glass Dragon
The Perfect Princes
The Loneliest Magician
The Wizard's Treasure

THE DRAGON NIMBUS HISTORY NOVELS

The Dragon's Touchstone
The Last Battlemage
The Renegade Dragon

SHORT STORY COLLECTIONS by Irene Radford

Fantastical Ramblings
Speculative Journeys
Steampunk Voyages
Magical Meanderings

NON-FICTION

Magna Bloody Carta
Committing Novel

ABOUT BOOK VIEW CAFÉ

Book View Café LLC (BVC) is an author-owned cooperative of over twenty professional writers, publishing in a variety of genres including fantasy, romance, mystery, and science fiction. Since its debut in 2008, BVC has gained a reputation for producing high-quality ebooks. BVC's ebooks are DRM-free and are distributed around the world. The publishing company is now bringing that same quality to its print editions.

BVC authors include New York Times and USA Today bestsellers as well as winners and nominees of many prestigious awards, including:

Agatha Award
Campbell Award
Hugo Award
Lambda Award
Locus Award
Nebula Award
Nicholl Fellowship
PEN/Malamud Award
Philip K. Dick Award
RITA Award
World Fantasy Award
Writers of the Future Award

Book View Café
304 S. Jones Blvd. Ste 2906
Las Vegas, Nevada 89107

FAMILY BEDROCK

<u>www.bookviewcafe.com</u>[1]

---

1.   http://www.bookviewcafe.com